About the Author

Victoria Rabould was raised in a tiny town in the middle of nowhere. She spends most of her time roaming the mountains for work and pleasure. She enjoys numerous outdoor activities, as well as gardening and simple indoor hobbies such as baking and sewing. The time spent out of doors and the fruits of her gardening and baking are shared with her family.

Tales from Utherion
Heaven's Stone

Victoria Rabould

Tales from Utherion
Heaven's Stone

Vanguard Press

VANGUARD PAPERBACK

© Copyright 2024
Victoria Rabould

The right of Victoria Rabould to be identified as author of
this work has been asserted by her in accordance with the
Copyright, Designs and Patents Act 1988.

All Rights Reserved

No reproduction, copy or transmission of this publication
may be made without written permission.
No paragraph of this publication may be reproduced,
copied or transmitted save with the written permission of the
publisher, or in accordance with the provisions
of the Copyright Act 1956 (as amended).

Any person who commits any unauthorised act in relation to
this publication may be liable to criminal
prosecution and civil claims for damages.

A CIP catalogue record for this title is
available from the British Library.

ISBN 978 1 80016 782 7

*Vanguard Press is an imprint of
Pegasus Elliot Mackenzie Publishers Ltd.*
www.pegasuspublishers.com

This is a work of fiction. Names, characters, businesses, places, events and
incidents are either the product of the author's imagination or used in a
fictitious manner. Any resemblance to actual persons, living or dead, or actual
events is purely coincidental.

First Published in 2024

**Vanguard Press
Sheraton House Castle Park
Cambridge England**

Printed & Bound in Great Britain

To my mother, brothers, and grandparents, blood and adopted, that taught me perseverance, love, and strength in the wake of life's storms.

Chapter 1

Rowan sat on his horse, overlooking the narrow pass below him. He had an excellent vantage point from which he could see almost the entire road. The Pass of Handuin had been safe in former days, but darkness had slowly been spreading its fingers from the north, making it unsafe for the average villager. Goblins had been seen creeping down through the mountains and among the white rocks of the pass, and the traders that often used the pass most likely would not be prepared for their assault.

That was why Rowan waited on the mountainside. The mountain, although steep and rocky most of the way around, had a few small paths that wound up the cliff faces. These small landings had been used in the early days as lookouts for the soldiers, but the posts had been abandoned due to the longstanding peace with the surrounding realms. Now, if Rowan spotted goblins, he could shoot down the side of the mountain and straight to the road with very few obstacles in his path. His surefooted horse, Fior, had been in this spot many times and knew the path well.

Alder, his friend, and protector his entire life, sat on his own horse behind Rowan and looked carelessly out across the pass, mountains, trees, and road, not particularly caring what was where only that there was potential for a battle that day.

Rowan and Alder were both quiet and still. The horses did not snort or whinny, nor did they paw at the ground as horses tend to do when they are bored. Their only movement was the flickering of their tails to keep the stoneflies away. A faint breeze blew across the side of the mountain, stirring the branches of the thin pine trees that clung to life in the same way their roots clung to the cracks in the mountainside.

"Thankfully it is blowing from the west today," Rowan thought.

A noise could be heard at the bottom of the pass along the gravelly road, although the cause could not yet be seen. Alder sat up in his saddle and peered down. Rowan strained to see as well, his eyes not being as good as Alder's. A large group was coming by the sounds that echoed up the canyon walls. A troop of soldiers on horses came into view. Two by two they appeared. After six soldiers came into view, a richly adorned man and woman appeared on expensive-looking horses. Behind them, was a man with a purple banner adorned with a gold eagle, and then came more soldiers. They were from the kingdom of Midland and appeared to be heading for Kingsford.

A flock of quail burst from a rock formation on the side of the hill. Rowan and Alder turned in that direction as a host of goblins appeared, silently charging toward the group. This would be a fine prize for them.

Rowan kicked his horse and Fior shot down the path, kicking up dust and gravel behind him. Rowan could hear Alder's horse moving at the same speed.

Rowan fitted an arrow onto his bow. Suddenly, a goblin was on the path before him. He must have been slower than the others or had been waiting for most of the dangerous work to be done before moving in for the spoils. Fior was not afraid and charged through him. Alder had unsheathed his sword but did not need to use it on that particular goblin.

The soldier's horses whinnied and reared and charged about. The clang of clashing metal echoed through the canyon. Rowan and Alder burst out onto the road and into the chaos. The guards had been taken completely unaware. Most of them were already dead. The remaining guards were gathered around the two royal persons who had no weapons.

Rowan fired his arrows as quickly as possible, shooting goblin after goblin. Alder charged back and forth on his horse, slicing through the goblins. Rowan was thankful that it had been a small group.

The guards, seeing that they now had the upper-hand, moved forward and fought back. When all were slain except a few, the goblins attempted a retreat. Rowan was too skilled and hated the goblins too much to allow that and picked them off with his bow. He would not allow them to live, only for them to kill a more helpless villager tomorrow.

"Hail, our saviors!" cried the royal man. "We would have been slain and raided if it had not been for your coming and for your bravery. Who are you, if I may ask?"

Although he was grateful for his head still being firmly attached, Rowan could hear the notes of anger in the man's voice. He sounded as though he was not thankful for Rowan's appearance and that he was more annoyed with his own guards for not being able to handle the situation. This was not a man that enjoyed showing gratitude or thanks, and Rowan did not believe that he would keep any word he gave to honor the deed Rowan and Alder had just performed, not that Rowan expected much for his deeds at any time.

"I am Rowan, son of Lionn, and this is my companion Alder, son of Adder. At your service, my lord, although you have not yet told us your name," Rowan said in his most polite and honorable tone. Hinting that the more-polite thing to have been done was for the man to have said his name first and, "'at your service'," seeing how Rowan had just saved his neck.

The man shot a piercing look that was wasted upon Rowan and Alder, most of all Alder, seeing how he enjoyed this type of banter, and sat on his horse smiling and staring directly at the man.

"I am crown prince of Midland. I am Prince Aineolach. This is my sister, Princess Uiall." With that, Uiall pulled her horse forward a few steps.

"We are ever grateful for your assistance, lords. We would have perished with all our guards had you not arrived so quickly. Surely, we are the ones that are at your service, but as we are in the Pass of Handuin, we cannot offer you much, but instead ask for your services. We would pay you most handsomely if you would be willing to escort us to the castle at Kingsford. King Amadan waits for our arrival and we do not have enough men to protect us if we are attacked again."

Uiall said all of this very graciously and smiled and bowed her head in sync with her words as if this was a performance she had practiced many times before. Her performance gave Rowan an uneasy feeling in his stomach and he was unsure what to think of the woman. But he remembered that he did not care for her brother, either.

"We would gladly escort you from this place, although I will say the chance of another attack is very small. The goblins have only begun to push their way into the pass and have not taken up permanent residence. Send your remaining guards first, then your highnesses, and then we will follow."

They arranged themselves how Rowan described. Only three guardsmen were left of the original twelve and they led the way, followed by Prince Aineolach and Princess Uiall, and finally, Rowan and Alder.

The group was dismal. The soldiers were unhappy at the loss of their companions and the royal siblings were unhappy at being delayed and being forced to ride longer in the hot sun. Rowan and Alder did not mind heading back toward the town, but they did not really care for the royal party. They did not expect any rewards for their efforts, despite the promise of a handsome reward.

They would have liked a dinner out of it, but they expected bowing at the doors of the castle and being told that if anything could ever be done for them to not hesitate to ask, which was the worst kind of thanks in their opinion. The wealthy, that had the most ability to give and show gratitude, often had the strongest grip on their purses. Whereas the poor, who scraped by season to season and often knew want, were the most generous in their gifts and thanks. Rowan and Alder usually refused these gifts, unless they happened to be a hot meal at a warm table with good conversation and good stories.

They carried on through the white, sun-bleached canyon until the pass opened upon the great moors of Mòran Monadh, but only referred to now as Moorland. Several rivers, the largest being the Eabar River, ran down from the mountains and into the low plain on their way to the sea, creating a large moor. The moors were unpassable, except by a few well-known paths that hopped along all of the higher hills to avoid the waters. In the center of the moors, was a large hill.

The white city of Kingsford covered the hill. The city rose up strikingly against the greens, browns, and greys of the moors. The stone that was used to build the city had been hewn from the Dìonadair Mountains and, in moving the stone, created the Pass of Handuin. Many of the townspeople referred to the city as the King's Tooth for the way the glistening white stood against the dark colors of the moors. Rowan always thought that it must be a poor king to have only one tooth and brown gums and preferred Kingsford or the seldom-used Elvish name. Alder sneered at the old Elvish name for the city which had been Caradh but thought the new Elvish name of Trìloblaid was more fitting than the old. He too usually referred to the city as Kingsford, none of the peasantries now remembering the Elvish names. Beyond the city and the moors, was the sea, where all the water from the mountains and the moors drained.

"What a perfect swamp!" cried Prince Aineolach.

"Surely if we were not eaten by the goblins we will be eaten by flies before we get to the castle," complained Princess Uiall, swatting at the mosquitos that swarmed the group.

Rowan heard Alder chuckle under his breath. Rowan glanced at him. Alder, tall and fair with dark hair, was smirking from ear to ear and his sky-blue eyes shone out with light and laughter. Rowan smiled. The royal pair obviously had never been to Kingsford before and Rowan began to question what their business actually was with King Amadan, but he knew better than to ask. Prince Aineolach had been grumpy enough about giving his name and would most likely cut out his tongue for asking such impertinent questions.

"Do you know the way, Rowan?" Princess Uiall asked. "We have never been this way and we do not want to lose our horses on the moors. I would also prefer to proceed with more haste to remove ourselves from this wretched place."

"So, she cares more for her fine horses than for the soldiers laying dead at the bottom of the canyon," Rowan thought.

"Yes m'lady, but the path that we are on is well built and well-traveled. I do not think we will have a problem as long as your guards stay on it," he said, trying to sound soothing.

"If it is all the same, I would prefer that you lead us now, especially since we will soon be in the city and will need you to guide us to the castle."

This was a command. Rowan was made more uneasy by her. She commanded in a way that made you feel as though she was giving you a choice when you really had none. He wondered what the consequences of choosing incorrectly were in her kingdom.

So the group reformed with Rowan and Alder at the front and the guardsmen at the back.

The flies were bad. It was a hot and muggy day with a dark storm from the sea on the horizon. The royal siblings complained horribly of the conditions. Rowan, Alder, and the guards did not say anything but continued on in silence. The guards knew their place well, and that was below the places of the horses.

"What a horrid place to live," cried Princess Uiall. "Who would ever want to build a city in a swamp? I can hardly believe the rumors of it being prosperous and wealthy! Surely it must be rampant with disease from all this muck!"

"The swamp, although inconvenient for weary travelers, offers a good deal of protection against attackers, and is one of the reasons the city has withstood the darker times so well, which influences its prosperity. If you notice, as well your highness, the waters here are not stagnant as those of a swamp, which reduces the harmful waters," explained Rowan.

He could feel Prince Aineolach's eyes piercing into his back. No one talks to them in such a way, explaining the obvious and discounting their misery.

"It is surprising that a woodsman is so learned in defenses, history, trade, and the natural world. Surely you must come from a noble line and are not only a simple woodsman," Prince Aineolach said pointedly. Rowan felt the eyes of Alder shift towards him as he clenched the reins of his horse.

"I am only a simple woodsman, your highness. I was only wishing to redeem the moors for their few good qualities. I am not so learned in the matters you state, nothing compared to yourself, but I do love this city and land and have pride in it."

No one spoke for a while. Rowan felt a slow glow inside him. The prince knew of his family and knew that he was shamed. He could never escape it, even in his good deeds. He regretted his defiant words.

They reached the city before sunset and the captain rode to the gates to announce the prince and princess. Of course, the guards had been expecting their arrival and had seen their approach. As they passed through the gates, the fanfare began.

"These people must be in high favor of King Amadan," Rowan thought. There had certainly been more important people in the city in the past and they had received far less attention.

Kingsford was built upon a tear-drop-shaped mound in the moors. The mound was lowest at the tip of the teardrop, creating an advantage for the defenders should the city be attacked. Walls ran around the mound and layers of walls within the city divided it as the road lead closer to the castle. The poorest citizens lived within the first section of the city. These were mostly drunks, gamblers, widows, and elderly with no family. Although the city was clean compared to most, this section was the dirtiest, and refuse could be smelled on most days.

The main road leading to the castle was paved with the white stones the rest of the city had been built with, but the streets leading off the main street in this section were perpetually muddy.

Weavers, potters, carvers, masons, and bakers lived within the second section. It was much cleaner than the first section and it was well known that the refuse from this section was often dumped into the drains in the walls that led to the lower section. The side streets were not paved but were not as muddy and smelly as the streets below. The most notorious building within the second section was a building owned by Madame Belladonna. It was a well-kept, but out-of-the-way place with curtains over all the windows and a large, heavy door. A guard usually stood outside the door or directly within and acted as gatekeeper and animal wrangler, should a disturbance occur inside. Men haunted it and only desperate girls dared go near it.

The elite lived within the third section of the city. Lord Hammel, the Earl, and keeper of the merchant city New Market to the south, had a stately manor in this section. The manor house was two times the size of the other houses in the third section and four times the size of those in the poor section of the city. The grounds contained a stable and a garden, whereas everyone in the poorer sections was content to have communal gardens and a pen for the few animals that could not be left out on the moors. Other court nobility had their homes here, as well as the merchants and more profitable craftsmen, such as the seamstress and town builders. All of the streets in this section were paved and kept exceedingly clean. Refuse could be disposed of outside the city walls through small drain holes. The minter's workshop was in this section and was surrounded by soldiers at all times. Recently, the gold and silver coins, bonns, began to feature King Amadan, rather than the Star of Speur.

The White Horse Inn loomed over the market square in the western half of the third quarter. The stuffy inn was perpetually filled with aristocrats and knights. The class-conscious second-section citizens would have done anything to be allowed into the inn, but most of the city residents were content to haunt the Grey Goat Inn in the first quarter.

The biggest attraction and source of income for the city, however, was the Temple of Cruthadair. The temple split the main road in two like a river running around a rock. It was the largest temple in Utherion. The colored glass that filled the windows had been crafted by the elves. The gold-plated turrets had been built by the dwarves. All races had come together during the building of the city to build a monument to the gods as a symbol of unity. That unity had not lasted even a generation.

A large fence separated the temple grounds from the outside world. The dormitories, kitchens, storerooms, and other necessary buildings for the manach dotted the grounds. The library tower rose high above the temple with a domed observatory at the top. The eldest and wisest of the manach spent their time studying the stars, searching for the teachings and inner workings of Speur, the sky god that had painted the stars and was the most powerful of the Diathans.

People from all of Utherion, rich or poor, would travel to the temple for the sermons on the evening of the new moon. They would bring tributes and offerings to be burned during the morning bonfire and hope that the Diathans would grant their wishes.

The castle and its ground took up the entirety of the fourth section. Due to King Amadan's constant state of paranoia, this section was heavily fortified and held one garrison of soldiers at all times. A barracks, a training area, a very large stable and riding area, and a large kitchen and storehouse made up the outside perimeter of the grounds. The castle itself was a huge rectangular building with a smaller rectangle on top. Everything about the outside of the castle and out-buildings was plain and King Amadan hated all of it, having only ever drooled over the stories of the grand castles that had once been the houses of men in the east.

People hung out their windows and waved as the group passed by. The doors, which were painted the colors of the moors, were open and welcoming. The horses clip-clopped on the stone streets. Children jostled each other to get near the prince and princess, waving and shouting in the hopes that they would throw a coin. Rowan and Alder did not enjoy the great commotion that surrounded them. Rowan blushed at the idea that people were noticing him and Alder was stiff, feigning to keep aware of his surroundings, despite the uproar. Rowan kept his head down, but slowly navigated his horse to the castle. Prince Aineolach enjoyed every minute of the parade and held his head high and dignified. Princess Uiall waved and smiled.

Finally, they reached the castle steps. Banners hung from every place a man could reach to hang one. Guards stood at attention in full regalia. Surrounded by a dozen soldiers, King Amadan stood on the stone steps outside the great castle doors. He was fat and bald but wore many robes of fine materials from different lands and a large crown beset almost entirely with jewels in an attempt to hide both his fat and baldness. His beard was thinning, but still had some streaks of red running through it. The redness of his hair had always been a great shame to him and his family, given that all the great kings of old had thick, golden hair.

Next to him stood his current mistress with a sheepish, yet welcoming, smile across her angular face. Fine silks from the Elven lands hung loosely around her swelling body. She wore no crown or tiara, for the king had given up marrying his mistresses long ago. It was harder to explain the unexpected deaths of so many queens, rather than the unnumberable mistresses no one could remember the names of.

Behind King Amadan and his mistress Rowan could not remember the name of, stood his two sons and three daughters. Magadh, the oldest son, was almost as pompous, cruel, and pretentious as his father. He was a decent warrior, but he had no tact, no intelligence, and no true courage. He could pull out his sword quickly enough when he felt that he had been slighted, but the honor that he defended was a sham. Rowan had heard many tales about Magadh's escapades with the chambermaids of the castle. Magadh spent an unusual amount of time in the second section of the city for someone of his social ranking. Although Rowan paid little attention to gossip, he admitted that an unusual number of disappearances occurred for a place so well-guarded. Magadh was tall and still trim from his youth, but no one doubted that he would become fat and bald like his father. He at least had his family's blond hair that they had been so admired for.

The second son, Bacach, was lame. He was the youngest of the king's legitimate children and had been born without the lower half of his arm. He wore long, flowing sleeves to hide his missing arm. He would never be able to wield a sword, which was a disgrace to his family since they had long been seen as the defenders of men. However, even without his arm, he was the best-looking of the children. He was tall, fair, and had thicker blond hair than his brother. He looked the most like his mother over all of his siblings.

It was told that his mother was killed after his birth due to her no longer being able to produce "'whole'" children. His siblings resented him for the death of their mother, rather than holding their father accountable for the role he played in her poisoning. Regardless of his mistreatment at the hands of his siblings, Bacach did not hold grudges against the other members of his house and he was often lost in thought in the library. Because of his deformation, he spent most of his time studying books, maps, scrolls, lore, and runes. He was the only friend Rowan had within the castle.

The daughters of King Amadan were no better than hags. The eldest, Azalea, had hair to match her fiery temper. She was known to beat her maids regularly for anything she deemed a slight against her disposition or her looks, which were fair enough for a princess, but were nothing in resemblance to her mother's. The other two daughters, Rose and Lilly, were generally not noteworthy. They were spoiled brats and had no qualities that were at all becoming them. They did little and said very little in the presence of other people because what they did say was often irrational, haughty, or cruel and they would receive a swift rebuke from their father. All the chambermaids that belonged to the girls were treated cruelly. Each girl stood behind their father, now, richly adorned with flowing silk gowns, jewels, fur robes, and tiaras from distant lands.

King Amadan's many illegitimate children served within the castle, their mothers being long deceased. No one acknowledged them as King Amadan's children for fear of losing their heads. Even the new mistress, standing smiling by King Amadan's side, young, fair, and beautiful, was with child and vainly wore a fur robe in the hopes of hiding her bulging stomach.

A look of astonishment, changing to dismay and perplexity, crossed over King Amadan's face when he saw Rowan and Alder followed by a very sour prince and princess without a flagbearer and three battered soldiers.

"My friends, I welcome you to Kingsford and the realm of Amadania! Surely the road has not been well to you, seeing how you are escorted by woodsmen and very few of your own men at your side."

Rowan quickly dismounted his horse and offered his hand to Princess Uiall to assist her. She smiled a half gracious, half-expectant smile. Her steel grip was icy and her eyes were cold.

"You are most right, King Amadan," started Prince Aineolach after he had been helped off his horse. "We were waylaid by a large host of goblins as soon as we entered the Pass of Handuin. Many of my men were slaughtered. Thankfully, your woodsmen were near and were able to fight. Without them, we would have been killed or taken for ransom."

King Amadan fidgeted at the news of the goblins, but more so at the prospect of having to reimburse Prince Aineolach for his dead soldiers. "Please come inside! You are weary and you may tell me of your troubles after you have had time to rest, eat, and drink! Our vineyards from the south produce the best wine in all of Utherion."

Both royal parties were escorted inside, leaving Rowan, Alder, and the three surviving soldiers.

"Sirs, please come have a word with me," called the captain. Rowan and Alder looked at each other before moving closer to the captain. He was tall and broad with grey hair. Despite him being at least fifty, he did not look too old for combat. He instead looked as though he would be a dangerous opponent. He wore a heavy steel plate and, unlike his soldiers, did not wear a helmet. He studied Rowan and Alder for a moment before speaking to them.

"Rowan, son of Lionn, and Alder, son of Adder, I was not able to speak earlier and I apologize for that. I would now like to thank you and offer you my services in whatever you may someday need. Without you, we all would have perished. Prince Aineolach is not like his father and does not know the price of his head or he would have valued you more when you arrived. I am Captain Caraid, son of Curaidh, and I owe you my life." With this, he bowed slightly and began studying them again.

"We thank you, Captain Caraid, but we want for nothing. We keep no possessions, and we have little need for any more gold or silver than what we need to secure food and lodgings in the winter. Our deeds today were not for want of glory or profit, but to protect those who needed protection from a ruthless enemy. At this time, however, we must take our leave. Already, darkness is falling and we must secure lodging for the night." Rowan bowed with his hand over his heart, trying to seem as polite as possible, but also not wanting to give anyone associated with Prince Aineolach more information than what was necessary.

"I am sure this will not be the last time that we meet," nodded Caraid. He turned with his two men and headed toward the barracks.

Alder looked at Rowan with a smile. "What a lot of noise. I was quite content sitting upon the mountainside today, but instead, we find this lot and get dragged into their mess."

Rowan smirked. "Something tells me that this mess will not be cleaned up for quite some time. But come, we must hope that the inn is not full already or we will be sleeping on the streets tonight."

Climbing back onto their horses, they meandered through the city until they came to the Grey Goat Inn. Although the inn was in the first section of the city, it was not badly kept and was large enough for some twenty patrons to have a room. The rooms were cheap and clean. In Alder's opinion, the inn also had the best food to be found in the city. Alder had been on good terms with the owner Òstair, son of Òsta since Òstair was born. Alder had been on good terms with the owners of the inn since the inn had been built, several hundred years ago.

Wooden chandeliers covered in candles illuminated the tavern with a warm, but cheerful glow. Roars of laughter and conversation filled the room as some forty people were crushed into the tiny space. Every table appeared to be filled with men drinking wild oat whiskey and shouting in good and bad humor. Margie, the owner's daughter, was carrying clay mugs of the liquid when Rowan and Alder stepped through the door.

"I was wondering when I might see you two in here again. It's been almost a fortnight. The corner table is open in the back if you can get through this lot." Margie was a plump girl with dark, curly hair that was always pulled back and covered with a cloth. Her loose dress was of the same thick, wool, homespun that the working class of Kingsford preferred to wear. Her eyes shone brightly out from her fair skin. Both of which, would flash in a second when she was angered. She was kind, generous, and always quick to laugh, but was quick with a rolling pin when she needed it.

Rowan and Alder waded through the patrons until they reached the corner table in the back of the room. It was a little more shadowy, but it was close to the fireplace that almost always had a merry fire crackling within it.

Margie reappeared with a pot of tea and set it down expertly in front of the men.

"We have meat pie tonight," she chimed, looking at Alder with a smile.

Alder returned the smile. "You do know the way to a man's heart, Margie," he joked.

"What will you be having tonight, Mr. Rowan?" she asked, noticing the downcast mood Rowan was in.

"Whatever you have on hand that is simple. Do not go out of your way to prepare anything special."

She nodded and whisked off to the kitchen. Alder turned and studied him for a moment before speaking.

"You're not still upset over what that weasel of a prince said, are you?"

"We had just saved the man's life and my past still could not be overlooked," murmured Rowan.

"And that shows more fault with him than with you," replied Alder, staring at Rowan sternly.

Margie returned with a large meat pie for Alder and a small bowl of cabbage soup and the heavy, wild grain bread made from moor grass for Rowan.

"Master Rowan, it's been a long while since I have seen you so down. Is everything quite all right?"

Rowan smiled at her and patted her hand. "Yes, Margie, I am all right. Don't you mind me a bit."

She looked to Alder and Alder gave her a smile and a nod. They ate quietly, Alder eating his whole pie and Rowan swishing the bits of cabbage around in his bowl.

"I will have to try harder," said Rowan at last.

"By doing what? Getting yourself killed? We kill goblins and wildmen when we find them. You do not take the rewards offered for their heads. We could have bought land and built our own castle with all the money we could have collected, but you only take enough money to keep us from begging on the streets or from working as mercenaries. There is no more that you can do. You are a good man. Do not let the mistakes of others cloud your path."

They watched the goings-on of the tavern for a while.

Alder began to chuckle, and Rowan looked at him questioningly.

"Did you hear King Amadan when we were at the castle?" Alder asked.

"About Amadania? I was wondering when he renamed the realm."

"The way he emphasized it, I believe he passed an edict relatively recently."

They both laughed. When King Amadan passed an edict, no one had a choice in the matter. The process was only a formality to make it appear to the people and his nobles that they were being represented. The votes were cast anonymously, making all involved assume that the edict had been passed honestly, but a quick discussion usually revealed that assumption to be false.

They paid Margie for the food and spoke with Òstair about a room. They were able to purchase a small room with one large bed. Òstair knew that they were not particular about lodgings and sent them to one of the rooms that was about the size of a large broom cupboard. Alder, who could sleep in almost any circumstance, slept soundly. Rowan, however, spent most of the night thinking about the past.

Alder was not surprised to see Rowan sitting in a chair by the small window when he woke in the morning. He was not surprised that Rowan had not slept a wink when he inquired, which was the polite thing to do. Rowan had watched the sun rise over the white mountains and had sat thinking about things while Alder rose and dressed.

"Since you have been awake, I assume that you have put thought into our plans for the day. Are we going to the Pass of Handuin?" Alder asked while putting on his boots.

"I was considering riding farther than the pass," murmured Rowan.

"Whatever for?" Alder asked looking at Rowan sternly. "If we go north there is nothing but goblins and giants. If we go south, nothing but wildmen and pirates. There are only two of us. We would need an army to besiege any of those hordes. There is little glory or honor for the dead if no one can find the bodies."

Rowan had started thinking again when there came a knock at the door. Alder, never moving into a vulnerable situation without a weapon, picked up his sword and went to the door. There stood a small pageboy in the dark blue and silver tunic of Amadania.

"Excuse me, sirs, I am searching for masters Rowan and Alder," the boy, not older than eight, stammered and looked imploringly from Alder to his sword, and then to Rowan.

"There is nothing to be afraid of young squire," Alder soothed. "I am Alder, and my companion, Rowan, is there." Alder nodded to Rowan in the chair and the boy seemed to perk up.

"King Amadan, at the request of Prince Bacach, wishes for you both to attend the feast at the castle this evening. You will be seated at the king's table." The boy clicked his heels and ran off down the hall.

Alder shut the door and turned to Rowan. "I wonder what that is all about?"

"I cannot be sure, but I am sure that the other two princes are not going to be happy about it."

Chapter 2

The castle was alight from courtyard to turret. Guards were stationed every few feet. Nobles arrived dressed in silks, furs, and jewels. King Amadan, unlike his fathers, did not feast with his people and make merry. His feasts were reserved for the few that he deemed worthy enough for his presence. Rowan and Alder were not the people he deemed worthy of his presence.

Nevertheless, Rowan and Alder arrived to accept Prince Bacach's invitation. They did not own more clothing than what they wore, but they had managed to convince Margie to wash their belongings before the feast. She happily washed them, but she did make fun of Rowan and Alder mercilessly for it, especially at them having to slide the bundles in and out of the room with the door cracked. The clothes now smelled of woodsmoke, having been hung by the fire to speed their drying. Alder and Rowan had washed themselves, which was of equal importance. Goblin blood and dirt did not do well at the king's table.

A crier stood at the entrance to the great hall as nobles drifted through. "Shall we enter one at a time or as a couple?" asked Alder.

"We may enter together, but I will not offer you my arm," returned Rowan, noting the couple in front of them, dressed in deep-purple robes and glimmering with jewels in the torchlight.

They reached the crier, and he screamed their names to a room of people that were not paying any attention but were looking up and down the tables at all the delicacies that had been prepared and the many casks of alcohol that lined the walls. Rowan stared straight ahead, not wanting to meet anyone's eyes in case they were staring at him. Alder met the gaze of everyone that dared to look at him. He was well known throughout the city, being the only elf in their midst, but he did not speak to anyone and went out of his way to avoid being the center of attention. But many people were often enamored by his striking beauty and stature, and frequently stared at him.

Alder and Rowan reached King Amadan's table at the front of the room and bowed low. Prince Aineolach was seated with a scowl on his face on the king's right side, along with Prince Magadh and Prince Bacach. On King Amadan's left side, were his steward, his marshal, his mistress, and the four princesses.

"So you made it... Master Alder and Rowan," King Amadan said, not very excitedly. "Prince Bacach, my son, begged me to invite you due to his needing information. You may sit down at the end with him."

"Thank you, your highness." They bowed in unison. Alder locked eyes with King Amadan for a second, before the king adverted his gaze. Rowan and Alder found their seats next to Prince Bacach, who was quite happy to see both of them.

"It has been a long time since we have been able to have a conversation, Rowan! I hear that the goblins have moved into the pass. Can you tell me what you know?"

Rowan smiled at him. "Never a moment to spare, Bacach. We got word that the goblins had attacked some villagers in the pass and we decided to investigate. We did not know how the goblins were attacking or when, so we waited along the ridge with our horses. Prince Aineolach's people had just entered the pass when a group of about twenty or so attacked. We rode as fast as we could to help in battle and we were able to slay the entire host of goblins. I am not sure how many more goblins are in the pass. It may have been a small band of them for now, but they are emboldened enough to enter the pass and more will come. We will need guards within the pass to protect the villagers from the hordes that are bound to come. Otherwise, the pass will be overrun and no one will be able to cross safely. If we cannot guarantee the safety of the merchants and traders from Midland, our relationship and economy will be degraded; not to mention the lives that will be lost."

Bacach beamed at him. "You are better than any scout or advisor in this land. I wonder as to why the goblins are choosing now to move into the pass. As you said, they are emboldened. What forces are at work in the north that allows them to feel strong enough to move into our territory in such a way?"

"Has there been news from the dwarves or from the northern scouts? No news is ever good out of the south. The people of Whitecliff are always at war with the Spùinneadair and the wildmen still hold Sudland. Has this prince brought any other word?"

Bacach smirked. "This prince knows nothing of his own land or even the tales of his own forefathers. I questioned him about a few of his family's relics from the days of Roimhe Seo and he could not answer a single question and finally waved me off stating, 'True kings have no need to know the stories of the past. They only need to know how to move their line forward.' Which, if he means that his only job is to procreate so that his people may always have a king of his blood, then I have pity for his people and they surely want many things that he turns a blind eye to."

"Surely he does not have much to fear. The people of Daingneach battle with the dark forces of the south and he is protected by the mountains on all sides," Alder added.

Bacach again smiled. "But there are foes that may come out of the shadows of the north. The giants rule Fuamhaire and who can guess what creatures live in the Fae Forest."

Food was brought to the king's table now that the final guests had arrived and had been seated. It was a grand feast, with more food than most had ever seen and fountains of drink. After the food had been served, the servants danced at the king's orders.

Rowan glanced at Alder who prodded his remaining food with a chicken bone and stared absently at the table. Alder enjoyed dancing, watching or participating, but he preferred the loud, noisy, fast, and discorded dances of the taverns and festivals. He enjoyed the merry music and the breathless girls that were always happy to dance with him, him being extraordinarily beautiful. Alder was light-footed and nimble and did not grow tired or weary for hours, especially on such occasions. Rowan knew that it was his Elven blood that always moved him to music and dance, but Rowan did not discuss it. The dancing of the hall was slow, and rhythmic, and appeared as if it had been practiced many times over, which, knowing King Amadan, the servants had most likely been practicing since Prince Aineolach accepted his invitation.

King Amadan now, however, was becoming red in the face with drink and was laughing loudly at everything Prince Aineolach said, whether it was funny or not. His loud, boisterous laughter seemed out of place in the hall with the slow dancing and the monotonous music. He stood and the dancers left the room.

"With all the honor I may bestow upon him and all the blessings I wish for him, Prince Aineolach has asked for my daughter, Princess Azalea's hand in marriage and I have granted it. We may now join the two kingdoms of men into an unbreakable bond. Peace we will have for the long years to come."

A great roar of applause thundered throughout the room. Rowan glanced at Azalea who somehow did not know that this was the reason for Prince Aineolach's coming. She had turned deathly pale. The dancing and music again began, slightly more merrily this time. Princess Uiall and the princesses of King Amadan rose to leave, but King Amadan stopped Azalea.

"Do not be rude, daughter," he scolded. "He has done all of us a great service in taking you for his wife."

Azalea paled again and slowly approached her soon-to-be-husband. She curtsied and bowed her head.

"Thank you, husband," she murmured.

He smiled and nodded at her. He kissed her hand before bidding her good night.

"What a mess. Although there are few choices for us in the world, I daresay Azalea will be a fitting Queen for him. I am only unhappy that I will have to see that man multiple times a year now," Bacach whispered to Rowan.

"Has any lady been found for your brother?" Rowan asked in a low voice.

Bacach laughed. "He will have no ladies and no lady that is not held captive will have him. His reputation precedes him in every arrangement my father attempts to make. Magadh only wants the lowest scullery maid or seamstress he can find in the castle. He sullies them and then they are never seen again. Many an heir he would have throughout the kingdom if they were not lost upon the moors. I daresay that he will never marry unless my father buys a woman for him. But I do not feel that he should marry. I do not feel inclined to it myself, but not for the same reasons as him.

"But now comes the problem of Azalea's and Prince Aineolach's marriage. If my brother and I are to remain unmarried and have no heirs, then the lordship of Kingsford will fall to the heir of Aineolach and Azalea. The stewardship of Midland would most likely go to Uiall, for Aineolach would want his line to take over Amadania, which would technically be their birthright should it go uncontested. I am loath to think about what ruin would fall upon the kingdom if that day should come."

Rowan glanced at Alder and they all sat a while in thought, despite the thunderous noise around them. By this time, almost everyone was drunk and more than just the servants were dancing. Rowan had never thought about the fate of the kingdom from the inside. He had always been concerned with its defense and did what he could to keep outside evils well away from the borders. He had never considered the evil hearts of the children of King Amadan, and he had never thought about Bacach not marrying. His siblings mocked him, but he was still a prince and noble. Rowan was sure that many young ladies would be happy to marry him. But Bacach had said that he did not want a wife, not that he could not find one.

Still, he was young and Rowan was sure that Bacach would find a young maiden that would cause him to swoon. Bacach was younger than himself and Rowan avoided women in most cases. He found their company exasperating and he did not want to pull anyone else into his dishonor.

Alder, who had barely spoken, as was his way around the castle folk, stretched and yawned. Alder had spent several hundred years doing mercenary work for the royal family. King Amadan had been furious when Alder had given it up to raise Rowan, forcing King Amadan to show his hand more often in his own dirty work. The family believed that Alder had insulted the king, which was possible, given Alder's sarcasm, sneering, and general uncouthness. No one in the household spoke to Alder, save Bacach occasionally, and Alder did not mind.

Prince Aineolach and Prince Magadh rose from the table, whispering with devilish grins on their faces, and left the room giggling like little girls. King Amadan snored loudly with his head on the table.

Bacach looked to Rowan and Alder with a smirk. "Whereabouts are you two staying tonight?" he asked, knowing very well that they were homeless.

Alder returned the smirk. "Maybe on this table next to your father."

Bacach laughed. "I will have the servants prepare a room for you. You will stay as my guests and have breakfast with me in the morning. I may have an errand for you by then."

Bacach clapped his hands and servants appeared immediately. They whisked off to prepare a room. After Bacach finished his wine, he led Rowan and Alder through the castle to their room.

"Is there anything else you need?" Bacach asked before leaving them.

"Only to tell you that you are a fine friend and that I owe you a service far greater than my life," Rowan murmured, staring at their room.

Bacach laughed and turned away down the hall to his own quarters.

The room appeared to have been the royal nursery many years ago. Two large feather beds were across from each other with a small table between them. Heavy bedspreads and furs had been thrown back and perfectly clean sheets shone brightly in the candlelight. A short table with short chairs stood next to the window with long velvet curtains blocking out the world as if waiting for their tutor to throw open the curtains and begin Rowan and Alder's lessons. A padded armchair sat next to the fireplace, welcoming whoever wished to warm themselves. A fire crackled merrily in the fireplace, warming the damp room with its heat and glow. Tapestries, less gruesome than the tapestries in the great hall, covered the green-plastered walls.

"I am glad for your friend," Alder began. "He owes us nothing, but treats us like we are lords."

"That is the way of Bacach. Noble, wise, generous, and of the utmost humility."

"Well then you at least have the last in common," Alder smiled.

They had just begun to take off their boots and remove their belts when a commotion came from the hallway. Alder crept to the door and peered out for a second before sticking his whole head out. He frowned and shut the door.

"What was that about?" Rowan asked.

"Just the fine princes casting out the poor wretches they have spent the last hour with. I believe that they are withholding the poor girls' clothes and sending them off into the dark naked."

"I would like to hold my knife to his throat for what he does to them," Rowan murmured.

"You would be doing a great service to the women of two kingdoms if you did, however, his father might take offense." Alder flopped onto his bed and almost immediately fell asleep.

Rowan laid back on his bed. It was as if he was sleeping on a cloud. The furs and blankets were warm. The feather pillows were heavenly.

The morning came swiftly. Rowan stirred before Alder, as per usual. Alder had buried himself under his blankets and furs in the night and now appeared to be a large bear sleeping on the bed. Rowan let him sleep and went to the great windows at the side of the room. The day was grey. The sun was hidden behind the clouds and the sea was dark and tumultuous.

Rowan had always loved the sea, but he loved the trees and mountains more. He knew in his heart that he would never be truly satisfied without being able to roam in the woods.

Rowan looked upon the grounds and saw no one. A few guards wandered about the walls, but none of the castle residents or nobles had appeared. The entire population of the castle was still in their bedchambers or passed out in the great hall. Rowan stoked the embers that had burned down in the night, sank into the large and comfortable armchair that was still warm from the fire, and dozed off again.

He awoke to a knock at the door. Alder was still in bear form, but the rhythmic breathing had stopped. Rowan went to the door and opened it. An exceedingly pretty maid bowed.

"Prince Bacach wished to inform Lord Rowan and Lord Alder that there will be breakfast in the library in an hour. He wished to inform the lords that there is hot water in the bath hall if the lords wish to enjoy it." She glanced about the room quickly, and a slight look of disappointment came when she did not see Alder. She bowed and scurried down the hall.

"Does he mean to tell us that we smell?" Alder asked, emerging from the pile of blankets.

"He means to tell you that your hair looks as though you were a fledged chicken and that you smell like the henhouse," Rowan said, noting that Alder's hair stood in all directions. Alder began bawking and rested his head back on the pillow.

"Why are we not princes? Surely we would be better than any of this house, save Bacach."

"Maybe your elf mother is a great queen somewhere and you are a prince," Rowan proposed.

"If the elves are anything like the royalty that reside in Kingsford, it would not be unlikely that she is a queen.

But a sore king they would find me. Repentant they would be of their folly of forsaking children to the world when they are equally guilty in their shame." Alder was always angry when his mother was brought up.

"I intend to make use of the bath hall. Do you wish to join me?" Rowan asked, not wanting to think of his own family line.

"If I really look as frightful as you claim, then I must go before we meet Bacach, though how bad can I smell when we bathed yesterday?"

Rowan and Alder picked their way through the silent castle until they found a room on the lowest level with a great pool of water. Light shone through a few windows at the top of the wall, which Rowan assumed to be ground level on the outside. Carved pillars held up the ceiling and the statues of maidens danced about the room. The room was empty and the water was calm and clear. Steam wafted into the air and filled the room with the pleasant aroma of flowers. The men undressed and lowered themselves into the water. The water was hot and goosebumps shot across Rowan's skin as he sank into its depths.

"This water has healing properties. It comes from deep within the mountains and flows underground to the sea," Alder murmured as he relaxed deeply in the water.

Rowan did notice that his mood seemed to lift slightly and that his body seemed to feel lighter He dunked himself in the water, in an attempt to dissolve his worries. His mind seemed to clear and he felt that the day was full of possibilities.

After a time, they dressed and went to find Bacach in the library.

The library was not a large room, as Rowan had expected. It was slightly bigger than a bedchamber, but every inch of wall space was covered in bookshelves. The wall opposite the double doors was almost completely taken up by windows and blue, damask curtains. A fireplace broke open a spot on the wall to the right and warmed several blue sofas. The familiar aroma of old books and crackling fire hung about the room. Other than the snapping of the fire, no other sound broke the stillness. A table had been spread with a hearty breakfast in the center of the room.

Bacach stood by the fireplace, staring into the flames.

"Hello, friends," he called as Rowan and Alder entered the room. "Please sit down and we will eat together. I have been awake most of the night and have many questions for you."

Bacach's eyes shifted over them quickly and he seemed pleased at their clean appearance.

Rowan and Alder both sat at the well-laden table. Rowan ate a simple portion of bread and fruit, whereas Alder ate heartily of everything that was available. Bacach did not eat very much but smiled at his guests as they ate.

"Alder, you have lived in the city for several hundred years, aye since just after the city itself was built. Your father was a lord for the first king and helped in the construction of the castle. There are not many records of what our people did before that time, the elves being the only record keepers of that time. There are rumors of certain artifacts that are believed to have been given to the king by the elves as a token of his right to rule, but there is little proof of them existing at all. Tell me now, have you ever heard of the Clach Nèimh?"

Alder looked at Bacach with curiosity. "I had heard stories of it when I was a child. It seemed more like something from a fairy story they tell children than something that might actually exist. I was born after the elves visited the city and do not know anything about the gifts that they brought to Kingsford. You know my mother left after I was born, so I never heard the stories from the elves. I have heard that many of the treasures from that time, being extremely valuable, have been sold off by these lesser kings that do not honor the ties that used to exist between elves and men. If such a stone did exist, and if it were to be in Kingsford, I am sure that one of your grandfathers would have had it set inside the throne or in the crown," Alder scoffed.

"What is this stone?" Rowan asked, not having heard of it before.

"The Clach Nèimh, or the Stone of Heaven, was said to have been a gift from the creator to the elves for their hard work and diligence in the Roimhe Seo. Some say that it was a gift from the dwarves to the elves when the elves helped remove the first waves of goblins from the dwarven mines. Others say that it dropped from the sky from the sun and therefore shines with the sun's light. The stone is white and sparkles like snow in the sunlight. But the stone changes color to the color of the soul of the wearer. If one's soul is consumed by wrath, the stone will be redder than a ruby. If one's soul is good and pure, the stone will stay the glittering white. The stone is said to have all the powers of heaven within it and it can give the holder anything their heart desires. Yet there is no one alive today that has seen it, and most have forgotten that it ever existed if it did indeed exist at all. That is why I hoped that Alder had heard stories of it."

"Why do you ask for it? No good could come from such a stone in a world such as ours," Alder asked, somewhat pointedly.

"There are dark forces at work in these lands," Bacach explained. "If the stone does exist, and the last 'known' location of the stone was in Kingsford, the enemy's eyes will be looking in our direction. That may be why the goblins are beginning to push into our realm. That may be why the enemies have withheld any advance into our kingdom until this point. Taigheland is nothing but farmland to our south, and yet the wildmen have not entered our realm to plunder it as they did in Sudland. Why do they stay their hand? We have great armies and Kingsford and New Market are well protected, but seldom do our enemies cross our borders and when they do, they are always in small, desperate groups. They fear us. But why do they fear us?"

"If that is true, then when spies discover that we do not have the stone, we will be attacked," Rowan added.

"Or worse," Alder proclaimed. "If the enemies to the south believe that we have the stone and they desire it, they will prepare a great army and siege Kingsford."

"That is my fear," claimed Bacach. "If the stone is hidden within the castle, we must find it. If a great host of enemies attack, then perhaps we can use the stone to defend the city or perhaps even turn them away with them having the knowledge that we have the stone. But if the stone is not here and the enemy believes that it is hidden in the castle, they will tear it apart stone by stone and slaughter our people. I wish to discover news of the stone, but I know not where to look first. The elves are loath to speak to my kindred at this time and the dwarves to the north seem to be the least likely to have found the stone. Perhaps it was the dwarves of Fortar, them being the golden dwarves."

"But to send a host to chase a relic that may not exist is folly. Many would surely die along the road. Even if the stone is within the castle, who here can wield it?" Alder asked.

Bacach sat back in his chair and sighed. He knew the truth of Alder's words. He was the only person of the royal line that was pure enough to wield the stone and not fall slave to its powers. Yet, with only one arm, he could not fight and the enemy may not fear him even with the stone.

"Why do you fear hosts marching upon the city so suddenly?" Rowan asked. "There is little reason to expect it soon and there is a great distance between the Pass of

Puinnsean and Kingsford. We could form a great host ourselves before such an army could reach us."

"Our neighbors are weak against the enemies that constantly flow from the Plains of Hutuloth. If a great host were to march upon any of them, I fear that they would fall quickly. Once they fall and the enemies cross the Dìonadair Mountains, we will be trapped. We have no means of escape once the enemy crosses the mountains. I am ashamed to say it, but we do nothing to stop the waves that are rising around us. We sit comfortably within our castle and we turn blind eyes and deaf ears to the world around us that is begging for help. When they fall, we will be the only kingdom that stands in the way of complete darkness. My family has fallen into darkness and corruption. They lust for partners, gold, and drink. They do not care about what goes on outside the castle walls."

"You said that you had an errand for us, Bacach, tell me now, what you would have us do," Rowan said after a long silence.

"I believe that there is a book in the library of Kingsland that may have more information. The historian, Eachdraiche, went there in his exile many years ago to escape my grandfather. If there is information on the whereabouts of the stone, if it was ever in Kingsford, he would have written about it. He was an elf and was sent to help our kingdom, but he is now dead and no one ever knew what his errand was."

"How are we to get into the library?" Rowan asked.

"Perhaps if you offer protection to the royal wedding party on their return home you will be granted lodging in the castle," Bacach smiled.

"Are we invited to the wedding feast?" Alder asked, inquiring about payment.

"Of course," Bacach laughed. "You will be my guests and I daresay my father will not mind. He will be so excited for the union that he will not know who is present."

"What shall we do until the wedding? You have not told us when it is to be held," Rowan added.

"I have not heard a word of when the wedding will take place. My father will be eager to have it and I would guess that it will be as soon as possible. Until then, you are to stay in the castle as my guests. You may keep your room and go wherever you choose. We will be sending a garrison to the Pass of Handuin to protect it for the people of Midland and you will not be needed there. I do not believe that goblins would dare attack it with a company of soldiers camped within it."

"You offer us a mighty gift for such a small task." Rowan bowed. Bacach shook his head.

"I do not believe that this will be any small task. The road will be safe, I am sure. We will send many soldiers with you and surely Prince Aineolach will send for his own. The trouble will be in finding the book."

The day passed without much ado for Rowan and Alder. They moved their horses to the castle stables and spent much of the day wandering the halls. Rowan wanted to have a complete layout in his head, for he did not know when he would ever be given the opportunity again. He spent a few days searching for any hidden ways that could lead them to the stone.

From the great entryway doors of the castle, one walked through a small corridor that was filled with great carved pillars. The entryway then opened into the great hall. The great hall was a huge room with many windows lining the ceiling. White columns twisted up to the ceiling and formed arches, supporting the floors above. The white stone had been taken from the mountains and had been polished for the walls and the floors, giving the room an unnaturally clean appearance. Torches were attached to the pillars and walls and three gold, branched chandeliers hung from the ceiling with heavy chains. Great statues of former kings stood between the pillars. Each statue was slightly bigger than the last, showcasing the growing egos of the line. The banner of Amadania was dark blue and silver with two silver swords clashing above a silver star and hung from everywhere it could be hung. Many tapestries hung from the walls, showing the kingdom's history, but slowly these had been replaced with tapestries ordered by King Amadan and his father. The new tapestries showed events, real or unreal, that King Amadan and his father had thought important.

Alder was always disgusted by the sight of these tapestries, having seen the original tapestries and knowing that the new tapestries were lies. The tapestry that bothered him the most was of King Teigan and his son Prince Amdar ridding the city of elves.

A door with a spiral staircase at the end of the great hall led to the throne room. The throne room was a smaller version of the great hall. Rugs, tapestries, and the skins of animals and beasts that had been hunted by former kings covered every square inch of space. The king's throne sat at the top of a set of five stairs. On a lower level was a lesser throne for his mistress and another throne for the heir to the kingdom, which was currently held by Magadh. The dwarves had given the molded silver throne with deep-blue, silk cushions to King Taighe at the completion of the castle. Blue and white stones glittered from the top of the throne and were meant to represent the stars of Speur above the king's head. King Amadan, however, was not as illustrious as his forefathers had been. King Teigan, King Amadan's great, great, great-grandfather, had begun the downfall of his line when he forsook the Elven ways of peace, humility, and generosity, and began to seek wealth and became proud. He cast out all elves within the kingdom and forbade them to come hither again, stating that they were nothing but witches, charlatans, and gypsies out to prevent others from making a way in the world. Thus, the line of the king had fallen into black days.

Two passages ran away from the great hall with stairways at the end. The hallway to the left led to the armory, the treasury, and the guardroom. The hallway to the right led to the more important storerooms and to a secret entrance that allowed the servants to carry food in from the outside kitchen. The second level of the castle contained the royal families' bedchambers, the guest chambers, the study, and the library. The bath hall and the dungeon were on the lower levels of the castle. This dungeon was unoccupied, being the dungeon for political prisoners and the main prison being attached to the barracks. All the halls were lined with rugs, tapestries, and sculptures. A fair number of antiques and rare objects were on display in the hallways from the days before the downfall of the royal house.

Rowan did not know where the Clach Nèimh could be if it was within the castle. Even on inspection from the outside, he could not discern where any hidden chambers could possibly be located. The castle was square and the rooms met up exactly how they should. That would only leave the lower level of the castle or a hidden compartment within one of the rooms.

Alder had looked through the lower level and saw no indication of a secret room. To this, he only said, "If you were trying to hide the most powerful object in Utherion, would you not hide it beyond all sight of others, as well? I do not doubt that there is an enchantment over the true hiding spot. Perhaps that is the reason the elves were cast out. I am only half and do not have their eyes or wisdom."

"I do not believe the elves were cast out because of the stone. Only King Taighe would have known where the stone was hidden because he would have directed the building of the hiding spot. It does not seem that he told his children of the whereabouts because there is no other knowledge of the stone being here. The elves lived in peace with Kingsford for many generations after the death of Taighe and his sons."

"Only after the death of King Taighe. You may be right, but I have few other ideas as to where it could be hidden."

"The chambers, perhaps, but the only one of us that may enter them is Bacach and I am sure that he has searched the entire castle."

In the evening, a great feast was always presented, given that so many guests were residing in the castle, many of which were used to eating large amounts. Alder and Rowan were not used to having so much food so often and their appetites were small compared to that of King Amadan, Prince Magadh, and Prince Aineolach. Prince Bacach ate slightly more than Alder and Rowan, but still a much smaller portion than the others. A never-ending stream of whiskey and wine flowed from decanters. Rowan and Alder politely refused to have it even set in front of them. Bacach drank small amounts of wine. The others drank large amounts of whiskey and wine every night and King Amadan couldn't pass a single evening without becoming roaringly drunk.

"Why do you abstain?" Prince Aineolach called across the table to Rowan and Alder one night, quite drunk. Rowan and Bacach paled at the question, but Alder's eyes lit with fire.

"Aye, I know why you abstain Rowan, son of Lionn. Your father was a drunk and your mudder was a drunk whore gypsy. You fear that you will be a drunk, but a gypsy you already are. Homeless and wandering ceaselessly. Dare I say this is the longest time you've resided in one place? Dead on the moors your father is. Drunked and drowned he was, but where did your mudder go hither? Back to her whore gypsy ways, leaving you to the woods and beasts. Are you the eldest of your sisters or do you not know?" Prince Aineolach slurred and sloshed the dark red wine from his cup, his eyes never leaving Rowan. All the time Aineolach was speaking, King Amadan laughed and pounded the table.

Rowan stared at his plate, barely breathing. His stomach had dropped with his spirits and his mind. He gripped his tunic and then let go over and over again. He felt as though he could vomit and he tried to repress the nervous shaking he knew would overcome him if this assault continued. Alder was furious, but it was Bacach that spoke first.

"Sir, you attack, dishonor, and anger my guests and friends. Prince or no prince, such words in the days of old would have been grounds for a duel. Given that you are drunk beyond your wits, an apology and a swift removal from the table is all that is necessary."

Magadh, being drunk himself, laughed more loudly than his father at his brother's boldness. "With your words, you anger your elder brother and his friend, half-born. Get thee and thy guests away from the table of your king and future king lest we cut off the other arm, or maybe thy leg so that you will be half in form as you are half a man."

Bacach again paled and met Rowan's eyes. Rowan was now more grieved that his shaming had swelled to include Bacach. Bacach, Rowan, and Alder all rose from the table and left the great hall. Alder ran to their room and slammed the door, the sound echoing through the castle. Rowan and Bacach stood in the hallway in silence.

"I would like to apologize for my presence at your table," began Rowan. "I have brought shame and ill words upon you. You have only shown me kindness and I have repaid you by throwing you to the dogs."

"Rowan, you are my only friend in this world and you brought nothing upon me. The tormenting that was brought upon me tonight is the same tormenting that is brought upon me almost every day and every night by at least one member of my family. I am Bacach the half-born. My father only wished to give Magadh an Elvish name because he is the heir to the throne but could name me nothing else but lame, so he did so in the Elven tongue. Every time my name is said, I am mocked. My mother was ill-used by the time of my birth and it is little surprise to me, knowing what I know now, that I am the way that I am. But I do not blame anyone for it. It is my load to bear. I only hope that someday I can prove useful to my kingdom in some small way, though I know that it will not be in any feat of strength."

"What would you have me call you, if not by the name your father has given you?"

Bacach smiled. "I will go by my given name unless I prove useful in the future." Rowan put his hand on Bacach's left shoulder.

"You will do far greater things than any of your household and the elves themselves will give you a name worthy of your deeds."

Bacach laughed now. "And you, my dear Rowan, will have the highest kings of Utherion bowing at your feet."

Rowan smiled at this and felt his heart lift. Only two people in this world believed in him and saw him for more than what he was. He would protect them with his life. He looked into Bacach's sad, but smiling face and saw a strange flicker in Bacach's eyes. Bacach's expression changed quickly and, with a hasty goodnight, retired to his bedchamber.

Alder was firing arrows into the banner of Amadania with Rowan's bow when Rowan entered the room.

"I daresay that is treason," Rowan said as he shut the door.

"As I am a half-elf, I choose to be counted among my Elven line tonight and claim that I am not a subject of the fool king." He let loose another arrow and it struck the center of the star. "Let them come at me for treason and call death upon me."

"Elves are illegal, to begin with, but since you use my bow, I am now an accomplice," Rowan shrugged.

"Let them lay a hand upon you."

Another arrow whipped past and into the banner.

"What will we tell Bacach of the banner?"

"Tell him that his castle is falling into ruin and is plagued with moths that seek to destroy the very threads that hold this kingdom together."

"If King Amadan catches word of that he will have his men out burning moths rather than fighting goblins."

Alder lowered Rowan's bow at this and looked at him. "King Amadan's men do not fight the goblins. We and the other woodsmen fight the goblins. We and the men of Taigheland fight the wildmen to the south. The king's men fight boredom in his halls and about the city walls. Them being sent to the Pass of Handuin will be the first time many of them have been sent outside the city other than to collect firewood or to escort the merchants."

Alder now picked up his sword. "What do you mean to do with that?" Rowan asked, not afraid of Alder's actions or judgment, but concerned for the decorations within the room.

Alder looked at the sword in his hand, thinking about why he had picked it up. "I should go to the armory or else Bacach will find himself king in the morning and that he has two fewer friends in the world." Rowan stepped away from the door and let Alder pass. Alder slammed the door behind him, which took a great deal of effort for ordinary people, being made of wood several inches thick.

Rowan sighed and sat in the armchair by the fire. He rested his head against the back of the chair and closed his eyes. He tried not to think of what had been said. *Why should it be abhorred that I avoid drinking? It plagues the mind as well as the body,* he thought to himself. *It brings down kings and honorable men and creeps into their minds until it grips them. To that, they claim that there is no harm and then it is said that they hold their alcohol well. While those who wish not to plague their bodies and minds are considered shallow, cynical, and 'different'. But only because great kings and lords drink as much as they please and the lowest attempt to keep up with them is it accepted.*

Rowan tried to comfort himself but in vain. He would never be accepted or have honor and he would have to learn to accept that, despite his good deeds. The fire was burning low when a knock came on the door. Rowan opened his eyes. "You may enter," he called, thinking that it was one of the servants coming to check the fire.

A cloaked figure entered the room and removed their hood. Rowan was surprised to see Princess Uiall. He had not seen her since the great feast the day after their arrival. "I came to offer my apologies, Master Rowan," she said in a somewhat humbled tone. Rowan was aghast, but in his heart, felt something to be amiss.

"I need no apology from you or your brother, your highness. What was spoken was truth and although I would have wished for none to have known it, many do and it cannot be helped that you should learn of it as well."

"I had heard of the story in my own kingdom, well before ever meeting you. Yet, for a man of such low ranking in the world, you saved our lives and to that deed, we are bound to you. Before we can repay you, I would ask a service from you."

"What would that be, your highness?"

"The wedding of my brother and Princess Azalea will be in a week. After the feasts, we will return to our own kingdom. I ask that you escort us back to our kingdom. There will be a few nights of feasting and you are welcome to partake in those if you wish. My brother will not suffer you to be at his table, but you may surely sit at another table. Once in our own kingdom, there will be more ways in which we may pay you for your services."

Rowan thought about her words for a moment. She was asking him to escort her back to Midland and for his services, he would receive food. For saving her life, he had not earned a place of honor at the table, but somewhere in a dark corner of the room where he might not be seen by anyone of importance. She had not mentioned his lodging, which led him to believe that it would not be in the castle. But then he thought of Bacach and what he had said. In the library, there could be a book concerning the stone.

"I will do this for you. I only ask that I may be allowed to tarry in your library for a little while. I enjoy reading and have looked over many of the things in the library here, I spent much of my childhood in the castle, you know. I wish to see if there are any books that I have not yet read."

Princess Uiall laughed. "I did not know and I would not have thought you for a great reader, but you may look upon the books if that is your wish. I cannot say that I have seen the library of Kingsford, but I am sure that you will not be wanting new books in Kingsland. Now that I have your answer, I will leave you."

Rowan stood and bowed. "Good evening, your highness," he murmured. She only smiled and left the room.

After a while, Alder returned, and Rowan told him about the strange coming of Princess Uiall and of their conversation. "She makes me uneasy," Alder said, falling back onto his bed, still holding his sword.

"There is something in her eyes that seems piercing and she speaks as though you have a choice in her errands when you have none," Rowan added.

"It is very gracious of her to offer no true payment for our services besides a few meals. There are peasants that offer more and it means more, given that they have less to give," Alder sneered.

"The only consolation is that we will have the chance to go through the library and look for the book Bacach told us about."

"I have searched the library here and have found no clues regarding the stone. I am sure Bacach has read every book in the library and was dismayed over finding nothing. My hope is that the stone does not exist and that it has escaped from the minds of everyone within Utherion. But in my heart, I feel that that cannot be and instead, I will hope that there is a book in the library with the precise location of the stone and a clear description as to how we may use it."

Rowan chuckled. "If it were as easy as that, I would write a dozen books about how our lives may be improved and have you read them to our benefit."

The day of the wedding was bright and merry. The entire city bustled like a disturbed ant hill with anticipation. Flowers, ribbons, and wreaths adorned almost every home. Feasting, drinking, and all other forms of merrymaking were happening throughout. The castle was no less busy. Lords and knights were arriving from all across Amadania and Midland. They brought lavish gifts and were all dressed in their finest clothes and jewels.

Rowan and Alder would not be attending the ceremony. Being friends of the last-born prince did not hold a high enough esteem to be given two highly sought after seats. But they did not mind. They had no interest whatsoever in wedding ceremonies. Especially not that of Prince Aineolach and Princess Azalea. They sat upon the city wall, staring out at the ocean, far away from all the revelry.

"Do you really think it's out there?" Rowan asked.

"Is what out there?" Alder returned.

"The land they used to sing about when we were children."

"Tìr na Sìth? I cannot believe that it is, though it is pleasant to think about from time to time. A land of peace and quiet like the beginning of days. A land where all people are kind and good-hearted. Where people care about their fellow man and do not turn a blind eye, or only give when they are being watched. It cannot exist or it would have been overrun long ago. The forces of darkness are far more plentiful and eager than the powers of good."

"But the powers of good are always able to chase away the darkness."

"Only when those who do good mean to do good and do not outstretch a hand to give while taking with the other."

Rowan fell silent and stared across the sea, trying to imagine faint trees in the distance. He wanted to believe that a land could exist, but he knew that it never could in a place such as Utherion. Alder was right. There would always be too many people that used false generosity in order to bind others, to make others dependent, or vowed to them by oaths.

"If you were marrying Azalea today and becoming king what would be your first order of business?" Rowan asked.

Alder laughed. "To end one of our lives. Loath am I to think about marriage, but it would be dreadful indeed to be married to one such as her. Beyond burying her in an unmarked grave somewhere far to the south after an untimely death, I would hold a feast in which everyone is invited. Not just lords and knights, but even the lowest peasants. But it would be a feast in which everyone contributed and could show their prowess. Then I could eat the finest foods across the realm."

Now Rowan laughed. "Of course, your stomach would come first. Much, I expect, to help with the mourning of your dear wife. Though I say I would set her horse dashing across the moors."

"You have a plan for how you would kill her. I did not plan that much. What would be your first order of business?"

"My first wish would be to invite the elves to train the people in medicine. Many are afflicted in ailments of the mind and soul and I have heard that the elves know how to cure them, but they do not share their wisdom with the likes of men now and men long neglected their willingness to teach."

"Well, if that was your first order of business, perhaps you would not have to kill Azalea, only have her mind cured of its ailments."

The bells of the towers throughout the city began to ring. "So the wedding is over," Alder acknowledged. "What time is the feast to take place?"

"Bacach said a while after the bells. The marriage documents would need to be signed and the wedding party would ride throughout the city for all to see. It is likely that we will be able to see them from here," Rowan explained, looking over his shoulder towards the castle.

They both turned toward the castle and they could see the road that led to the castle gates. The gates were open and the entire city flocked to the road to watch the prince and princess exit the castle. After a short time, they appeared on their horses. Only the banner of Midland was carried in front of the wedding party, as was custom. Marriage was the final step for Prince Aineolach to take the crown in his own realm, his parents both being dead, and he was the happiest Rowan had ever seen him. He smiled and waved to the peasants and threw small coins. Azalea, dressed in pink silks and shrouded in flowers, smiled and waved, but was not happy. Rowan wondered who she had planned on marrying instead. Only a few princes were left in the world and there were far fewer that would be interested in her or her father's line. She would be a cruel and dark queen, most likely crueler and darker than Princess Uiall was in her own land. The wedding party turned out of sight.

"Shall we make our way toward the castle? It will most likely take a while with everyone carrying on in such a way in the streets," Alder advised.

"You are likely right. I do not believe we will be granted admission to the feast if we are not with Bacach to escort us."

They climbed down from the wall and began making their way toward the castle. Alder had been right. The streets were thronged with people dancing, singing, and drunkenly wandering. The smells of food came from everywhere and oat whiskey, and wines were spilled across the street. Flowers had been thrown from the windows and in front of Princess Azalea's horse. The delicate blossoms were now being trampled under hundreds of feet.

Rowan, trying to bump into as few people as possible, felt a small tug on his pocket. With the lightning reflexes of the hunter and warrior, he caught the small arm of a child, his small purse of coins in the boy's hand. Rowan wheeled upon him. The boy glared at him with a sour, yet defiant expression. A soiled hat that was too big for the boy covered his entire head, casting a shadow over his eyes. His clothes had been patched many times over and he was filthy. Rowan noted the boy's swollen pockets, the boy's healthy complexion and stomach, and the lack of dirt under the fingernails of a child that was supposed to be on the streets. This was not a starving boy.

"For less than thievery of my personal belongings have I taken men's arms. For less than the plundering of an entire town's pockets have I taken men's lives," he whispered clearly, fixing his eyes on the boy's. The boy's eyes became wide. Alder now stood behind Rowan with his hand on his sword. The boy looked from their faces to Alder's sword, to Rowan's bow and his dagger in his belt, and then back to their faces. The boy dropped the coin purse and slipped his small hand through Rowan's now relaxed grip and fled into the crowd of people.

"He soiled himself, Rowan."

"I had not intended for that to happen."

Chapter 3

After a long while, they reached the castle. The commotion within the castle was slightly less than that of outside, but it was easier to walk through the halls than the streets.

"Why does nothing ever befall you?" Rowan asked Alder. "Always when a drunken man gets aggressive, it is with me. When there is an attempt at robbery, it is from me. Why is it never you? Not that I wish them to befall you, it is just that there is an equal chance for these things to befall you, but it only ever falls upon me."

Alder laughed. "It is the ears," he said, tugging on his pointed elf ears. "People see my features and assume that I am an elf sorcerer and will do some great harm to them. They assume that I must be great to defy the will of King Amadan. But it is quite the opposite. He can do as he wills to me, for I care little. We had our little disagreement, but he will keep me around for as long as he thinks me useful, working for him or not. People also see me as… something or another for being the only person to ever insult the king and keep his head. It helps that most people fear swords, as well." He laughed and patted his sword in his belt.

"There you two are!" came Bacach's voice from behind them.

They both turned to see Bacach in all his royal splendor coming toward them.

"You look quite marvelous," Alder said with a grin.

Bacach, who was never adorned, was wearing a dark blue silk tunic with silver embroidery and a long fur cape. He was wearing a sword, a coronet, and a large gold necklace, all of which he never wore.

"If you were given your father's scepter, you would look like a king," Rowan smiled. Bacach, however, frowned.

"Unfortunately, I am to remain dressed like this for the remainder of the evening. My father 'requested' that we all dress for the occasion, and by that, he means the arrival of the guests from Midland. Do either of you have anything else to wear?"

Alder and Rowan both stared at him without answering.

"Right. I apologize. If you return to your room, I will have some things sent up for you for the feast. I do not mean offense, but—"

"We are dressed as woodsmen and your father and the groom will be displeased if we appear as such, especially seated at the high table with your kin," Alder finished for him with a smile, providing the words he struggled to express.

Bacach exhaled and smiled. "I will come up after a while to escort you to the feast."

Alder and Rowan both bowed and went to their room.

Within minutes, a host of chambermaids appeared at the door with fine silk clothing.

"Just leave the clothing. We are able to dress ourselves!" Alder cried out after being cornered by four women that pulled at his belt and shirt. Rowan noted the look of disappointment on their faces as they left the room, but said nothing.

"They came at me like wolves," Alder murmured, dressing in the new clothing. He had been given a silver tunic, black tights, and a long black fur cape. Under the pile of clothing, he found a wreath of silver. It was not fine work, like that of elves or dwarves, but Alder understood the meaning of it. No one would see him closely.

"They mean for me to look like an elf lord come to pay respects to the king," he stammered with notes of anger in his voice.

"What do you mean to do?" Rowan asked, looking at Alder who glared at the wreath in his hands.

"What I mean to do is not what I wish to do. What I mean to do is to not disappoint our friend who would never have consented to this if he had had a choice in the matter. What I wish to do cannot be uttered within the castle walls."

Rowan turned to his own clothing. It was a simple black, velvet tunic with silver embroidery. A gaudy gold necklace beset with diamonds had been provided for him. He felt that he could not wear such a thing, but then he thought of Alder and how they shamed him. He would pretend that he was more than what he was on that night, as well. For Bacach.

After they had dressed, Bacach appeared to escort them to the feast. Neither Alder nor Rowan made any comment about their costumes but followed Bacach down the corridor and into the great hall. Bacach had not commented on their clothing, which was unlike him, and only spoke more to that he had been unwilling to ask them to wear the costumes.

A small change in seating at the royal table had occurred. Aineolach now sat to the king's left and next to his new wife. King Amadan's mistress was missing, and she was not brought up in any of the conversations. Her stomach had grown beyond hiding, so now King Amadan contrived to hide her or had possibly already disposed of her.

Once all the guests had settled and before the food had been brought out, King Amadan rose to give a speech.

The room was completely silent.

"On this day! We toast! My daughter and her new husband! Soon to be king of Midland! Prince Aineolach and Princess Azalea!" Tumultuous applause shook the room. Alder, however, looked at Rowan for the horrid way in which King Amadan had given his speech. Bacach smiled at both of them. Prince Magadh was downing a goblet of wine with more haste than Rowan had ever seen.

The feast was larger than on the night Prince Aineolach had arrived. The drink seemed to rain from the sky. The servants danced unceasingly. The nobles presented their gifts to the newlyweds, making a grand show of each gift and the name of which noble family had presented it. King Amadan was the happiest Rowan had ever seen him. He could not see Prince Aineolach or Princess Azalea but assumed that they were equally pleased. Bacach smiled upon everything. He was finally rid of Azalea and Rowan wondered if he would be sending messengers out to find suitors for his other sisters.

Alder was unhappy. He hated hoarded riches, and the pageantry of gifts was unlike anything they had ever seen. The dancing was slightly more enthusiastic, but still, the mechanical dances that had been seen previously. King Amadan had a very select taste for food and much of the food that was presented on this night was the same sort of things Rowan and Alder had been eating for a week. Rowan assumed that Alder would have preferred to have been in bed. He knew that without Bacach's errand, they would have been on some adventure out in the world and he knew that was where Alder really wanted to be.

"It will all be over soon, and we can go back to our ways of the woodsman and the hunter," Rowan thought.

A faint rumbling sound grew over the sound of the party. The music stopped and everyone looked from one to another. The king set down his unnumbered glass of wine and squinted out across the room as if someone in the crowd was making the noise. The torches that were mounted to the many pillars in the room began to burn lower and lower until they seemed to be smoldering. A wisp of purple flame shot out of the floor at the center of the room and all the dancers fled away from it. The fire grew larger and larger, and a figure emerged from the flames, hooded with a heavy black cloak.

"Torradh, the great and powerful sends his emissary to you now. He who harbors the Clach Nèimh, surrender this now or face the extinction of your people. No king of men, elves, or dwarves will remain alive as long as the stone is withheld. Surrender it to him and you will be well rewarded. Harbor it in folly, and you will die at his sword. The dead will rise at my hand and the living shall join them." The specter seemed to look about the room. Alder slowly pulled his dagger from his boot and in a lightning stroke, threw it at the base of the figure. A blinding flash illuminated the room with a snap like a lightning bolt hitting the ground. The figure was gone.

Everything was still at first. The torches returned to normal. Not a sound could be heard. Then crashing and thuds and the noise of people came from every corner of the room as nobles and servants alike began to upturn cups, plates, tables, and benches in an attempt to flee from the castle.

"So much for great heroism in the face of evil," Alder murmured.

After only a minute, the only people that were left in the room were King Amadan, Aineolach, Magadh, Bacach, Alder, and Rowan. Amadan, Aineolach, and Magadh had been roaringly drunk and were now trying to sort their wits enough to understand what had happened and what had been said. Bacach stared at the spot on the floor where Alder's dagger stood. Rowan stared at Bacach waiting for him to speak.

"What is the meaning of this?" Amadan roared at last. Everyone looked at him, mostly out of confusion over the vagueness of his question. The meaning of the overturned tables and dishes? The meaning of the uninvited guest? Everyone waited for him to speak again.

"Torradh? What Torradh? And what stone? If it is stone they want, then they best find themselves a quarry!"

"Father, Torradh is the evil one that rules over the Plains of Hutuloth. He is the leader of all the darkness to the south and the wildmen of the south, pirates of the west, and all the other evil things of Utherion. The stone he speaks of is the Stone of Heaven."

"Stone of Heaven. Nothing but a fairy tale! I would expect nothing more from an elf! Always after other people's wealth and always chasing legends and children's stories!"

"This is a very real threat!" Bacach cried.

Amadan slammed his fist on the table, spilling his goblet of wine. "It is nothing more than the work of the elves! They wanted to spoil the wedding party to make me look like a fool!"

"Father, we must not waste time! We must find the stone or we will all be doomed!"

"And I say it does not exist! We will do nothing! The soldiers guard the Pass of Handuin and there they will remain. Prince Aineolach and Azalea will be returning that way in two days and the way must be safe!" At this

Amadan's eyes grew wide. "That is what they want!" he shouted. "This is goblin work! They want me to pull my guards from the pass so that they may ransom the prince and my daughter back to me! Well, they will not get anything from my hoard! They will not get a hair from my head!"

Bacach, Rowan, and Alder looked upon the king in dismay. The sorcerer had not been after the riches of Kingsford. They were after one single object and they would tear the castle apart stone by stone until they found it. Bacach looked to Rowan and Alder and then stood. They rose with him and left the room.

"What was that last bit the sorcerer said?" Bacach asked Rowan and Alder in the hallway.

"The dead shall rise at my hand and the living shall join them," recited Alder.

Bacach stood for a moment in thought. "So it is a necromancer that joins Torradh."

"What power does a necromancer have over the dead?" Rowan asked, looking at both of them.

"A necromancer can bring back any of the dead, as long as part of their body remains. They could have a finger and bring back one of the greatest foes Utherion has seen throughout history. As long as there is something that can bring the soul back, they can be brought back," Bacach murmured.

"How could they teleport into the great hall from such a great distance?" Rowan asked, starting to become embarrassed at asking all the questions.

"I do not believe that that was the actual necromancer," Alder began. "When I threw my dagger, I struck something that had been placed in the flagstone. A token, as you will. Something personal that belonged to the necromancer. The necromancer has been here in the castle. They could be anyone and are in hiding. They most likely came here to look for the stone themselves and discovered that they could not find it on their own or without being noticed sneaking about, so they went with a different plan."

Rowan suddenly became anxious and looked around. The hallway was dark and appeared to be empty, but it was dark. "Maybe we should continue this conversation in a more private setting," he whispered. Bacach looked around and the darkness seemed to grip him as well and he shivered.

"We will go to my bedchamber. I do not know if the library is safe."

They followed Bacach to his bedchamber. Bacach sat on his bed, Rowan drew the shutters and curtains at the window, and Alder stood sentinel at the door, which was now locked.

"Who is Torradh? Who is he actually?" Rowan asked.

"The stories say that he was once a great elf. He was high among the first elves of the Roimhe Seo. Then I suppose he quarreled with the high elves, and he left the elves to find his own kingdom in the south. They never seem to tell the small details, even though they are most likely the most important. He went to the realm to the south which was mostly uninhabited. Under his rule, the wildmen were born and a whole host of other evil things came into being. They say he is a great sorcerer and that his powers have not been seen since the Great Wailing when so many people died. But the lands to the south changed with his rule. It became dry and scorched by fires. The water dried up and now only the Dead River flows out, but even it dries up before it ever reaches the sea. The stories say the land itself has become dead from the great darkness he has brought to it, always ripping the earth open to take what he can and never allowing it to heal. There are no plants, no birds, and no living things. All have fled or perished under his reign. If any being is capable of ruling all of Utherion, it is him," Alder explained.

"You two must go to Midland and find Eachdraiche's book," was all Bacach could muster. "It has the key to all of this. If we have the stone, we can fight, or at least parley. But without the stone, we are doomed."

"Even with the stone Kingsford is doomed!" cried Alder, slightly red in the face. "There is no one in the kingdom that can wield that stone. Even if they could wield it, they would have to march to Dorchadas and kill Torradh. He will not stop until he has it, and he will create whatever evil he needs to get it. The only hope the world of men, elves, and dwarves has is to find the stone and find a captain that can wield it and hold the hordes of Torradh at bay long enough for someone to kill him."

"But where are we to find such a man?" Rowan asked, dismayed.

"Perhaps among the elves?" Bacach proposed.

"We would have to have the stone in our hands before the elves would stick their necks out of their hiding places. Even then, no one within Kingsford has had contact with the elves for several generations. We do not know what state their kingdoms are in or if their leaders have fallen to the same dark ways as the kingdoms of men."

"Then we will find the stone at all costs," Rowan resolved.

"The book must be found first. Then we will be able to find the stone," added Bacach.

The kingdom was eerily quiet during the following days. Children did not play in the streets. Women did not sing. Men stored provisions within their homes and braced what defenses they had. The blacksmiths were busy restoring swords that had not seen combat for generations. The armor and shields had been sold long ago.

The guards that remained within the city were on high alert, looking at every dark cloud as an ominous sign. They wore full chainmail and were armed with everything the armory could spare. Much to Rowan and Alder's displeasure, King Amadan had stationed more guards around the castle than the perimeter of the city.

"Much good it will do if the dark hordes reach the castle. The necromancer will be able to double their army with the amount of dead that will be in the street," Alder raged. Rowan said nothing. Alder had been in a rage since the necromancer had appeared and he thought it best to allow Alder to say what he needed to say. Especially because most of what he said was true.

Rowan and Alder spent much of their time preparing for the journey ahead. Bacach provided them with everything they would need from the castle armory. Rowan's quiver was filled, his dagger sharpened, and he received a spare set of chainmail that he wore under his tunic. Alder's sword was sharpened and he was offered a set of chainmail, but he rejected the offer claiming that it was too heavy and awkward. Alder tended to the horses, making sure they were shoed and packed for the journey. Rowan learned all that he could from Bacach about the book he would be looking for. He received little information that he deemed helpful, though he did not let Bacach know.

Rowan would be looking for 'an old, very thick book that would be written in Elvish'. If the library had many thick, old books, Rowan would have to go through each of them to see which were written in Elvish. If more than one was written in Elvish, Rowan was not sure what he would do since he could not read Elvish.

Rumor spread that Princess Azalea had refused to leave the castle without many of her personal objects and that several carts had been procured to move her belongings. The conversation about Azalea's dowry to be paid to Prince Aineolach was a point of debate and Aineolach refused to leave without settling the matter. King Amadan was loath to give away anything of value, but Prince Aineolach rivaled him with his greed. A deal had been made and there would be a cart for the dowry.

All of this made Alder and Rowan anxious. The party would be slow-moving and would have several carts full of high-valued treasures. The soldiers of Kingsford were only stationed in the Pass of Handuin and no further, the other side of the pass being the realm of Midland. Goblins or thieves certainly had room for an attack where one army ended and the other began. More soldiers of Midland had arrived for the escort, but Rowan was unsure of how many soldiers would be needed against an unknown enemy. He was prepared for an uneven battle at any moment.

On the morning of the third day after the wedding, the party was gathered outside of the castle. Besides Rowan and Alder, twenty guards had arrived from Midland for the escort. Captain Caraid, who had been left in the barracks for two weeks with his few remaining soldiers, was at the head of the party. Rowan and Alder preferred the back so that they could watch the progress of the group and the hillsides. Very rarely was the first person attacked. Attacks usually came toward the middle of the group.

After Azalea said a long and tearful goodbye to her father, sisters, and Magadh, they were off through the city and headed through the moors toward the Pass of Handuin. The day was cloudy and the tops of the mountains were shrouded in mist. Rowan hoped that the mist would not be low within the pass. Very few bugs attacked them, which led Rowan to believe that a storm was coming. The wind racing across the sea and moors seemed to confirm it.

After four hours, they reached the pass. To Rowan's dismay, the mist was low and he could not see up the sides of the cliffs. They halted at the mouth. "Hail! Soldiers of Kingsford! I wish to know if the pass is safe before we enter, for we cannot see! Can you answer?" called Captain Caraid. A moment of silence passed before a soldier was seen on the road ahead. He approached cautiously.

"We are happy to see you finally! A long while we have been stationed here. There have been goblins, but we have slain them as they have appeared. The road is safe. We have guards stationed all throughout the pass and there have been no attacks for a few days. Strange it has been, for they were coming frequently enough until then."

"That is strange, indeed," Captain Caraid murmured.

"I would be happy to escort you through, seeing how there is such a dreary fog today. Then I can give the signal and you will not have to name yourself at every checkpoint."

"We would be grateful if you did so. We would like to reach Kingsland tonight, if possible. I do not wish for us to camp in the fields, even if we are in the realm of Midland."

"Certainly, lord," the soldier cried. "Follow me then!"

The soldier led the way through the fog. Every so often he would give a whistle and every time there would be a diffcrent whistle in response. The group did not have to stop in the pass, as the soldier had said, thanks to his whistling. Rowan strained his ears at all times to hear throughout the canyon. He could hear the soldiers muttering and the occasional fall of gravel where someone's foot had slid out. If goblins or raiders were waiting for an attack, this would be the perfect opportunity.

But after several more hours, they reached the end of the pass without incident. A small group of soldiers waited along the road and checked people before they went into the pass from the Midland entrance. They reported that they had not seen any sign of goblins for several days. The soldier that had guided them now took his leave, not being permitted to leave the pass.

The group dropped out of the fog as they descended into the plains that were the realm of Midland. On the right were the ruins of the Watchtower of Faire and the Fae Forest. The group skirted around the base of the mountain along the road. Rowan and Alder seldom went into the forest and when they did, they did not go far from the road.

There had once been a safe road that went through the forest, but that was now long ago. The road ran along the Òrail River and had been the main route for the merchants of New Market and the farmers of Taigheland to reach the lands on the east side of the forest. Now the only safe path from Taigheland and New Market to Midland was the Shore Road from New Market to Kingsford and from Kingsford through the Pass of Handuin. Kingsford was in danger of having their trade routes blocked, should the threat of the goblins persist.

Still, a few brave souls would try to take the old road through the forest to save time. The road was well established, but many paths would appear or disappear as they pleased. Any paths off of the road were not to be trusted. Sometimes one might be able to reach the other side of the forest along one of the paths and a traveler may have learned to use the path often, but then one day they would disappear without a trace.

It was said that strange beasts lived in the forest. Some of the farmers that lived along the forest's edge often said they heard great wailing noises as if women were being tortured somewhere within, but no women were ever found on the brief and superficial searches. Children were kept far away from the edge of the woods for fear of ghosts, goblins, or unnamed dark creatures.

Rowan and Alder had once chased a small band of goblins into the woods and away from the pass. Rowan and Alder had stopped their horses, the undergrowth being too dense. The goblins, however, disappeared when they had been only a few yards away. The goblins had never let out a cry or screech. It had seemed as though a great hole had opened up under them, swallowed them up, and closed again before they realized what had happened to them.

Rowan and Alder had seen strange lights within the forest on a few occasions. The lights had been different colors and had appeared and disappeared. Rowan, more susceptible to magics than Alder, had felt a strange urge to run after the lights and had made a movement toward them when Alder pulled him quickly away from the forest's edge.

None of the soldiers wanted to tarry so close to the edge of the forest, so the group moved briskly onward.

Farms dotted the fields that led to Kingsland, the capital city of Midland. Wheat, barley, and rye covered the plowed-over hills. The farms did well, though no major rivers ran through the farmland except for the Airgead River far to the south. Rain usually fell often enough for the want of the farmers.

It was late afternoon and the sun beat down upon the party. Azalea, never having traveled this far in her life, began to tire and grow weary of the endless road.

"I am tired of this horse!" she cried. "I am tired of the sun and the heat! I wish not to go back into the fog where all was quiet and dreary, but I do not wish to carry on in the heat of the day like this!"

"We must reach the castle by nightfall. We do not have much time to tarry," Princess Uiall soothed, though Rowan could hear the notes of annoyance in her voice. Uiall was much to the same mind as Azalea, hating the journey, but would not have dared to complain about it in front of her soldiers or anyone else besides her brother, perhaps.

"Can we not stop and take tea?" cried Azalea after a few minutes. "We have not eaten since early this morning and I say that we will not have the chance to eat until very late this evening if we do not stop. I daresay it will be ten o'clock before we reach the castle!"

"You must learn to mind your tongue! Your father may have allowed you to say and do as you please in your own kingdom, but Midland is *my* kingdom and these are my soldiers! If we are to stop, it will be at my command. Your whining will not change their or my course!" Prince Aineolach lashed.

Aineolach's reprimand was harsher than Rowan thought necessary. He felt a 'no' would have been sufficient. Aineolach was obviously weary and tired of the journey as well, but would not suffer his treasures to be on carts in the fields longer than they had to be. Rowan looked to Alder who was squelching what would have been roaring laughter. Rowan was glad that they were at the back of the party.

No one spoke for a while and then Azalea began to weep.

"Why do you misuse me so? I am your loving wife! Pray lord, let us stop only long enough to stretch our legs and have some of the food the peasants sent for our journey. If we do not eat it, surely it will spoil. Peasant food is not good if it is not eaten quickly!"

Aineolach choked on his rage, making a queer gurgling, grunting sound. Aineolach and Azalea rode next to each other and Rowan almost expected him to throw her from her horse. Instead, his grip loosened on the reigns of his horse and he called out to the group to stop. No one's expression was that of amusement, except Alder who did everything in his power to hide it.

Azalea had stopped weeping at once and a soldier was now helping her down from her horse. She did not thank him. Uiall smiled graciously but did not thank Captain

Caraid when he helped her. Aineolach almost leaped from his horse. The foodstuffs that had been given to the party from the citizens of Kingsford were numerous. The villagers had prepared many fine cakes, fruited loaves, and other delicacies that no doubt cost the poor people much of their saved stores and money. The royal family turned their noses up at it.

"You will eat, for all the racket you made along the road!" Aineolach ordered Azalea as she picked at a fine-looking honey cake.

"They have not candied the fruit and there is no cream!"

"I suppose I ought to send my men off to the dairy country now and barter with a farmer about cream!"

They carried on in such a way for several minutes. Rowan and Alder sat along the side of the road, looking out over the fields. Alder grinned and chuckled under his breath with every outburst as he ate his fruited loaf. The soldiers sat on the other side of the road and quietly ate their rations. Rowan could not tell if they were having whispered conversation, but the movement of their backs as they laughed silently said they found it humorous, as well.

"They must hate Aineolach as much as we hate Azalea," Rowan whispered to Alder.

"They should not find it so funny. We are free men in a few days and they are stuck with both of them!" Alder whispered back with an ear-to-ear smile.

Aineolach stormed off down the road on foot, carrying a particularly toothsome-looking cake. Azalea was quiet once he was gone. She would not complain directly to any of the guards and Uiall had already moved some distance away before Aineolach had walked off.

Azalea now stood among her subjects, mocked and made a fool of, though she hardly knew it. She had prevented everyone from taking anything she *might* have wanted, so she now had a small pile of goods on the wagon in front of her. Knowing no constraint, hunger, or lack of plenty, she ate from many of the things and left many half-eaten or with only a few bites taken from parts. She ate the best parts from some of the finer pastries and picked all of the candied fruits out of others. She licked, but did not eat one cake that had been generously covered with flower-infused honey.

"I have never seen someone do that," Rowan murmured.

"Lick a cake and set it back among food meant for an entire group? I have not either. Nor have I seen someone tear apart or bite into a dozen cakes that were meant for an entire group. But I find that there are no surprises with the line of Amadan," Alder laughed in a whisper.

After a while, Aineolach returned and ordered that everyone get back on their horses and that they set out at once. This was done and the group was silent as the horses plodded along the road. No one spoke within the group. The soldiers, Rowan guessed were not allowed to speak. Alder and himself would not speak with other ears so near

Prince Aineolach, Princess Azalea, and Princess Uiall all rode in complete silence with coldness and disdain for each other. The word 'love' did not exist between any of them. As Rowan had feared, the storm had risen over the mountains and raindrops dotted the dusty road.

"What a fine marriage, though I say they will take out their frustrations upon their servants," Rowan whispered.

"They will both be well off enough. They will tarry with others behind the other's back. Perhaps after Azalea has a few children she will go the same way that her mother did," Alder returned.

"It is almost as if they were meant for each other," Rowan smiled.

"It is a reassuring thought, is it not? If they can find their true love then what prevents us?" Alder had a gleam in his eye and Rowan smiled, knowing all too well that they would kill each other and Alder and himself had no intentions of finding companions.

Well after nightfall, they reached Kingsland. The city was silent as the rain poured down. Lanterns were lit and the guards hailed them, but no parades or pageantry welcomed them as there had been in Kingsford upon their arrival and upon the day of the wedding. The guards bowed as they passed and if people were about, they bowed, as well. But the songs, cheers, and laughter of the people were missing and left an eerie quiet in the rain. It was late, yes, but no one came out of doors to see the return of their crown prince, his new wife, or their princess.

The castle, when they reached it, was well-lit, but silent. It was a much smaller castle than that of Kingsford. It was cylindrical with only one hallway branching off. No balconies or columns adorned the exterior or interior of the castle. No stained glass or large windows allowed the light to illuminate the dark and hostile environment. The great hall was simple and had purple and gold banners hanging from the ceiling. A staircase wound around the back of the room and up to the throne room and chambers. Fresh rushes and flowers covered the otherwise dirt-floor. Another staircase led down into the storerooms and armory. To the left was the guardroom and to the right was a small hallway.

A large table stood in the great hall and mounds of food had been set out. Servants stood along the walls with their heads down and hands behind their backs. The soldiers departed to deal with the horses and treasures once the prince and princesses were inside. Rowan and Alder stood in the doorway, dripping with rain, not sure if they were invited to this feast or if they were to go to the barracks with the soldiers.

Aineolach went to take his seat at the table without so much as greeting a single person in the room. He shed his soaked fur onto the floor and appeared to be quite dry underneath. Azalea followed him towards the ornate chair that was smaller than Aineolach's but was clearly meant for her, dropping her cloak onto the floor. Uiall began to go in that direction, but then recalled that Rowan and Alder were not servants or soldiers and were standing behind her.

"Ah, Masters Rowan and Alder. I almost forgot that you were among us. The day has been so long and weary and you two are both so silent. We are grateful that you accompanied us, though your services were not needed. Still, you may enjoy this meal with us. I daresay there is more than enough for the three of us and I do not believe that an extra two will make any difference. Chairs for them, now!" she screeched.

Two chairs were promptly brought out and were set at the end of the table. "Thank you for your generosity." Rowan bowed before sitting with Alder. Uiall smiled her cold grin at them. They ate in silence.

Aineolach turned to one of the servants. "Where is Hiroval?"

"He retired to his chambers an hour ago, my lord." The servant bowed.

"Did he not know that we were coming?" Aineolach asked bitterly.

The servant paled. "Why, yes, your magnificence. He ordered that this dinner be prepared and ready for your arrival."

"Then as steward, did he not think that I would wish to speak to him upon my arrival?"

The servant stammered, but could not articulate a sentence.

"Wake him, before I have both of your heads." Aineolach waved.

The servant scurried up the stairs wild with terror.

Rowan and Alder looked at each other in amazement, but otherwise ignored the scene taking place in front of them. This was no different than what usually occurred in Kingsford. They both ate heartily, for they were weary from the day, but they did not eat as much as the others. Princess Uiall had been right in saying that the addition of the two of them would not make a difference. Enough food graced the table for all the escorts, though they had not been invited. Rowan, as he became full and stopped eating, became dismayed at the amount of food that had been wasted in preparation for the return of the prince and princesses. Only three seats had been placed at the table, so no others had been expected to be eating. Rowan was afraid of how much more would have been wasted if the servants had known that Rowan and Alder would be eating, as well.

Hiroval, the steward, padded down the stairs in front of the servant. He did not look amused at having been woken up but was intelligent enough to know that his life depended upon his appearance.

Aineolach reprimanded him and a long discussion about the events in the village during the royal party's absence took place. An elderly man died from a fever, his house had been burned to prevent the fever from spreading and his family had been 'sent into the country'. A baby had been born and the parents were waiting for Aineolach to name it.

Aineolach asked a few questions about the baby and its parents. Upon hearing the surname, he frowned.

"Do they not owe me twenty pounds of barley as tax?"

"Yes, your highness."

Aineolach thought for a moment with his tongue in his cheek. Then a sly smile appeared on his face. A cruel smile.

"Then the child is to be named Barley and you shall take it tomorrow as payment for their taxes. Take the child to the penial farm and make one of the women there feed it and raise it as a laborer. If there are no women with milk, arrest a different woman whose husband is delinquent on his taxes and send her to the farm. You are dismissed."

Hiroval bowed and returned to his chambers.

Uiall snapped her fingers, and a servant came immediately to her side. She whispered in the servant's ear, the servant bowed and left through the front doors. After a while, Captain Caraid entered the hall.

"You wished to see me, your highness." He bowed.

"Yes. Masters Rowan and Alder have finished their meals and I would like you to find them room in the barracks for the night."

"Yes, your highness." He bowed again.

Rowan and Alder looked at each other, stood, bowed, and followed Captain Caraid out of the great hall. The streets were empty, and the entire world seemed to be quiet. Captain Caraid said nothing as they followed him down the streets and to the barracks. Two guards stood outside and bowed as he walked past them. They stared at Rowan and Alder as they walked past. The door was shut behind them. A spiral staircase led down from a long corridor once inside the barracks. At the bottom of the stairs was a very heavy door. Caraid turned to Rowan and Alder with a smile but still said nothing. He swung open the door and warm light flooded the dark stairwell.

And noise rushed out at them like a hurricane.

The soldiers inside were laughing and singing and talking. Some soldiers were telling jokes and riddles, and others playing games. All was merry in this dungeon far away from the cold castle.

"I apologize for not speaking to you along the way," Caraid said with a smile. "The prince and princess do not like the sounds of their people. They only enjoy the sound of their own voices. They hold no feasts, nor parties, or any form of celebration. The people of Kingsland lock themselves in their homes to sing and dance and celebrate, but long has it been since they have had much to celebrate. The prince taxes them ruthlessly and takes a portion of all goods that are to be sold. Peasants barely keeping themselves from starving to death must hand over precious food. The weavers hand over their best clothes that they could sell to the merchants, the smith hands over weapons made from the best ores that he could trade to wanderers, and shoemakers go without shoes for the princess' wardrobe. Then tonight, upon that table was enough food to feed the lot of us. And who shall it go to? The pigs! The pigs will be made fat so that they may live another day toward the slaughter."

Rowan and Alder stood in amazement. On the day of their first meeting, Captain Caraid had stood between

Prince Aineolach and the goblins, prepared to give his own life. He bowed graciously, and said, "Your Highness" with no malice or contempt, but before them now, stood hating the people he served so wholeheartedly. They did not consider telling him about Aineolach taking people's children.

Alder laughed a hearty laugh that sounded from deep within him. Rowan smiled at the sound he so rarely heard. All the men that were near Alder smiled. His laugh was that of the elves, with all the jingling and merriness that those people were renowned for. Rowan seldom heard this laugh, but it always gladdened him when he did.

"I do believe that you would be an admirable adversary, Captain! You serve like a slave. You bear your burden without a sigh. And yet, you would not mourn their deaths if they were hacked to bits where they sit right now!"

Caraid only half-smiled at this. "I will not confirm or deny what you say, for my head depends upon it. Come! Let me show you to your beds. We have plenty. They insist on having a heavy guard at night, so many of the beds are empty." Caraid took them through the great room to where a row of empty beds were. "You may choose any that you like. It will make no difference which. All of their owners are on duty until dawn. You may hang your clothes to dry, as well, otherwise, you will catch cold in this dreary weather."

"Thank you, Captain." Rowan bowed.

Caraid smiled at them. "It is the least I can do for you men. You have done us a great honor. First, you save our lives and then you escort us all the way back here. And for nothing more than a few dinners." He bowed and left back the way they had come.

Rowan and Alder both sat on empty beds. Alder began to remove his belt and sword. Rowan set down his bow and studied the room. From the outside, no noise whatsoever could be heard. The room, however, was noisy and loud as if all the noise that should have been throughout the city all day was now occurring all at once in this one place.

And Rowan was happy for them. Rowan was glad that they could still find it in their hearts to be happy and joyous and sing and dance and do everything their hearts needed to do throughout the day, but could not because they found themselves caged by the evil lords that were their prince and princess.

Rowan undressed and lay down to sleep. He was surprised that, despite the noise, he was not having any trouble drifting off.

Chapter 4

Rowan awoke as the men moved about to prepare for the changing of the guard. Alder was already awake, watching the movement around him. Alder always had trouble with other people's movements, though he could sleep through anything Rowan did. Rowan quickly prepared himself for the day. It was before dawn, as Captain Caraid said the owners of the beds would not be back until then. Rowan worried that he would not have enough time to search the library and still make it back to Kingsford before nightfall.

"Rowan," Alder began. "If you find the book you need, how do you plan to get it out of the library without anyone noticing? Guards and servants were stationed every few feet within the hall. Somebody is bound to notice you carrying off a large, heavy book."

Rowan stared blankly for a moment. He had not thought of it. Nor had Bacach. Rowan was upset that Bacach had not bothered to come when he could move about more easily and knew precisely what he needed.

"Perhaps there will be windows," Rowan said after a while. "Perhaps you can wait outside the window and catch the book. I can then find something that is old and useless and feign interest in it and ask that it be my payment for our services."

"What if I am seen sneaking around the side of the castle with a book?"

"You will have to make something up, I suppose. All the guards know that we are here by this time. You will not be arrested. Just questioned. I am not sure that anyone will care all that much, either," Rowan said.

"I suppose it will just have to work," Alder sighed.

Captain Caraid appeared. "Thanks to you two, I will be receiving breakfast this morning." He smiled.

Rowan and Alder again followed Caraid through the streets and back to the castle. Few people had ventured outside, being so early in the morning, but they were all mute. No one greeted their neighbors with, "Good mornings" or "Good days," just a head nod or adverted eyes. The streets were mud. No one had bothered to pave them and the rain had made them slick. The houses were small, wooden buildings that had no windows. The whole town seemed abandoned.

They reached the castle, and the doors were opened for them. Princess Uiall was the only one at the table, but the table was laden for an army. None of the dishes were cold leftovers from the night before. Everything was hot and had been made fresh that morning.

"Good morning, Your Highness," Rowan said, and all three men bowed. Caraid had already said his good mornings with his initial summons.

"Ah, there you are. I had some things to discuss with you two and thought we might eat while we talk things over," Uiall said, not acknowledging the pleasantry.

The three men sat at the table but did not touch anything. She smiled at this and seemed to nod that they could begin eating before she spoke.

"My brother's coronation is today. He has filled all the requirements to become King in the laws of my people. The last stepping stone was for him to be married, which he has done. Usually, there would be celebrations in their honor, but he does not see the need for it at this time. So the coronation will be today and your oaths will be fulfilled, having delivered him safely back to his kingdom. I wanted to invite you to the ceremony today. It will be short. Everything is in order. He only needs to be crowned in front of the castle doors and in front of our people. He may then give a short speech, though I doubt he will. There will be some song, I suppose." She did not seem happy about that but went on. "After that, all will be dismissed and he will begin his rule. His true rule anyway. He has been ruling since the deaths of our parents, but that is of little matter. I believe that you wished to see our library, which you may do after we finish breakfast. The coronation will be sometime this afternoon. My brother and his wife will be along late, I am sure. You are more than welcome to stay in the barracks again tonight before you return to Kingsford in the morning."

Rowan wondered at what point there would be a discussion. Princess Uiall said everything that needed to be said and it did not sound as though they had any choice in the matter. He thought everything over for a moment.

"Thank you, Your Highness," was all he could muster.

She smiled and nodded as if she was doing him a great honor. Her look soured suddenly. "Master Alder, do you know the common tongue well?"

Alder looked strange for a moment. "Yes, your highness. Why do you ask?"

"It is always Rowan who pays the courtesies and never yourself. You do not thank, you do not speak at all. For many days we have dined together and only a few words have I ever seen you whisper to Rowan. It is as if he is master and you are servant, which would be a strange course of events given the stories I have heard in Kingsford. I was only curious to know if you spoke the common tongue well or if you were afraid of speaking in a fragmented language, mixed with the Elvish tongue, which I presume is your native tongue."

She stared Alder straight in the face. She had felt insulted that he did not thank her for what she perceived to be the utmost generosity.

Alder's face was blank as he processed the words. It was an insult blanketed with insults and Rowan knew that Alder did not take these things lightly. Rowan knew that he could not speak, yet he was afraid of what Alder might say. Even Captain Caraid stared wide-eyed at the food in front of him, terrified to make any noise or make eye contact with either party.

"I do not speak because my customs are different than that of the people of today. I am almost a thousand years old and I do not keep up with the customs that seem ever-changing to me. The lives of men are short and, in their lifespan, they alter many things, and I wish things to be the same. They take offense to things that used to be a compliment and it is difficult for me and it makes me anxious to speak. Therefore, I allow Rowan to speak on my behalf for he is more aware of the current state of things, and he is more aware of the emotions and customs of men. I can only guess at the things he can easily see. I mean no offense to you, Your Highness. In the days of old, before elves and Elvish was banned in Kingsford, it would have been very courteous for me to thank you in the Elvish tongue, but now it is a very loath thing to do and I could be imprisoned for it. But I will address you now, how I would have in the days of old. Tha mi gad mhallachadh gu bàs leis an fhear as motha a tha earbsa agad. Tha mi an dòchas gun tig crìoch air loidhne d'athraichean mus leudaich i." Alder put his hand to his heart and bowed his head.

Princess Uiall was quite pleased by this. "Here, here!" Captain Caraid smiled. Rowan smiled, but he could not continue eating and neither did Alder. To everyone's relief, Prince Aineolach entered at that moment.

He said nothing to anyone, but sat at the table and began heaping piles of food onto his plate. He looked a mess and as though he had not slept.

"You look a fright, brother," Uiall stated coolly. "I hope that you will have time to remedy yourself before your coronation today."

"There will be time enough. It will not take place until I am good and ready. I am King. It is only a ceremony," he grumbled.

Uiall said nothing but sipped the contents of her goblet.

"With your leave, Your Highness, I will go to the library now," Rowan said, standing and bowing. Uiall smiled and waved her hand. Aineolach stared at the pile of eggs in front of him, not processing what was happening around him.

"Tha fuath agam ort." Alder bowed. Uiall nodded with a smile.

"Show them to the library!" she screeched.

A servant appeared and escorted them to the library.

"Well, now we are both in here," Alder murmured as the servant closed the door behind them.

"What did you say to her?" Rowan asked, spinning on Alder.

Alder smiled. Not a good smile. He had done something. "No less than what she deserves," was his reply.

"I cannot speak Elvish, but I know enough of it to know that you did not say anything gracious."

"I cursed her and her kin," he replied, still smiling and beginning to glance over the shelves.

"You *what*?" Rowan demanded.

"I cursed her," he said more firmly.

"To what end?"

"I shall not tell for pain or death, but it was along those lines." He laughed, looking over his shoulder at Rowan.

Rowan continued to stand in the middle of the room and stare at Alder who was scanning over all the books. Elvish curses have a way of coming true and Rowan knew that whatever Alder had said now had strong power behind it.

"Are you going to help me or shall we wait for the coronation?" Alder asked with a grin. Rowan started searching on the other side of the room. He pulled several old books, but they were all written in the common tongue. He could hear Alder doing the same on the other side. After a while, they met without having found any books in Elvish at all.

Rowan was disheartened but said nothing. This was the only way they could stop the attack on Kingsford, or at the very least, delay it. Alder looked back across the books with a frown. Then suddenly stopped dead. He quickly looked to the window and rushed towards it. With lightning reflexes, he reached down and pulled something into the room.

It was a gnome. He was bald but had a long white beard that he had tucked into a gold chord that served as his belt. He wore a brown tunic and brown boots. His nose was large and round and his eyes appeared beady behind his beard, but he was not unpleasant.

Rowan had never seen a gnome and now one was struggling in Alder's hands. "Cha dean mi cron ort. Feumaidh me fiosrachadh," Alder soothed. The gnome stopped struggling and turned to look at Alder as he set the gnome down.

"It has been a long time since I have heard anyone speak in Elvish around here," the gnome said in a raspy voice.

"What did you say to him?" Rowan asked.

"I told him that I would not harm him and that I only need information," Alder replied.

"And what information would you have from me elf Lord?" the gnome asked, not at all afraid.

"Tell me about yourself, first. I find it unlikely that the prince or princess are tolerant of you digging about the grounds," Alder joked, squatting down.

Gnomes are always happy to talk about themselves because they feel that they are the most overlooked of the creatures and that they are the most useful. They are good at digging and mining like dwarves. They are skilled in the creation of jewelry and the cutting of gems. They live extremely long lives and have a wealth of knowledge, given that they are small, hard to see, and can easily eavesdrop wherever they find the information easy to obtain.

"My people have lived to the back of the castle since before the castle was built. Of course, we had to remodel after the big oafs built the castle on top of our city, but we still have many networks right under the castle floor," he began proudly. "These people do not notice anything. They never walk in the fields or gardens, so they have never noticed us and I do not think they would know what to do if they found us. They would throttle us, I am sure, but our tunnels go deep underground and we can always dig deeper or farther in any direction we choose. Many things we hear, being under the castle floor and most of it never sounds to be wholesome. Always plotting and bickering these people are. Always discussing riches and power. Do you know that Uiall cut off her chambermaid's hand because she pulled her hair too much while she was fixing it? A terrible racket it was. All the screaming and wailing. Uiall slit her throat for all the racket. Things became awful silent in the castle after that day. Awful silent. No one dare make a peep when Uiall was about. They say she keeps a poisoned dagger about her all the time, but she does not like to use it for fear that tongues will wag. We can hear her pacing the floor at night when all others are asleep. She must have suitors come to her room, for sometimes there are men's voices that are not the prince's." The gnome seemed as though he could raddle on forever about the goings on in the castle. Rowan was dismayed to hear any of it because it seemed to prove Alder's response correct when Rowan had been hesitant to approve of it.

"What do you know about the elves that used to be here?" Alder asked.

"Elves were outlawed in Midland long before they were outlawed in the other countries of men. Midland is closer to the Elven realms and their perceived threat is greater, though Midland is always slow to share its news with others. I think they were a wee jealous of all the attention the elves paid to Kingsford, the first kings being rivals and all.

"After a while, King Sannt got the people so worked up that they shut up the doors to the elves or chased them out of the city with swords and dogs. Anyone that said anything against the King was killed most terribly and in public. One night an elf from Kingsford came upon the castle. There had not been any guards about, so he was able to walk right up to the doors. He banged on the doors and asked for sanctuary. King Sannt let him in and, seeing that he was an elf, bid him stay here in the library. The elf told him his name, as well, which was Eachdraiche, if I remember well enough. King Sannt knew that Eachdraiche had been wise and intelligent and that's why he bid him stay in the library. When Eachdraiche went to leave the room in the morning, guards pushed him back inside and locked the doors. They kept him locked in the library for many days until he had grown weary from lack of food or water. Then, they placed him in bonds, stripped him, and drug him through the streets until they again arrived at the castle doors. There they killed him in all his shame, dishonor, and mud and blood." The old gnome shook his head.

"You know the story well," Alder whispered.

"I ought to. I was a young lad when it happened. It was a shameful day and this land has felt evil ever since.

To give sanctuary to a creature and then to shame it and kill it is evil no matter what that creature is."

Rowan looked at Alder's face. He had never seen the unguarded mixture of emotions that were playing across it, but Alder quickly regained his composure.

"Lord Gnome, I am not an elf spy, but I am here seeking something that Eachdraiche may have hidden before they killed him. There is a great deal of weight upon this object being found, but my quest must remain secret. Princess Uiall does not like me, but I have cursed her name in Elvish. Still, she is an evil woman and I do not wish for her to find the heirloom of my ancestors, especially when they died at her hands. Do you know of any hiding spots within the library where a book may have been kept for these long years?"

The gnome brightened at once. "Of course! We do not touch their things for fear of them hunting us, but I know where there is a chamber beneath the floor." The gnome began walking about the room, listening to his footsteps on the floor. Under one of the chairs, he stopped and pressed his ear against the floor. "Right, here it is!" he called.

Rowan went to the spot and moved the chair, minding that he did not harm the gnome or make any noise. He pulled out his knife and began pulling up the tiles. A small, hand dug hole was beneath the tile. In the bottom of the hole was a leather sack.

"There is an enchantment on it," the gnome said to Rowan. "No *man* can reach into it or else he will be cursed."

Alder knelt down next to the hole and reached in, muttering something in Elvish the entire time. He pulled out the bag and looked inside. He pulled out the book with a grin. A few other things clinked around the bottom of the bag, but Alder did not remove them. Noticing something before closing the bag, he pulled out a small sapphire ring and handed it to the gnome. "I offer you this ring, in repayment for your help and honesty."

"This is a great gift, Elf Lord," the gnome squeaked. "I will ever remember you and sing glad songs of you to my people. What is your name, good Lord?"

"Feàrna leth Fuil," Alder answered.

Rowan was shocked. He had never heard Alder refer to himself in his Elvish name.

"And who is this, Lord Feàrna leth Fuil? This is a man who does not speak and appears humble and not proud like the others."

"He is my companion and friend. He is Caorann Meallta."

Rowan bowed his head to the gnome. The gnome suddenly got a queer look. "Someone has turned down the passage. In haste! Restore the room or they shall know!"

Rowan quickly replaced the tiles and the chair. Alder hid the bag under a cushion on the chair and helped the gnome out the window. He had just flopped down on the chair and Rowan had just grabbed a book at random when the door opened.

Princess Uiall entered the room. "I thought you would have finished in here by now, Rowan," she said, slightly annoyed that he was still in the castle.

"I apologize, Your Highness," he said with feigned shame. "I was carried away by this book. It is a fantastic tale. Have you read it?"

"What book is it? Surely I cannot answer without knowing what it is," she said haughtily.

"It is *Dragons of the Roimhe Seo*, Your Highness. The writer seems to think that dragons were real! It is quite exciting to think about!"

"Surely for those who wish to bring themselves out of shame and indignity can imagine doing great deeds such as fighting dragons, but for those who must worry about the well-being of their people, imagining dragons is quite loathsome. I daresay you have had enough time to rummage through my library. The coronation will be soon and you must leave before people start to gather. You are not dressed as royal guests or even as nobles and I do not wish for either of you, especially you Alder, around the castle. You may attend the coronation from the crowd and I daresay the back, where you will go unnoticed. But make haste!" She spun out of the room and did not close the door.

"That was uncalled for," Alder whispered as they both stared at where she had been.

Chapter 5

Sneaking the sack out was easier than Rowan had thought it would be. The castle was in a silent uproar as the servants scrubbed every surface and prepared the doorway for the coronation. The royal family needed to be dressed and both crowns needed to be polished. All three members of the royal family were demanding baths and hot water must be brought.

Rowan and Alder simply drifted out of the castle without anyone paying any attention to them. "Where can we go that is safe?" Rowan asked.

Alder shook his head but thought for a moment.

"Perhaps the guards will all be going to the coronation and the barracks will be empty?"

Alder was correct. As they approached the barracks, guards began to appear in full regalia, marching toward the castle. None of them looked happy. Rowan and Alder stood by the door and waited for all the soldiers to exit the barracks. When the last man had marched out, they entered and shut the door. They ran down the staircase and entered the great room they had slept in, making sure to shut the heavy door behind them. They were alone.

Alder looked under the beds to make sure that no one was attempting to hide from the coronation and might overhear their conversation.

They sat on one of the beds at the back of the room and dumped the artifacts out. Inside was the book, a parcel that may have contained food at one time, an old water skin, a pen, and an Elvish medallion.

Alder, with the book lying in front of him, took a sudden interest in the medallion. Gold dragons intertwined themselves with their heads coming together in the center. Their eyes were tiny white gems and many runes had been carved along the dragons' backs.

"I have seen this before," Alder murmured.

"You have? When?" Rowan asked, surprised.

"My father wore this for a time. One morning when I woke, it was gone. I asked him about it and he told me that he had given it to a friend that he held dear. I had forgotten that it had existed. I was only very small then and my father died a few years later."

"Well then you must wear it! If it was your father's then it now passes to you as it should have many years ago," Rowan smiled.

Alder looked at it hesitantly and thumbed the gold dragons. Alder did not frequently think of the past and it appeared to Rowan that many distant memories were now finding their way into Alder's head. After a few moments, Alder slipped the chain over his head. He stared down at the medallion on his chest.

"Maybe I should keep it hidden until we leave. The royalty will most likely think me a thief if they should happen to see me with it."

"That may be best. Now let us look at the book." Rowan picked up the book as Alder tucked the medallion under his shirt. It was very old but had been well preserved under the enchantments. Rowan timidly opened the cover as if a curse would be laid upon him.

"There is nothing to fear. There are no enchantments. I do not think he had enough time," Alder smiled sullenly.

Rowan sighed and opened the book fully. It was written completely in Elvish. He handed the book to Alder with a laugh. "I cannot understand a bit of it."

Alder looked over the pages. "It is a history of Utherion. A very long history. This book begins shortly after Torradh left the Rìoghachad and Aonaidh. Torradh was the first historian, so Eachdraiche must have taken up the task when Torradh left."

Alder read over the histories very quickly and it seemed like a long time before he found anything.

"Here." He stopped, pointing at the paper. "The stone that fell from the heavens, the gift of Smaoinich and Cruthadair unto the mortals and held by the immortals for safekeeping, has been severed. The rising threat of Torradh in the south is too great and many fear that he will seek out the stone.

"The severing of the stone was not an easy task. The elves most skilled in smithing and gem lore arrived and the elder smiths had a great debate amongst themselves as to how it should be done. They labored for many weeks to severe it in such a way that it would fit together again and could again be whole when the threat in the south is overcome.

"They say that the stone has been split into three pieces. One for the leader of elves, one for the dwarves, and one for the men. The stone for the elves will remain hidden here. The lord and lady are taking great pains to conceal it and they will not tell any what is to become of it. There is some debate as to which house of the dwarves the stone will go to. Lord Iarann of Fortar will be the one to take it in the end, though his cousin, Copar, of Da Shuil claims it would be safest at the farthest reaches of Utherion. The stone for men will go to King Taighe in Caladh.

"King Taighe knows nothing of the stone, for it has been hidden until this time. The dwarves did not know that it was real, only believing that it was a legend and they have repeatedly expressed their fear of having a shard. They do not wish to keep it but know that all the powers of Utherion will be needed to protect it. Men have never heard of it and care has been taken to never speak to them before this time, the elders not believing that a suitable ruler existed amongst the species of men that would be able to wield the stone as Cruthadair would have wished. King Taighe is the mightiest of men and he must be suitable to withhold his section from Torradh."

Alder stopped reading aloud and began to skim through the entries again. Rowan waited patiently but was burning with questions. Alder found another entry and began again.

"On this day, a great host has left the city to take the severed stone to Caladh. I am traveling with the host as well, wishing to document what takes place in Caladh. The Lord and Lady wished to wait until the city was finished and we now go with many of the women and children that we have harbored during the war. The group is slow for there are not enough horses and there are many children that tire quickly. We have brought much food and it does the women well, but the road is long and weary. Taighe still has not been told of the stone. There will be a secret council upon our arrival and he will be bidden to hide it. Some who helped hide the Elven stone are in our company to offer their services to Taighe in the hiding of his stone."

Alder again shuffled through the pages, growing impatient.

"The stone has been hidden within the castle. The castle is within the heart of the city and the stone will be safest there. I know not where. Everyone was cast out of the castle for many days while the smiths worked. Upon our leaving, the only man that shall know of the stone and its location will be Taighe, for he will not tell even his remaining son. The secret will die with Taighe and perhaps that is the right course, for men are weak in morals and quick to arms and the stone may prove too much of a temptation to these people. It was unfortunate to hear of the passing of King Taighe's second eldest son. May the Diathans protect the young one, the only remaining heir, and may he continue to lead his people as his forefathers have done."

Alder continued to look through the pages. He stopped and read one entry very intently, but did not read it aloud. He continued flipping through the pages.

"But why did he return?" Alder was muttering.

A sudden noise came from above and Alder shoved the book back into the sack.

Guards were reentering the room. The coronation ceremony was over. They all muttered under their breath and began to take off their regalia. Over their steel armor, they wore purple and gold tunics. They wore purple capes and shiny helmets with purple plumes arcing from the top. The loud clanging of metal echoed throughout the barracks as they cast down their armor upon the stone steps. No one spoke until the barracks were full and the doors were shut. When the doors had been closed, a great deal of muttering took place, but many remained silent as they finished casting off their regalia. Captain Caraid was not with the group.

"I feel uneasy," Rowan whispered to Alder. Alder said nothing for a moment but nodded that he felt the same.

"What time is it?" Alder asked one of the nearby soldiers. "We have been in here since the start of the coronation and we rested so that we would be ready for our return home. We have lost track of the time in our sleep."

"We have been at the coronation for two hours. The coronation was only an hour, but we were present for the arrival and departure of the citizens. It is about four now, and if you are not in too much of a hurry, we will soon be going to the table," the soldier smiled.

"We thank you for offering to share what little you have, but we would not take it. Two more stomachs would be unwelcome guests, I am sure. We only wish to rest a while longer and then we will leave for our own country."

"Why leave at night? Do you have reason to fear the light?" another soldier asked.

"We have no reason to fear the light or anyone seeing our going. You look upon us now and see that we have nothing. Our only reason for leaving at night is that it is cooler. We have a long journey before us and it is very hot this summer. We would both prefer to ride in the cool night air." Alder stared firmly at the man, but his words had not been unkind. The man looked Alder up and down but said nothing.

"Breage!" another soldier shouted and the man turned, ending his staring at Alder.

The two soldiers began their own conversation. Alder turned back to Rowan with a strange look in his eyes. "Rest now, Rowan. I feel that we will need all we can get ere we arrive in our own land."

Rowan laid down to rest and somehow fell asleep. He had harsh dreams of marauding men. Alder woke him when all the soldiers were asleep.

"Come, Rowan. It is time we are off and I should say that we need to go as quietly as possible. I get a strange feeling from Breage and his friends."

Rowan and Alder quietly snuck out of the room with the bag. Rowan had used it as a pillow and, though he did not know it, Alder had lain awake and watched over him.

They crept without a sound, both being able to walk about without noise due to their time hunting in the woods. They pulled the heavy doors open and slipped out. They moved up the stairs slightly faster and stopped before exiting the barracks. Both took a deep breath. Rowan slipped the bag on.

"We mustn't look like thieves in the night, escaping with a bag of plunder. We are not thieves. So we must look like we are only leaving to return home," Rowan whispered. They took another moment to compose themselves before Alder pushed open the door.

They casually strolled out into the night and waved to the guards, but said nothing. They walked a few paces before Rowan stopped as if remembering something. He turned back to the guards at the door. "We did not see Caraid, but when he returns, please give him our deepest thanks for providing us with lodging during our stay. We must return to our own land and we prefer to travel in the cool night air, rather than the blistering sun of the day."

The guards nodded and Rowan and Alder walked toward the stables. Their horses were waiting for them and had been well tended to. Rowan and Alder quickly saddled them and rode out at a fair pace. They tried for speed but did not want to look as though they were fleeing from a crime.

It was a dark night. Clouds filled the sky and rumbling could be heard in the distance, though it did not feel like rain. The air was cool and a low breeze that seemed hardly noticeable brushed past them. The road was dark before them, but their horses were surefooted, having wandered long distances in the dark before. Rowan sighed once they were outside the city and away from the gates.

"I have this overwhelming feeling of dread about me," he said in a low voice to Alder.

"I do as well, but it is fading with every foot farther we are from that castle and that woman. But there are some that are loyal to her within the barracks and they spied on us most of the evening. They may have even watched our going. But that cannot be helped and we have nothing except an old book that no one within the city can read."

"Do you think Princess Uiall can read Elvish?" Rowan asked.

"No. I do not believe that she knows a word of it, or surely, she would have had me killed when I spoke to her. She would not have suffered my words."

"Eachdraiche was afraid of them finding his book or he would not have taken such pains of hiding it."

"He was, but I do not know why other than he knew he was about to be killed. This was many years ago, as well. Maybe the old king knew Elvish and Eachdraiche was afraid of him reading the book. We cannot be sure what his true fears were, however."

They rode in silence for some time.

"I wish to go faster," Rowan murmured. The feeling of dread had not dissipated, and he wished for more distance between Kingsland and themselves. They pushed their horses on faster through the night. The rumbling clouds persisted and lightning could be seen across the hills, though no rain came.

"I have the uneasy feeling of being followed or being spied upon," whispered Rowan. He and Alder rode side by side and slowed their horses again. The moon was hidden behind the clouds and no lantern light appeared across the fields from the scattered farms. They could hardly see their way except for when the bright white flashes broke across the sky and illuminated the fields. A wind from the storm whisked the grasses in the fields and they rustled uneasily. Still, no rain fell and the thunder rumbled across the plains.

"I have the same feeling and often I have glanced back at the road behind us when the lightning has flashed, but I have not seen anyone upon the road. If I knew where we were, I would think that perhaps we should stop. But there is no shelter here and if we are truly hunted, they will see the horses."

"We cannot be halfway yet. I watched as we traveled and I was unable to find a suitable shelter after we left the Pass of Handuin. We must still be several hours' ride from there. I feel that leaving during the night was a mistake, though I know not what dangers the morning would have brought."

"We would have faced many dangers if we had stayed. I do not believe we would have gotten out of the city with—" Alder stopped mid-sentence and peered ahead into the night.

Several flashes of lightning lit up the world around them. On the road before them was a dark figure. Another flash and the figure was gone. "I know not what evil is before us, but pull out your knife and ride with all haste," Alder whispered.

They kicked their horses and the sudden change in their riders made the horses bolt down the road. Alder and Rowan stayed close together. Rowan had his dagger in his hand and Alder held his sword. They passed over where the figure had been and no assault came. Another flash of lightning. Nothing appeared on the road ahead, but three figures had entered the road behind them, and they appeared to be following them.

They were dark and appeared shapeless. They were bigger than a man but did not have the same structure. They moved on all fours, with long drooping arms in front and shorter legs in the back. They moved quickly. Rowan could not distinguish their faces if they had any.

"Faster!" Alder shouted. Rowan looked at him and shivered. Alder was terrified. Rowan kicked Fior. "Faster my friend! We need haste!"

"Cabhag! Cabhag, Luath!" Alder pleaded.

Another flash of light. The road before was open, but now five were behind and they were charging as quickly as they could. One stumbled and knocked into another. A hideous cackling came from the beasts as the one that had been knocked bit into the other.

The quarreling and cackling became more intense. Hideous croaking, moaning, and growling reached their ears. Another flash and all the creatures had fallen back into a pile of fighting beasts.

Still, Alder and Rowan pushed the horses. Rowan did not know how far they had ridden. He did not know where they were when they slowed the horses.

"What were they?" Rowan asked when he and Fior had caught their breath.

It was a moment before Alder spoke. "Bugbears, I think."

"From the children's tales? Even in the tales, they were creatures of the forests and caves, never on the plains and in the fields."

"It seems that many things are beginning to emerge from the children's tales, but I learned of them before and have seen one only once. It killed many men. They have the strength of trolls, and they can run as fast as horses with their short back legs. They appear to run like rabbits if you see them in the light. The old stories say that they are a cross between goblins and trolls, but I always seemed to think they were a cross between evil men and trolls. Their faces do not look like that of goblins'. Hideous to look upon. They resemble men, but they are deformed into animal shapes. Their limbs are covered in hair. But it is their grins that fill me with dread. They are always smiling, wide, toothy grins. Their teeth are not sharp, but flat and far apart. They do not kill with claw or fang, for they have neither. They kill with crushing and snapping. They will throttle any they can get their hands on and they eat small children almost whole. But only almost, unless the children are very small…" Alder trailed off and Rowan did not say anything for some time.

"Why were they down so far into the fields and why did they hunt us?"

"I do not know. They seldom travel in such groups. The males, as we saw, are territorial and hostile. Males tend to stay far away from other males. For one to come after us would not be unusual, but there have not been any sightings north of the Òrail River for at least a hundred years and now they come in a pack and they find us. I do not know."

Rowan could hear Alder's voice quivering and did not want to question him any longer. Lightning flashed behind them. The monsters were not on the road behind them, but the white mountains of the Dìonadair rose before them. "We are almost to the pass," Rowan said in a soothing voice. Alder did not reply.

"Perhaps we should rest a while in the watchtower until it is light. I am worried that there may be goblins within the pass and we are weary," Rowan offered.

"I think you are right, though being so close to the forest makes me uneasy."

Another hour went by, and they reached the ruins of the watchtower. It had been mighty several hundred years ago and had served its purpose well. But with the changing of kings came the changing of opinions and the watchtower was abandoned and left to ruin. Still, the goblins believed it was haunted by the spirits of the ancient soldiers, ever ready to perform their duty, and they did not go into the ruins.

They led their horses up the small hill and into the ruins through a hole in the wall. The grass had grown up through what had been the floor and the horses were pleased enough. The horses bedded themselves in the grass. Rowan and Alder backed up against a pile of stones and buried themselves the best they could. They rested but did not sleep. The storm had passed, but the clouds blocked out the moon and very little light was able to penetrate. Every stirring of the grass had them lifting their weapons.

After what seemed like an eternity, the sky began to lighten with the coming dawn. Birds in the forest began to chirp as they woke. The horses lifted their heads and looked toward their masters.

"Should we go while the dawn is upon us? I do not believe that the goblins will be stirring at this hour," Rowan proposed.

"I hope that you are right," Alder murmured.

They led their horses back to the road and mounted them. Alder still held his sword and Rowan saw that his hand was white around the hilt. Rowan, knowing that the pass could be dangerous, readied his bow as the horses began to plod along quietly.

The pass was clear and quiet. Rowan strained his ears for any sound, but no noise came to them from the road. He was weary, wearier than he could recall being in many years. Alder did not say anything. They rode through the pass without incident. After many hours, they reached the end of the pass.

Rowan felt a vast weight fall off his shoulders when he looked out across the moors. Nothing had changed since they had left, being gone only three days. The marsh birds twilled in the grasses and ducks quacked merrily in the swamps. The bugs were still rampant, as usual, but they could not bite through their leather tunics. The smell of wet earth wafted about and toads croaked and splashed into the pools.

"Do you notice that the pools are not as high and the road dustier?" Alder asked in a low voice. Rowan looked about. He had not noticed. The horses kicked up more dust as they walked and the water level in the marsh did seem lower. "I had not noticed, but I do now. It must not have rained since we left, which is unusual," Rowan stated, not quite knowing what Alder was getting at. Alder, however, did not elaborate but kept his stern gaze fixed upon the city ahead.

Rowan did not know what to say to him. He was in some dark place Rowan could not begin to understand. He realized that he seldom thought of the many years Alder had lived without him. Alder had known the entire line of kings of Kingsford. He had watched the downfall of the kingdom. He had seen monsters and beasts of myths and legends and had watched them disappear from the land. Kingdoms had risen and fallen, fields tilled and then burned, and populations grow just to be killed by the darkness in the south.

The city was bustling and nothing was out of the ordinary. It was just as clean and cheerful as the day they had left. People still sang and greeted each other and children ran through the streets.

Rowan and Alder made their way to the castle. A messenger had gone before them to find Bacach and tell him that they had returned. Now the horses meandered up the streets at a slow pace. Rowan and Alder had put their weapons away once they had gotten to the moors, but Alder's hand still rested upon the hilt of his sword. He still held tightly onto the reins of his horse with his left hand.

When they reached the castle, Bacach stood smiling upon the steps, looking strangely like his father when Rowan and Alder had escorted the royal party from Midland.

"My friends!" he called. "I am glad to see that you both are well. Come inside. Your horses will be taken care of."

Rowan smiled and dismounted his horse, handing the reins to the stable boy. Alder did the same, but his face was still sullen. They were led to Bacach's room. Bacach was still fearful of the other rooms of the castle and preferred to only do business concerning the stone in his own room.

"How was the road?" Bacach asked once Rowan and Alder were inside and the door was shut and locked. He smiled at them, but it quickly disappeared when he saw their faces.

"We were hunted by the bugbear, Bacach," Alder stated bluntly and slightly irritated.

"But bugbear are not—" Bacach murmured, shocked and confused.

"They are quite real, Bacach. I have seen them before this occurrence, but it has not been for over nine-hundred years. I daresay there used to be a tapestry of one within the castle, but your grandfather most likely had it removed."

Bacach stared at Alder, not sure what to say, but vaguely understanding that Alder was waiting for an answer.

"What happened?" was all he could whisper.

"We left Kingsland yesterday as soon as it was dark. The clouds were thick in the sky, and it was extremely dark. I felt uneasy within the city or else I would have stayed until morning. From the time we left the city, we felt as though we were being watched. From the flashing of lightning, we could see shapes appear on the road before us. Then we found that we were to be assailed by five of them. Why they did not attack us from the front, I cannot say. I do not know why they hunted us in such great numbers or from whence they came. We were able to outrun them and we took refuge in the Watchtower of Faire. Nothing else came for us and we arrived here just as you find us now."

Bacach was silent for a long time.

"How did they know, Bacach? How did they know that we would be on the road and why were they after us?

A group that size could have assailed Kingsland and would have had a lot of success. But they came for us."

"I do not know, Alder. Perhaps they were after the book."

"None knew of the existence of that book besides the three of us and perhaps some of the lords of the elves. Torradh himself should not have knowledge of the contents of that book! There is no enchantment, no magic about it that would call to the forces of Torradh! Someone knew that we had found something and they knew when we would be leaving. They set a trap but placed their faith too high in creatures that cannot be controlled. If it had not been for their lack of judgment in the numbers that would be needed to assail us, we would not have been able to outrun the bugbear. Our horses would have tired long before the bugbear and perhaps they would have chased us into the pass where a host of goblins awaited us. Our doom was near at hand and we do not know who to thank for it or why."

"Alder, I did not intend for you to face such dangers upon that road. Nor you, Rowan," Bacach implored, turning to Rowan with the look of a rabbit corned by a wolf. Rowan could not think of anything to say to deter Alder. Again, he spoke the truth, though Rowan had not understood the fullness of the peril they had been in.

"But you found the book?" Bacach asked, timidly. Alder chuckled a very dark and silent laugh. Rowan was taken aback by him. He had never acted so boldly before and in the darkness of the room with only the firelight, he looked almost evil.

"We found it. It is written completely in Elvish," Rowan answered.

"Did you read it?" Bacach asked.

"Alder read it. I do not know Elvish."

"What did it say of the stone?"

"That it is hidden within Caradh and the only person that knows its location are the two elves that helped hide the stone and the king of Caradh," Alder interjected.

"Caradh, being the ancient name of Triloblaid, which is now the ancient name of Kingsford, and the king being King Taighe," Bacach stated. "So where in the castle did he put it? I have searched everywhere! Every chamber! I have sounded the floors and walls. My family and the servants think that I have gone mad, crawling about the floors and tapping upon the walls, but I have searched!" Bacach now paced about the room.

After some time, he calmed down. "Did the book say anything else of use?"

"I did not have the chance to read much else, save why my people were cast out."

Bacach stopped pacing and stared at Alder. "I apologize, Alder, but little can be done for the past."

Alder stared into the fire. "That is all you have to say about that? All you have to say about the killing of my people in the streets? It was lust and greed that sent my people out of the city! They had lives here and ever only strove to help the city. Cursed it was before it was renamed

Triloblaid and long it will remain cursed, regardless of how many times your kings change the name! Their blood flowed in the streets and to this day I have been willing to shed my blood! I was left an orphan because my mother could not reside here for fear of death, but did not wish to deprive my father of his son! My father stayed because he swore an oath to protect the kingdom until his death, and how did he die? A man too old for combat, but faced with nothing more than a bugbear! But little can be done for the past..." Alder trailed off.

"Alder, my friend. Why did you not speak of this?" Rowan whispered.

"I did not know. My father never spoke of it. My father was building Taigheland with King Taighe when I was born. When he returned, I had been left with a woman in the second quarter, in a building that now belongs to Madame Belladonna, and my mother was gone. He never received word from her and he was wroth and would not search for her. If he learned wisdom in death, surely he regrets not seeking her out."

"Alder, I am sorry for what happened to your people, but we lack time. I must know if the elves have written anything else in the book!" Bacach interrupted, impatiently.

Alder looked at him quizzingly. "I told you, Eachdraiche did not know the location of the stone. The elves made an effort that no one should ever find it. The book says nothing about the location."

"But you didn't read the entire book! What if there is more information later on? What about when he returned to Kingsford and Midland? Did he write about why?"

"He did not. He only wrote that King Urram gave him a special task and that he must leave with all haste. He then discussed the witch hunt that followed him from Kingsford and his captivity in Midland."

Rowan stared at Alder. Alder had lied. He had not read through the book and had already told Bacach that he had not.

But Bacach paced about the room in silent anger. "Why could the fool not write anything of importance before he died?" he was muttering.

Alder's face twisted slightly in the firelight, but he turned so that Bacach could not see his expression.

"Bacach, my friend, we are all weary. Surely we can discuss this more after we have had some rest? We have been in this room in the dark for some hours and Alder and I have not eaten," Rowan persuaded. He could feel the charged atmosphere and knew nothing good could come from Alder's mood and the strangeness that had overcome Bacach.

"Ah, yes. I apologize. I have forgotten that the road was hard. I will call the servants to prepare a meal for you," Bacach stated, coolly.

"Do not trouble your household. We will go to the inn tonight. I am afraid that we are both overwhelmed with the splendor of castles and great halls and rich foods. Send for us as you will, but we will be in the Grey Goat for the night."

Bacach called for a servant and Rowan and Alder were shown out. Bacach had closed the door and they could hear him pacing about the room as they walked down the hall.

It was a sunny afternoon and quite hot. Alder and Rowan squinted at the outside world with the change from the dark room they had been arguing in for hours. A haze was about everything and the white stone reflected the light mercilessly in all directions.

"I do not wish to leave the horses so far away," Alder said, stopping before the doors of the castle.

They retrieved their horses and slowly drifted down the streets. Without a word, Alder passed Rowan and headed toward the city gates. Rowan followed but did not question him. They passed over the moors toward the sea.

Most of the beach was wet and covered in marsh and seagrasses, but a few small islands rose up and forced the water around and towards the sea. Alder dismounted and allowed Luath to graze on the sedges and rushes of the moor. Rowan allowed Fior to do the same and he sat next to Alder in the sand.

The waves crashed and the sea birds cried overhead, dipping and hovering in the faint breeze. Salt spray brushed Rowan's face as the waves came down in front of him. He always enjoyed the sea, but he seldom had time to sit and enjoy it. He mulled recent events over in his head. They had been so busy, but everything came and went in waves, just like the sea. The events were crashing down upon him, then came the ebb in the tide, the build-up, the arc, and the crash once more. Great things were happening around him, but the other moments were filled with nothing and waiting as the waves built up again.

Their life before rescuing Aineolach and Uiall was steadier like a stream. The days flowed together with occasional bumps or obstacles but peacefully moved along. But like the stream, they had reached the sea and were now being pulled out with the tide. Where the tide went, and where it would bring them, they did not know, but Rowan knew if they did not swim, they would drown. The whole world must learn to swim or drown.

"Bacach seemed strange today, did he not?" Alder asked, interrupting Rowan's thoughts.

"He seemed more on edge, but he was still kind to us when we reached the castle."

"After that. When I brought up the outlawing of the elves and the killings. He became very agitated as though he knew something that he did not want us to know."

"Well, it is most likely an uncomfortable topic, between the two of you. He knows or should know, that what happened was wrong, but it cannot be amended."

"Perhaps you are right, but he was very concerned with me having read the book."

"The stone is very important to him. It is very important for all of us. He most likely would have wanted you to have read the book thoroughly multiple times to examine all the details. Why did you lie about the end of the book? I know you did not read it."

"Bacach was not listening. I had told him that I had not read very much of the book, but then he questioned what happened at the end. We all knew that Eachdraiche came to Kingsford first and was refused entry to the castle before running to Midland. I only told him the information he already knew because he was acting strangely. Even if I had read the ending, I would not have told him what was really in there. I wish to understand why he was behaving in such a manner before I tell him anything more if there is anything more to tell."

"But it is Bacach!" Rowan scolded.

"And a necromancer appeared in the great hall. We do not know where the fiend is. Whoever it is, they are skilled in dark magic beyond either of our knowledge. Perhaps they have bewitched Bacach in our leave, perhaps they were disguised as Bacach. I did not detect magic, but whoever is hunting the stone is aware of our every move. It may not be a bad idea to distance ourselves from Bacach until we can find more information for ourselves and keep our knowledge to ourselves the best we can. Bacach mutters to himself a lot when he is thinking. Perhaps he has muttered too much to the darkness."

"What shall we do?" Rowan asked in dismay.

"I know not, but whatever we do it must be done with caution and secrecy."

They sat a little while longer, staring out across the sea. The sun began to touch the sea as it lowered in the sky.

Rowan suddenly got an idea. "Let us head to the inn."

They tied their horses in the stable, providing them with plenty of wild oats and grains collected from the moors. The wild grasses were saved for livestock and were eaten by the poor of the town, but most saved their money or goods to trade for the grains grown in Taigheland or Midland. Herbs and spices grew in the moors, and these were often collected by children to flavor the heavy bread of the city. A few of the older lads of the city tended the collective herds of sheep and goats that grazed on the moor grass. Game birds and their nests were frequently pillaged by the same bands of marauding children. Alder had been one of these children in his own day, only he did not have a home to return his spoils to and many of the other children had been afraid of the pale, wild, Elvish boy that roamed the moors unceasingly except for when he came to trade his prey for food he could not acquire on the moors.

One of Alder's more frequent customers was the innkeeper of the Grey Goat. For generations, he had sold his game to the always-willing innkeepers. Hungry mouths were always present at the inn and those mouths usually were not partial to what type of meat was in their stew or pie, as long as the meat was present. The wives of the innkeepers were very happy with the herbs and spices that Alder would bring and often paid him to bring them specific things such as quail eggs. But the most highly sought-after food was the golden cloudberry. They came from bushes that grew almost on top of the still and deadly water. Many responsible parents would not allow their children to pick the sweet and juicy berries for fear of their children falling and drowning. But Alder, light and nimble, was able to pick large quantities of the berry and had plenty to trade after taking his fill. Thus, the pies and cakes of the inn had been adorned with the tantalizing berries and many a noble was persuaded to venture into the 'unsavory' inn.

Alder and Rowan now stood outside the door and a great commotion could be heard within. Rowan only smiled at Alder as he pushed open the door. A flood of warm light flooded the now-darkened street and music and mirth poured out, along with a drunken man who staggered out into the mud.

They stepped inside. The tables had been moved to the shed, chairs lined the walls, a band played in the corner and dancers spun about the room. Hardly anyone danced the same steps, but all the couples spun together at the same speed so as not to be trampled by the next group. The familiar smell of Margie's cooking, woodsmoke, and whiskey filled the room. Smoke from many pipes drifted hazily about the ceiling.

Margie was behind the bar with Òstair and waved to them as they entered and shut the door. They pushed their way to the bar and sat down with smiles.

"You boys come to see me less and less, nowadays," she scolded with hands on her plump hips. "I suppose it has to do with all the ruckus at the castle. I say the inn has been busier than ever, though. Father started trading for new hops and barley from the merchants in New Market.

They say they are getting it from past the Troich Mountains, but heaven knows I don't know much about what lies where. Costs a pretty penny, I'll say, but we are the only inn in town with beer! We have folks from all over coming here now to taste father's beer! The lads weren't able to keep up with catching things on the moors, so now we are buying pork from those merchants. Can you believe that? Salted pork from Taigheland! I'll say that the men enjoy the pies a lot more and hardly seemed to notice that we started charging more for them. But I always keep some of them game birds in the kitchen, especially the eggs, just in case you boys come in. I know you don't prefer anything more than quail eggs in your pie and ducks in your soup."

"Aye, you're a good lass, Margie," Alder smiled. "Maybe I should hunt up some cloudberries for you just like old times?"

"You haven't done that since I was a wee lass, Mr. Alder. Even then you only ever brought them for me, never enough to make anything out of. You were already doing mercenary work by then. Though I'll say I'd rather never taste another cloudberry than for you to go back to that line of work. Such a changed man you are since you took up company with Mr. Rowan." Margie smiled and patted Rowan on the hand.

"Well if Mr. Rowan had been born a few hundred years earlier, perhaps I would not have taken up that line of work, to begin with," Alder joked.

Shouts for beer arose on the other side of the bar. "If I haven't talked your ears off already! I best be back to work! I'll get some supper for you boys as soon as I take care of that lot. Men from the south, I'll say. They don't speak as gently as the men from Kingsford and I can't say they remind me of the farmers from Taigheland, either, but serve them I will as long as they keep paying." Margie whisked off toward the brewhouse.

"We have only been missing from society for a month and look how things have changed!" Alder shouted above the roar of the room.

"Margie was right about crowds coming for a taste of the beer. Most everyone in the room has a pint in front of them and a good amount of them are on the lines of being drunk."

"A lot of new folks. I've never seen most of the people in the room."

"You're right. A lot of strangers. They don't appear to be farmers. Maybe some sailors or merchants out of New Market?"

"I am not sure," Alder shouted in a less happy tone.

Margie reappeared with two large bowls of stew and a loaf of bread. "Sorry, Mr. Alder, about not having a pie for you. I wish I had the time to make one for you, but my father needs all the help he can get out here with the lads. I hope you like it."

Margie really did look upset about not having a pie for Alder, knowing that they were his favorite. Although Alder had always been part of her life, Rowan suspected that she had the same tinge of hopeless feelings for him that many of the other women of the city had, though they lie deep within her and she was not a woman to dwell on fantasy. She was sensible and busy.

Alder smiled at her. "I love all your cooking, Margie, especially those spice cakes I know are hiding in the back."

Margie flushed but quickly regained her composure. "Have you been rooting through my pantry? How did you know I have spice cakes saved in the back?"

Alder tapped his nose. "I can smell those beauties from here. Although, it seems that you have started buying spices from the merchants, as well."

Margie flushed again. "It must be your Elvishness, begging your pardon, Mr. Alder. We started buying cassia from them. They say it is from far to the east and better than what used to come from the south. They say it is guarded by winged serpents and only by making offerings can they get it, a bunch of offal, I'll say. I don't much mind how they come by it, but you should smell the cakes as they cook. The honey and that new cassia make the room smell like what the heavens ought to smell like."

"Why don't you go bring us one of those cakes?" Alder smiled with one of his irresistibly dashing grins. Rowan laughed as Margie frowned and turned toward the kitchen. No one could resist that smile. Alder seldom used it, but when he did, he received what he wanted. What he wanted was usually cake.

Margie reappeared with a small cake, set it down, and spun away as if to avoid Alder's face entirely. Alder smiled at Rowan and sliced the cake in half. He began eating his soup with a sly grin on his face. Rowan smiled and ate his soup.

The music and dancing continued. The dancing sometimes changed, whether it was a song that required specific dancing or whether it was left for interpretation, it was always a mess. Many people were not native to Kingsford and did not know the local dances, but they danced regardless which caused frequent jostling and mixing of dances and dancers throughout the room.

Rowan and Alder finished their food, paid Margie double the cost of the food, and purchased their usual small room from her father. They now sat with their backs to the counter and watched the dancers. Alder's mood had completely changed, and Rowan was glad for it. He felt Alder's low moods in his heart and he always had an overwhelming feeling to cheer him, though he seldom knew how and often lacked the right words to say. But he knew that Alder loved this chaos. The laughter, the dancing, the music. Good food, a full stomach, and the smell of woodsmoke about a room.

Alder rose from his stool. Rowan looked at him, but Alder was staring at a young woman in the crowd. She had blonde braids wrapped around her head and wore one of the wool dresses that were common to the young women in the town. Then Alder was through the crowd and offering his hand to the girl. Rowan smiled. Of course, she accepted. Her eyes widened when she looked into Alder's face and Rowan was surprised that she did not swoon.

Alder was now spinning her about the room with the easy grace that belonged to his race. They spun quickly, but easily around the other dancers. When the song was over, Alder bowed to the girl who was flushed and out of breath and really looked as though she might swoon. As quickly as he had appeared in front of her, he disappeared and was offering his hand to another girl.

Rowan smiled as he watched Alder but then felt eyes watching him from behind. He looked over his shoulder to see Margie staring at him with her hands on her hips. "Why are you not out there, Mr. Rowan?" she questioned.

"I am a poor dancer. I am not as light-footed as Alder, nor am I his equal for looks to have a partner for every dance."

"Well there isn't a one in the kingdom that is a match to Mr. Alder, and I don't know that you'll find one anywhere except the Elven lands to the east. But you can't be any more clumsy than these other men who are as fat and drunk as they are! You're a hunter, Mr. Rowan! Go have a dance. There are plenty of pretty girls over there and some not as pretty that I'm sure would be happy enough to have a partner as handsome as you! Blond hair as long and thick as yours and you being rugged and twice the man as any out there! And them brown eyes of yours, soft like fresh bread! They'll swoon for you just like Mr. Alder!"

Rowan laughed heartily. "Only you can compare eyes to bread and make it a compliment, Margie! I will dance, but only if you are my first partner."

"Why, I couldn't Mr. Rowan! Father needs me back here!"

"Òstair, will you spare Margie for a dance?" Rowan called down the bar.

Òstair looked surprised but happy. "Aye, I can handle this lot for a jaunt. She should get out and have a jolly for a bit, always working so hard my wee lass."

Rowan turned back to Margie who was red in the face and scowling. "Either we dance, or I sit here," Rowan laughed.

The band was settling in for a fast one. Alder had selected his next victim but laughed heartily when he saw Rowan lead Margie to the floor. Rowan smiled at Margie, but his smile flickered when he saw the sparks in her eyes. The music started.

Margie, as plump as she was, was hardy. She worked all day and well into the night. She was quick on her feet and could march miles if she had to. Now she danced effortlessly around the room with the same speed Alder danced with his partners. Rowan and Margie never missed a step, for they both knew all the dances well. They laughed merrily and all the cares of the world were gone from the room.

When the song was over, Rowan stepped back. Another song started and Alder snatched Margie into his arms before she could say a word. Rowan watched them as they careened about the room, Alder laughing the whole time and Margie looking as though she was scolding him, despite moving with all haste. Again, she never faltered or missed a step. She had watched the dances her entire life and knew every beat by heart.

After many dances, the lot appeared to be at the end of the night. Most were drunk and were staggering to their rooms or out into the night. Rowan had danced with many girls. He had been surprised that all the women he offered his hand to smiled at him and accepted it. They all bowed at the end of the dance and stared after him. Now he was again sitting at the counter and watching as Alder finished the last dance with a very tired-looking woman.

Rowan yawned and smiled as Alder approached. He could see that Alder's eyes were heavy, although he did not show it as much as mortal men. He smiled almost wearily. "Ready for bed?" he asked happily.

They headed to their usual small room and locked the door behind them. Alder, who had been carrying the bag with the book inside all night, even while dancing, now took it off and set it behind his pillow. Rowan placed his bow and quiver next to the bed and slid off his boots. "How do you talk to women like that?"

Alder looked up, questioningly. "Talk to women?"

"When you dance with them. What do you say to them when you approach them?"

Alder laughed. "I do not say anything to them. It is all about how you do not ask them. You approach them, broad-shouldered and tall. You outstretch your hand, give them your best smile, but not too excited of a smile or too kind, and stare into their eyes. If you ask them to dance, then it is a question in which they can say aye or nay. No decent girl will deny the outstretched hand of a decent lad, or even a somewhat indecent one. If she does, she is usually haughty and full of herself and you simply shake your head as if you did not mean to ask her and take the girl next to her."

Rowan laughed. "That plan can work for none other except you."

"Aye, and probably any other Elvish men among human maids, but it would most likely work for you, as well," Alder chuckled, flopping down on the bed. He had removed his sword, but it lay in bed next to him. One arm was under his head and the other rested on his sword.

Rowan blew out the candle and lay down next to him, staring at the ceiling. "What do you suppose will happen next?" he asked.

"I know not, but it cannot be as good as this night," Alder sighed.

Chapter 6

The dawn flooded the shabby room and Rowan was surprised that he had slept soundly all night. The inn was quiet, but every so often he could hear Margie and Òstair moving around downstairs. Rowan rolled over and found that Alder was sitting in bed reading Eachdraiche's book.

"Anything of interest so far?" Rowan asked, propping himself up on his side.

"Most of it is political nonsense. It discusses the improvements in the Elvish armor and weaponry, the formation of new towns and villages, the destruction of those towns and villages, the ever-changing threats in the south, and the discovery of some new beast from that region. Very little of it is of any importance, though it most likely seemed important at the time. The stone is never discussed again, but with the amount of detail Eachdraiche wrote in, I doubt it had slipped his mind."

"Perhaps he was forbidden? It did not seem as though the elves wanted it to be remembered."

"Perhaps. But we write things so that they can be read and remembered. So by writing even one page about the stone, he is accepting that the information will be read and used. But who can tell what his purpose was when he included or excluded information. Thus, history is in the hand of the author."

Alder continued scanning the pages and flipping through the book.

"I think I will go see Margie about breakfast," Rowan offered.

"You certainly treat me too well," Alder chuckled.

Rowan slipped his boots on, scooped up one of Alder's, and threw it at him. Alder swung lazily at it and knocked it to the floor with a smile. Before Rowan closed the door, he turned back to Alder. "I said I would see Margie about breakfast, not that I would serve you in bed."

The main room of the inn smelled wonderful. The windows had been opened to allow the morning air to chase out the pipe smoke from the evening. The fireplace had not been lit, but the kitchen fire was roaring. Margie bustled about the room, carrying pans and stirring pots. She frequently sniffed the air, smelling her many dishes for doneness.

"Ah! Good morning Mr. Rowan!" she called when she spotted him.

"Good morning, Margie. What do you have for breakfast?" Rowan asked with a smile, noticing the flour on her cheeks.

"Anything you could be hungry for! Porridge in the pot, fresh bread coming out the oven, salted fish, cold mutton, or pheasant. There is no cheese, though. Merchants say something has prevented them from getting anything from the dairies. Not sure what all that means, just that we don't have no milk or cheese for the table right now. Might be nice if someone would raise milk goats on the moors instead of all of them meat goats."

"All is well, Margie," Rowan smiled. "The grass out there makes bad milk, anyhow. I'll take a loaf of that bread."

"You best take two, or else I don't know Mr. Alder," she said, spinning toward the oven where several golden loaves could be seen against the fire. She quickly returned with the loaves wrapped in two pieces of cloth. "Now I don't want a penny more from you now. You paid more than double what you should have last night. I do want my good kitchen cloth back when you boys are finished."

Rowan nodded and took his prizes back to the room. Alder was in the same spot and barely looked up when Rowan entered. "This is boring," he murmured. His nose twitched and he stared pointedly at Rowan.

"Bring me one of those loaves at once," he drooled.

"Yes, Your Majesty," Rowan smirked.

Alder curled his legs up and Rowan sat at the foot of the bed. Alder shut the book and Rowan plopped the wrapped loaf down on top of it. They both unsheathed their daggers and carved large slices off the hot, steaming loaves. Margie had sweetened them with honey and flavored them with some of the sweet flowers that were blooming in the moors. It was pure heaven. Neither spoke as they downed the bread, savoring every slice before the bread cooled.

"What do you suppose we should do?" Rowan asked as they sat in silence.

"We have an unnecessary sense of duty to a kingdom that has all but destroyed our families. They are thankless in all that we do. They provide us with rooms that are empty and food from an overflowing table. We have no reason to continue down this path in their name."

"But if the necromancer comes, they come to destroy the people. The people of Kingsford know nothing of what is happening or going to happen. The king will not protect them. He will use them to buy time in an attempt to escape. I cannot allow these people to be slaughtered without even a warning," Rowan implored.

"But how will we save them?" Alder asked, heatedly. "What good are our weapons against those of the dead? How shall we know when they come besides waking to find specters gathered about us? We know nothing of this magic. Perhaps they will march upon us like the living, or perhaps they will rise around us like shadows. How will we fight shadows?"

Rowan stared at the dingy wall for some time. If weapons passed through them like dust, what could they do? Would the weapons of the dead pass through the living as well or would they slay that which is within them?

"Does the book say anything about magic or someone who may know magic?" Rowan asked.

"Like a sorcerer? No. The elves have their own spells and white magic, so to speak, and it is not discussed in here. Most likely it was too common to even be worth noting. This black magic was created by Torradh and was only ever practiced by his followers. I was always told and had believed that all of his followers and all that were capable of performing black magic had been killed in the War of Bàs Pianail. Either one of his followers survived and crept back to him or he has found a new student."

"What if we went to the elves? Surely they would listen about the necromancer. It would frighten them just as much and perhaps they would be concerned for the stone and they would be able to help in some way."

Alder thought about this for a long time. Though he was more accepting of his Elvish lineage, the idea of going to the Elvish lands had never crossed his mind. Finally, he spoke. "It is not so much a matter of if we should or should not go, but if we have the time. We know not when the necromancer will strike. What if we reach the Elven lands and return with a host, but the city has been reduced to ash already?"

"Perhaps we should ask Bacach what he would have us do?"

"No. I will not include him in this. Whatever we choose to do, we do it in our own time and way. Do not forget that we were hunted by bugbear. We do not know who in the castle knew of our errand. I do not suspect Bacach, but perhaps one of his servants. The servants have just as much access to the rooms of the castle and perhaps they have been listening to his mutterings or following his movements. They would have known when we left and where we were going before and I do not wish for them to know the same information if we are to leave. We must tell no one if it is to be our plan. We may wait a few days and be seen moving in and out of the city as was our custom. If we disappear for a day or two, then we shall not be missed until we have a great enough distance behind us and then they shall not know where we are headed."

"What shall we do with the book? It is not safe with us if we are taken upon the road, but if the castle is not safe then it is not safe within the city."

"You are right. I think it would be safest with us. If we are searched no one will think anything of an elf having a book written in Elvish. Unless we are hunted for the book, no attacker would guess the importance of it. Not that it seems to have any importance, besides the few scribblings confirming the existence of the stone."

"I agree. Even if we tried to hide the book within the city and it is attacked while we are gone, the book would be found or destroyed. If we reach the elves, perhaps we can tell them that we mean to return the book to them and seek council with their lords."

"That would gain us an audience," Alder smiled. "Let us rest a few days here and do as I said. We will move about the city and outside, as we have always done and then we shall be off. But let us not be caught as if preparing for the journey. I made a promise to Margie and let me be destroyed if I should not keep it to her."

The morning was warming quickly when Alder and Rowan left the inn. Folk from the city were already about in the streets, carrying out their business. Loriman, simply called Lori by everyone, walked sullenly past on the street. He was a fat man with white whisps of hair that floated about his head in the slightest breeze.

"Lori, what upsets you so?" asked Rowan.

"Well, Mr. Rowan, I am just returned from Merchant-Town, and heaven help me if they says theys can't get no skins for shoes. As you knows, I buy all dat is from around town that folk wish to sell to me and then I make me way to Merchant-Town and buy all they will sell to me. Now they says they have no leather and how shall I make shoes if there is no leather? Says there is something wrong with the supply, they do. Sounds like to me that ain't no one willing to stick their fine necks out either to find out what the matter is. I be hearing there is a lot of things theys ain't supplying to our craftsman. Maybe theys have found a new market with better prices and theys just don't wanna tell us for fear someone will go tell it to King Amadan. Wroth he would be for its our guards that protect their sorry lot. Perhaps I ought to take it up with the king, not that he has ever bothered much with what the people keep on their feet."

"Perhaps we could help, Lori. We are hunters and we have been planning on spending some time on the moors. I am sure the animals we can catch will not have the same quality of skins that you are used to, but if you are in want of leather, we can at least provide a little," Rowan offered.

"Why Mr. Rowan! I'd be ever grateful for whatever you could bring me. I'd pay you the going rate for anything you'd bring me. I'll have none say Loriman doesn't pay for what is brought to him."

Rowan smiled. "We will bring what we can and you can pay us for the price of moor-rabbits for I am sure that is all we will catch."

"Thank you greatly, Mr. Rowan!" Loriman waddled off, much happier than he had been.

"Well that should keep us occupied for a few days," Alder chuckled.

"I am more curious about how hideous rabbit boots are going to be once they are all stitched together," Rowan murmured.

A warm breeze was blowing across the moors from the sea. The sun beat down hotly and the moors were muggy. Alder tramped ahead, looking for cloudberries. He could easily recall where all the bushes were and was happy to find that the people of the city still would not allow their children to hang over the edges of the stable ground to pick the berries where they floated right above the water. Alder opened Eachdraiche's bag and peered inside and then shrugged. He pushed the book flat on the bottom and then laid down flat on the ground and began picking berries, tossing them inside the bag.

Rowan left him and went to find one of the large boulders that dotted the moors. Some of these had come down from the mountains before the days of man and others were stones that had failed the builders of Kingsford and had simply been left in the moors. Rowan found one of the larger boulders and perched on it like a scarecrow. He stood very still with bow and arrow in hand.

Catching rabbits in snares was much faster and easier, but he did not have any rope on his person. The hunter within him enjoyed hunting this way. The rabbits were fast and would notice any sudden movements which meant that his own movements must be fluid, fast, and accurate. He stood for a long while before his eyes caught a slight movement in the brush. A fat moor-rabbit was nibbling on the bottom of one of the bushes about fifteen paces from where he stood. It hopped behind the bush and Rowan used the few minutes that it was eating behind the bush to aim his bow. He stood in position for several more minutes before the rabbit crept out, still nibbling. Rowan exhaled and released the arrow. The rabbit was struck and flew back into the brush. Rowan did not move from his rock to retrieve it but scanned the surrounding area. He saw no other movement and he retrieved his rabbit.

The day proceeded in this fashion. Rowan hunted rabbits from his high pedestals, missing some and shooting others and every so often Alder would appear, move to a new berry bush and then disappear again as he picked on his stomach from the safety of the bank.

When the sun began to approach the sea, Rowan collected his rabbits and went to find Alder. He whistled the song of the honey-wren that lived in the forest. It was a small bird that would lead those it deemed worthy to beehives. The hunter could take as much honey as he liked as long as he left a honeycomb for the honey-wren. The call had been Rowan and Alder's call on the moors for many years. When they were in the forest, they would mimic the call of the blackbirds that lived in the moors.

Alder mimicked the call from where he lay in the bushes and he stood up out of the brush. Eachdraiche's bag was half-full of the delicate golden berries that were so highly coveted in Kingsford.

"It would most likely be full except that many were not fit for Margie," Alder smiled slyly.

"It is nice that I have been baking in the sun all day shooting rabbits and you have been lying in the shade eating berries," Rowan laughed.

"I could have shown you how to pick them, but you offered your hand to Loriman and who was I to interfere with such a noble quest?"

"I wished to help the poor man, being treated so unfairly by the merchants. We are low on money and I feel that we may need some along the road. We have been paying Margie a bit too handsomely I fear," Rowan chuckled.

"It has been some time since we have worked or since we have been paid for our work. Our last few tasks were repaid with warm beds and warm meals."

"Do you remember Farmer Curran's house? His wife made that lovely stew."

"Aye, that house was full of carrots like I have never seen. All different colors, but they were all delicious. Hopefully, he has not had any more trouble with those imps digging up his beds. What a mess it was trying to uproot them. Then his son was laid up in bed, them having got the best of him and beat him with his own shovel. Rather pretty daughters he had, as well. Auburn hair and pale skin," Alder nudged.

Rowan swatted him. "And you would sooner find yourself buried under a carrot patch than get a second look at those girls if the father thought you meant to take one of them. His wife could make a lovely stew, but she was as cross and sharp as a blade. With that son laid up you'd most likely be expected to take up residence in that house and become a farmer yourself."

"I'd sooner die than lay down my sword to become a farmer. Then to consider joining her household and becoming a farmer under her father, I would sooner perish by being beaten to death by imps with shovels," Alder smirked.

They reached the gates as the sun sank into the sea. The streets had quieted, but light now poured out from every window, and smoke curled out of the chimneys. Merrymaking could be heard from within the houses and smells wafted out into the streets. Children were singing songs and every so often a hearty laugh would echo out of a house. Rowan smiled at all the soft noises and warmth that pushed through the darkening streets. They wound their way through the streets toward the second quarter where Loriman lived.

The house was much the same as all the other houses within this section of the city. His door was painted brown and over the door hung a wooden sign in the shape of a shoe. The sign did not have writing upon it, for Loriman did not know his letters and would not trust a man to write upon the sign when he would not know what it said.

Rowan knocked firmly upon the door, and he could hear the loud scrape of a burdened chair on the wood floor within. Heavy footfalls could be heard approaching the door and it swung open, filling the street with light.

"Mr. Rowan! Why I did not expect you tonight and with six rabbits! Come in, come in!" he shouted, unblocking the doorway and waddling back to his table. Rowan and Alder entered and shut the door firmly behind them.

The living area was small. To the right of the room was a stairway that led up to the second floor. To the left was a table with many chairs and a fireplace crackled respectably against the back wall. A doorway at the back of the room led to Loriman's workshop where he made the shoes. The room was very clean, and the walls had been whitewashed. A plump woman dressed in dark purple was tending a pot over the fire. She turned when she heard the extra boots on the floor.

"Well bless my soul! I was not expecting company tonight, but you are welcome here young masters!"

"We thank you. Rowan and Alder at your service." Rowan bowed as formally as he could. Mrs. Loriman promptly puffed herself up like a hen and smiled with rosy cheeks.

"Sit! Sit! Have a seat boys and supper will be ready shortly!" she turned back to her pot and stirred it viscously.

"Where would you like the rabbits, Loriman?" Rowan asked.

"Ah! I nearly forgot! Give them here and I will take them in back to the workshop. The wife will skin me if I make a mess in her quarters." Loriman waddled to Rowan and took the rabbits while his wife grimaced at him from the fireplace.

Rowan and Alder sat at the table which was expertly crafted. Mrs. Loriman hummed a song as she unceasingly stirred the pot. Noises could be heard from the workshop as Loriman cleaned the rabbits. Rowan looked to Alder who seemed to be deep in thought.

"What in the name of Speur is wrong with this fire?" cried Mrs. Loriman.

Rowan glanced back to where she was stirring the pot. The fire was lowering, despite having plenty of wood. Rowan glanced quickly about the room to see that all the candles were in fact dimming until they snuffed out into thin wisps of smoke. Loriman had stopped making noises in his shop. Alder, like lightning, was at the door, barring it.

"Quick, woman! Drown the fire so that there is no light!" he cried to her in a whisper.

Mrs. Loriman emptied a kettle of water onto the fire and shrank into the corner, whimpering.

"Hush, woman!" Alder hissed.

A scream cut through the night air. It was long, shrill, and cold, but sounded somewhat distant. The scream faded and the following silence was deafening.

Another scream, but closer.

The following silence was broken by the waddling of Loriman. "What is going on?" he wheezed as he hurried from the shop.

"Hush!" Alder glared.

Another scream, still closer.

"The shutters are open lads!" Loriman panted.

"Leave it and get down! Don't look out the window!" Alder warned.

The scream came from the end of the street.

Loriman, in his panic, had waddled to the window to shut the shutters.

"Loriman! Move away!" Alder begged.

Rowan stared at Loriman as he was reaching to shut the shutters. Alder had been about to tackle Loriman but saw Rowan's fixed gaze on the window. Alder jumped to Rowan and covered his face.

The scream echoed shrilly from right outside the house. A heavy thud came from the window. The next scream was Mrs. Loriman's.

Many people had died. Some said that they had seen a banshee, others swore it had been Bean Nighe, the death omen. Some claimed that it had been both together, walking hand in hand. Of course, those who knew the truth had not survived to put the rumors to rest. Rowan and Alder had been quickly chased from Loriman's house. Mrs. Loriman had screamed almost like a banshee herself at the very sight of them.

The city was in an uproar with guards at every corner and the cartwrights wandering up and down the streets to collect the dead as if there had been a great plague. The bodies, young and old, were taken to the moors and burned.

Rowan and Alder walked about the streets in silence and looked upon the devastation. People wept openly outside their doors and mothers cradled the young children that had been bold enough to peer out the window from their hiding places.

The scene in front of the Grey Goat was that of a battlefield. In their drunken stupors, many of the patrons had rushed into the street in an attempt to make it to their homes. The ever-present drunks and the few homeless that sat outside on crates were lying in heaps.

Rowan and Alder were about to step across the grisly wall when they were surrounded by palace soldiers. "Rowan, son of Lionn, and Alder, son of Adder, you are both under arrest by the order of His Majesty, King Amadan."

Rowan instinctively grabbed Alder's arm as it had been moving toward the hilt of his sword.

The guards moved in quickly, having saw Alder's movement. They were both knocked to the ground and placed in bonds. The soldiers pushed them through the streets toward the castle.

Rowan could not hide his shame, though he made every attempt to hide his tears. Alder stared forward with fixed eyes that seemed to be cutting through the stone of the city.

A woman who had been holding a child earlier and was now weeping on the street, raced towards Alder and clawed at him. She tore at his face and his clothes. He did not flinch or even seem to notice as the soldiers flung the woman away and hurried Rowan and Alder on.

Some threw rocks at them, and others cursed them. Some stared in wonder and questioned why these two men were being arrested. Rowan wondered why they were being arrested, but he would not ask the guards.

They reached the wall that stood in front of the castle and a great black spot was just in front of the gate as if a bonfire had been lit there. The guards pushed Alder and Rowan through it, but they would not walk through it themselves. They then continued to march them to the throne room where King Amadan waited.

Rowan and Alder were pushed to their knees in front of the throne.

"Long have I allowed the two of you to reside within my kingdom, though doom in my heart I often felt. Rowan, son of Lionn, your line is a disgrace. Your mother was a gypsy whore and your father was a drunk. He was a disgrace to my ranks as a knight. I banished him and your whore mother and he took you with him. Now I wish that you had perished upon his death in the woods.

"Alder, son of Adder. I do not know where I should begin. Why you were allowed to reside in Kingsford by my forefathers, I know not. Your father was an esteemed

Captain, but he mated with an elf-witch and now you stand before me. We have harbored you and you have never repaid your debt to this city or to me. Ever have I practiced patience and allowed you to stay within the city. Ever have I stayed my hand from carrying out the death sentence that is owed to your kind by the laws of my fathers.

"Now you both kneel before me as traitors and murderers. I allowed you to eat from my table and you send demons into my household and ghouls into my streets that threaten and murder my people. Your sentence is death! Get them out of my sight!" King Amadan roared.

"Do not touch me!" Alder demanded. "If my mother was an elf-witch and if these demons you claim I brought upon your household are truly mine, do you think it wise to declare death upon me here in your halls?"

Everyone in the room hesitated. Rowan looked at Alder, wide-eyed. His heart seemed to be ready to burst from his chest.

"Elvish souls do not simply disappear into nothingness. We come from the gods and therefore are the gods. The gods were sent to serve their time on Earth, and we were born to be their stewards. My soul will remain within these walls. If you think the havoc upon the city has been great, wait until my soul walks these halls restlessly. Black are thy hearts, but blacker still will be my own if my immortal blood is spilled on the execution block. Banish us and no more danger will come to you. I will go to my own people and I will take Rowan with me. But if you kill us now, a necromancer will be the least of your worries."

No one in the room spoke or moved toward Alder and Rowan. Everyone seemed to be contemplating his words. No one had had time to know whether or not Alder was the true cause of the city's misfortune, but now he was here saying that worse would come if they killed him. Would more problems really come or was it a bluff? No one knew anything of elves or their black magic. Alder had always been uncouth, but never violent.

"You are hereby banished from Amadania. In the event of your return, you will be publicly tortured until your death. You have one hour to remove yourselves from the city."

They were released from their bonds and thrown out of the castle. Rowan almost had to run to keep up with the quick agile strides of Alder. Rowan did not attempt to speak to Alder as they went to the inn to retrieve their horses.

Alder stopped in front of the doorway.

"What is it?" Rowan asked timidly. Rowan was involuntarily shaking and could not regain control of himself. Alder did not speak but went inside. Rowan followed a few steps behind him.

The inn was empty except for Margie. She sat at one of the tables with her head in her hands. She looked up as Alder and Rowan entered.

Margie sprang up with a shout of joy and with tears streaming down her face. "They arrested you! I saw them do it! Why? Why did they do it?" Margie, who was so steady, was now shaken, with her nerves in shambles.

"We do not have very much time, Margie my dear. Take these." Alder had grabbed a mug from the counter and was now dumping the golden cloudberries into it.

"What is to happen to you? Where are you going?" she pleaded shakily.

"We are banished and we only have an hour to leave the city. I do not believe that we have a full hour, so we must make haste," Alder told her coldly.

Margie wailed and clutched onto Alder. She pulled him into a bear hug and held onto big handfuls of his tunic. "It cannot be!" she wailed.

Alder pushed her away gently. "Margie, dear, we cannot dwell here," Alder soothed.

Margie's resolve came back like a great wave. Her face stiffened and her eyes grew steady. "You boys will take everything I can spare in the kitchen and not one word about it! I say you'll need a bit of money on the road as well!"

Margie hastened to the kitchen and was back in less than a minute with a sack of food.

"Margie…" Alder began.

"What did I say, Mr. Alder? I won't hear it!"

Margie handed the sack to Rowan and crushed him into a hug. "There are some coins in that bag, so don't be getting holes in it! It's a shame there isn't more time to clean your shirts. You boys always stink and you'll stink all the worse at the end of the road! Now get yourselves gone or I'll call the guard!"

Rowan opened his mouth to speak, but the words would not come out. He felt sick and dizzy and like everything was a bad dream that would not end. Margie patted them both and shoved them out the door, closing it firmly behind them. They heard her bar the door and then the sound of weeping from within.

They packed the horses as quickly as possible and galloped across the moors. The horses knew the way across and Rowan and Alder did not have any fear of them stumbling into the water at their speed. Rowan frequently looked behind them to see if they were being pursued, but no one came after them.

When they reached the Pass of Handuin, they slowed their horses. They were not so upset as to forget the dangers of the pass. Alder pulled his sword from its sheath and Rowan readied his bow. The pass appeared to be deserted, the guards having left after seeing the royal party through to Midland. The horses' hoofbeats echoed up the canyon walls, creating the only sound in the empty canyon.

Rowan scanned the top of the cliffs. Twisted pine trees that grew in the cracks and fissures of the cliffs did not give one much room for hiding. Most of the danger was at the end of the pass where the mountains began to slope more and more vegetation grew.

Alder stopped his horse. The sound of hooves was coming from behind them. Alder wheeled his horse to face the coming group. Rowan fitted an arrow onto his bow.

A group of soldiers were now coming toward them through the pass, but they did not have their weapons ready. Bacach was with them.

"Friends! You made haste, indeed! I was hoping to catch you before you entered the pass, but we were not able to catch you for all we could ride!" he smiled and looked very uncomfortable on the horse he was riding.

"I did not know that you had a horse or that you could ride, Bacach," was all Rowan would say.

"Ah, yes. The horse is not mine. It is borrowed from our captain until my horse is received from Cunnart. They have the finest horses, as you both know. The horses from Greenfield truly are inferior. I have been learning to ride recently in case there is a reason to flee the city. I am afraid it has occupied my time more than I wish and that I have not been able to continue the discussion we had upon your return."

"I did not know that you were so opinionated on horses, Bacach," replied Alder.

"Friends!" Bacach cried in dismay. "I am grieved at how you have been treated by my father. I scrambled the men as soon as I heard what had happened so that we may come to you now!"

"Bacach, we are banished. You cannot undo your father's will. Nor can you undo that we were marched through the streets in bonds. Alder was attacked by a citizen!" Rowan stammered. His stomach felt twisted and he felt like he was trembling on his horse. He hoped that no one could see his weakness.

"I understand. Please, at least give me the book. It will be safer in my keeping," Bacach said coolly.

"This is a relic of the Elven peoples that used to call this realm their home. It is an heirloom of my kin and you shall not have it. You cannot read Elvish and therefore it is of no use to you. Besides, it is most likely full of dark Elvish magic," Alder sneered.

"If the necromancer is coming, surely the book is not safe within the city, Bacach," Rowan added.

A change came over Bacach and he ignored Rowan's comment. He sat upright on his horse and stared at Alder. "I have only ever wished to be your friend, elf, but never have you given me the proper courtesies of my title. Now I will say it again, give me the book. That is an order."

Alder chuckled. "I have never pledged my allegiance to you or your line, Bacach. Surely now that we are outcasts you don't expect me to follow orders. I seldom followed orders when I was allowed in the kingdom and your father used to have to pay me most handsomely to get any use out of me. Have you come to barter?"

Bacach raised his good arm and the guards unsheathed their swords.

"Bacach! What are you doing?" trembled Rowan. "This is madness! The book says nothing and it is in Elvish! No one in the city can read it!"

"I do not believe that Alder is telling the truth. There must be documentation of what happened or a clue or something!"

"Does the castle historian write about every young maid your brother spoils? Does he write about every mistress your father poisons or how many bastard siblings are scrubbing the floors of the castle? One of Azalea's own chambermaids was your half-sister!" Alder mocked recklessly.

"Silence *muc fuil*!" Bacach shouted in a tantrum.

Rowan's eyes grew wide and his mouth dropped. He looked at Alder who was burning with cold fire. His carefree countenance had turned to stone. He held his sword out away from his horse, challenging the soldiers. Bacach had used the old term for elves that had been used during the killings. It was rarely uttered and never directed toward an actual elf.

Alder said nothing. A charged silence permeated the pass as Alder and Bacach glared at each other. Rowan still held his bow at the ready with the arrow on the string, but he did not know if he could shoot Bacach if the time came. But no force would separate him from Alder's side.

"The quest for the stone has driven you to madness. Do you hear what you are saying?" Rowan implored.

"I am not mad! I am sick of everyone saying that I have gone mad! My own father sent for the doctor to bleed me for madness! The fate of the kingdom, the fate of *my* kingdom depends on this!" Bacach roared.

Bacach, seeing that Alder would not waver, motioned his soldiers forward. They seemed hesitant. Alder had just been banished for the practice of black magic and they were unsure if this was true. They had never fought an elf and Alder was a renowned warrior within the kingdom. Now he looked as though he would slay them, horses and all with his very gaze. But they did not have to be scared for long.

A black-feathered arrow whizzed past them and into a soldier's chest.

"Goblins!" another soldier screamed.

Rowan and Alder spun their horses around in a fan shape, dodging arrows while the other soldiers fell to the ground. Goblins appeared along the cliffside and from behind boulders. A few were scrambling down the sides and onto the road. Rowan fired his arrows at the goblins along the cliffs and they toppled down onto the road.

"You cowards!" Alder screamed.

Rowan looked behind to see that Bacach and his remaining soldiers were retreating out of the pass, leaving Rowan and Alder to fend for themselves.

But the look on Alder's face was not one of anger. He wore a smile. A cold gleam that showed he wanted nothing more at that moment than an entire battalion of goblins between him and his road.

Alder kicked his horse into a charge and rode forward with a cry and sword held high.

"Alder!" Rowan shouted in dismay. He had never seen Alder so reckless. Rowan shot arrows as quickly as possible, making sure that no arrow was wasted.

Goblin after goblin fell down the cliffs until all that was left was the group that had formed a line on the road. Alder had reached the group and had sprung off his horse.

He slew them all with a vehemence Rowan had never seen. His movements were so fast that the slow, fumbling strokes of the goblins never had a chance to hit him. They all lie dead in a heap on the road.

Alder stood looking at the pile with his sword at his side. He didn't move. Rowan kicked his horse forward and grabbed the reins of Alder's horse, leading it to Alder. Rowan slid off his horse and went to Alder's side.

"Let no one stop us from leaving this place," Alder said, still staring at the pile.

Rowan put his hand on Alder's shoulder, but Alder did not look at him. The sun was hot and beat down upon the canyon mercilessly. Flies caught the scent of the baking goblins and began to swarm. Rowan collected his arrows and as many of the goblins' as he deemed acceptable. Alder finally turned and mounted his horse.

They left the pass and stared out into the fields.

The watchtower where they hid less than a week ago now glowed white in the sun. The world was still around them except for a faint breeze swirling the brittle yellow grass. The air became very hot once they exited the pass.

"Where would you like to go, Rowan? The whole world is before us and we are officially out of King Amadan's reach. I will not support the idea of heading to Kingsland, but if you choose to head east, the road takes us there, regardless," Alder smiled.

"We could head south. Margie's words keep going through my head about disruptions in the markets. Loriman was having trouble with the market. We have no money and perhaps there could be some work for us," Rowan offered.

Alder looked at him with an eyebrow raised. "When has mercenary work interested you?"

"It does not interest me. Money does not interest me. I do not know what we should do. We have never ventured outside Amadania or Midland. We have never been without a city to return to if things went wrong. The goblins are attacking in larger groups from the north. We were chased by bugbears when we were in the east. We cannot return to the west. That only leaves the south and we know that there is trouble there, but perhaps it is trouble that we can help with. Very few people in Taigheland know us and those that do, at the very least, like us. New Market is busier, yes, but there is less likelihood of anyone knowing us. If we can make enough money, perhaps we can buy passage from the dwarves to allow us through the mines and not risk the mountains and we can make our way to the elves and receive council."

Alder sat quietly for a moment. "Seeing how we are on the east side of the mountains, and not the west, we will have to go through Fae Forest if we wish to reach Taigheland. I doubt we will be able to reach the other side before nightfall and we will have to camp within the forest."

"Our lives matter little at this point," Rowan murmured.

"Well if you are in agreement, then I propose we do not dwell here and we press onward," Alder grinned devilishly.

They turned their horses off the road, around the ruined tower, and into the trees.

Chapter 7

Dim light filtered through the thick forest canopy, creating the appearance of early evening on the forest floor. Moss completely covered the ancient trees that were the size of four large men around. Vines wrapped around the trunks and hung from the branches. 'Hangman's nooses' is what the villagers called them for their almost magical ability to tighten themselves around unsuspecting victims' necks. A faint mist hung in the air, obscuring the distant trees.

The ground was soft and covered in thick brambles and knotted roots. Rowan and Alder dismounted their horses to lead them through the thick growth. Alder whispered soothing words to his horse in Elvish and Rowan frequently patted his horse's neck.

At any time, there could be steep drop-offs hiding below the ferns and brambles. Although it could be deadly, Rowan and Alder trusted their abilities to save themselves if they fell rather than falling with the horses and almost ensuring that they would be crushed.

The forest and the outside world created two contrasting, but equally forbidding backdrops. The forest was humid, slick, dark, and mysterious. The fields had been bright, dry, and sun-scorched with the overbearing threat of men and goblins.

The brambles and ferns swished as the party moved through them. Birds did not chirp or flitter through the trees. Bugs did not buzz up from the grasses. Nothing seemed to live within the forest, but Rowan and Alder knew that that was not true.

The forest had once been named the 'strange' forest in Elvish, for no one knew what lived within. The creatures of fairy tales appeared and disappeared, leaving hunters and naturalists baffled, and usually dead on their quests to locate the animals. Every account from those that survived the forest was different. Some had not run into anything at all and others claimed that they had seen trees uproot themselves and move about. Others had seen giant insects or snakes. More had fumbled for words when attempting to describe what they had seen while they sat half-mad in the inns.

Rowan and Alder had listened to these stories, neither believing nor disbelieving the travelers. Many scoffed and made fun of the travelers, but none of those men would venture into the forest.

Now they were alert, searching the dark places for any sign of trouble. Alder had his sword at his side and Rowan carried his bow. Rowan was glad for the silence. If anything moved, they would hear it. The trouble came from their inability to navigate under the trees. They believed that they were heading southwest, but they knew it was easy to lose their way.

At the southern end of the forest ran the Airgead River. The dwarves would often send boats down the river with goods from Beairteach to New Market, but the legends claimed that the dwarves had spells and enchantments upon their boats that prevented the beasts of the forests from harming them. Rowan had never seen a dwarf and had heard very little of their myths and legends.

The forest began to darken and Rowan was unsure of how far they had traveled. He was weary, but it had been a weary day.

"Are you tired?" Rowan asked, noticing Alder's face.

"This forest weighs heavily upon me. There is so much evil within it, and it is unhappy that we are here. I do not wish to stay in this forest longer than we must, but I do not wish to make camp in the dark when we do not know what lies ahead. Let us return to the base of the hill and make a camp there."

They turned and went back to where they had come down a small hill with a slight clearing in the trees. They cleared an area in the bracken only large enough for the horses to bed down. The horses were uneasy and preferred to stay closer to the trail.

Rowan untied the sack that Margie had filled with food from the horses and brought it to where Alder sat with his back to a rock. He sat next to Alder with the bag between his legs.

The bag was full of bread and cakes. The cakes had been wrapped delicately in cloth and tied. Rowan, readjusting to what had been their way of life, split one of the loaves in half and handed the other piece to Alder. Rowan was about to eat his half of bread and was setting the bag down when he heard the clink of ceramic on a rock under the bag. He reopened the bag and dug to the bottom to find two small pots wrapped in cloth and tied with string.

"What do you suppose these are?" Rowan asked, removing the pots from the bag.

Alder stared at the two pots with his lips pursed together.

Rowan gently removed the lids and felt tears well up in his eyes. One pot contained butter and the other contained plum preserves. Alder said nothing and Rowan struggled to speak.

"This would have cost her a fortune. She could not have gotten plums even from New Market at this time of year. She must have bought the preserves from a southern merchant. I doubt we were the intended recipient of them."

"It does not matter how she got them," Alder murmured. He had turned very pale and looked away from the pot. "We cannot repay her or even thank her. She gave us this gift, knowing we would never see each other again. Let Smaoinich bless her and keep her safe in the time that is to come."

Rowan took a small bit of butter and a small bit of the plum preserves and then served Alder the same small amounts of each before carefully wrapping the pots and tying them as expertly as he could. He placed them gently in the bags so that they would not shift on the horses. They quietly ate the bread, thankful for the gifts Margie had provided.

"Do you think the food will be safer with us or with the horses?" Rowan asked after a moment of thought.

Alder thought for a moment. "Perhaps with us. If the horses scare in the night, then they will have all our food. They refuse to bed down which means that they are already uneasy from the forest."

"Do you sense anything at all?"

"I cannot sense anything under this veil. The animals sense more than us because they were here when the first magic entered the world. We came after and cannot feel the depths of the world. That is why the birds do not come here and why the horses do not wish to sleep here."

They were both silent for some time as the forest grew darker around them. The horses were silent and uneasy and only nibbled at some of the easy-to-reach ferns, but did not fully lower their heads into the undergrowth.

Nightfall in the forest was darker than anything Rowan had ever known. No light penetrated the forest canopy. They did not dare build a fire, lest it should attract strange beasts or powers to them. Rowan and Alder huddled together and stared out into the darkness.

"Your eyes are better than mine. Can you see anything out there at all?" Rowan whispered.

"No. I cannot see anything. I can hear something slithering about, though. It does not sound like a snake because I sometimes hear crunching as if there are footsteps, but it slides through the grasses and bushes like a salamander of sorts."

"Does it come towards us?"

"I am not sure. Sometimes it sounds near and other times it sounds distant. Perhaps it does not know that we are here. Or maybe it is just trying to discover if we are predators or prey. If you are tired, sleep now and I will stay awake. I do not believe that I will be able to sleep tonight."

"You must sleep and if you grow tired or weary, wake me and I will take the watch. We still have some distance to go tomorrow and we do not know what is ahead of us."

Rowan lay down next to Alder and fell asleep. It was still dark when he woke.

"How long have I been sleeping?" he asked in a whisper.

"A few hours, but be quiet now," Alder hushed.

Rowan heard a creaking noise and realized that that was what had woken him. He sat up very quietly, taking his knife from its sheath.

Very faintly, in the distance, blue, red, orange, and yellow lights shone through the din. They seemed to be hovering in one place. When the lights would move, there would be an occasional rumble or creaking noise.

Rowan and Alder watched the lights for a while. They did not come closer, but they did not go away. The colors never changed, but would sometimes move up or down or side to side.

"Do you suppose that these lights are the same ones we saw before?" Rowan asked.

"I believe that they are, but I do not know what they are. I feel the same strange feeling I had the first time we saw them."

"I feel the same pull that I felt before. They seem to pull me in towards them like I should run toward them this very moment."

Alder moved in the darkness and Rowan felt something slip around his ankle.

"What are you doing?" Rowan asked.

"Tying you to myself. If you become enchanted and run toward the lights, the rope will keep you bound to me and you will not get very far. I do not believe that we will be able to find each other again if we get separated."

"Then tie it tightly so that neither of us will be able to break free."

Alder had just finished securing the knots when Rowan noticed that the lights had stopped moving. They seemed to be stuck in space. The creaking and rumbling sounds had ceased. The only thing in the world seemed to be the lights hovering several feet above the ground. Rowan began to feel very tired.

"Alder," he mumbled. He fell back to the ground.

Rowan awoke with a start. He was very wet. But it was worse than wet. He was slimy. He tried to sit up, but Alder's arm forced him down. He turned his head to meet Alder's horrified gaze. Rowan could hear the gulping noise of something coming from their feet and something slid past his boot. He shifted his gaze toward his feet.

A great pale salamander stood at their feet. It was as long as a horse, but stood on squat legs, dragging its belly on the ground. A green slime wept from its body, clinging to everything the salamander had touched. It was trying to eat their store of provisions whole with a gaping mouth and long pale tongue that wrapped around the sack like an arm. Hundreds of very small tentacles lined the inside of the monster's mouth and seemed to be pulling in the bag of goods while the armlike tongue pushed. Its large, pale, tail swished back and forth, flinging slime in all directions. Everything was quiet except the horrid gurgling and gulping noises the creature made as it ate the bag.

Rowan looked to where the horses had been. Very little light was able to penetrate the canopy this early in the morning, but he could not make out the shape of the horses. He was certain that they had bolted long before the creature had entered their camp. He was happy about that. They were safe at the very least.

He turned his attention back to the monster at their feet. It was getting close to finishing its meal, but he could just make out a beady eye towards the front of its head and could not tell if the monster could see them or if it was more interested in its current feast.

Alder was not trembling as he had been when they had encountered the bugbear, but Rowan knew that he was afraid of the salamander. Alder had his sword at his side but had made no move to attack the monster.

The gulping noise stopped and the huge mouth closed slowly. The salamander's already dragging stomach stretched out at the sides and the beast seemed as though it could hardly walk. It slithered away into the bushes, hardly paying attention to Alder and Rowan.

When several minutes had passed, Rowan turned to look at Alder.

"What was that?" he asked.

"Alp-luachra. That was only a baby. It must have been what I heard last night in the grass."

"Why did you not kill it? It ate all our food," Rowan asked angrily.

"It was a baby. Which means its mother is somewhere in the forest. Should it cry out, or should she smell the blood of her baby, I am sure that she would come to greet us."

Alder sat up, covered in the same green slime. The slime stuck to everything they tried to use to brush it off and it smelled like rotting flesh.

"This slime worries me. It will not come off and it smells of dead flesh. Who knows what carrion beasts will smell it and come for us," Alder grumbled after several different attempts at getting the slime off.

"Then what should we do? There are no creeks nearby and I am not sure that I would dare climb into any water in this forest even if we were able to find it."

The slime began to sink through their clothes and it itched and burned like acid. They could think of no other alternative. They took off their clothes, took their weapons and the bag with the Elvish book, and began to walk through the forest.

They walked in silence for a while. "I do believe we have hit the bottom, my dear friend," Alder laughed. "We are currently in Fae Forest, without horses or food, and completely naked. There is no one to look for us if we should not return. There is no chance that our horses will return to us while we are inside this place. It is unlikely that we will make it out by nightfall on foot and it is very likely that we are being hunted by whatever those lights were last night."

"Then it sounds like all we have left to fear is death," Rowan laughed.

"Well we still have our weapons and, until those are gone, I will not accept death readily. Not in this place and not naked."

Slowly the trees began to change into swamp trees, with giant buttress roots extending out like pillars. The brambles and bracken transformed into reeds and sedges. Rowan and Alder were approaching a swamp. Frogs croaked ahead, but the croaks sounded like large drums being beaten upon with clubs. A huge splash came from somewhere in the reeds. Alder stepped forward and sank through the moss layer up to his waist in the swamp water. The black, thick water was stagnant and smelled of dead fish.

"It clings to me like mud, but it does not hurt. I do not suppose we have any alternative, but to go through it. Only dip one leg in first, to make sure that it does not hurt you," Alder warned.

Rowan gingerly slipped his leg into the water. It did feel like mud clinging to him, but it did not hurt. It was cool but smelled horrible.

Alder tied the bag more tightly across his back so that the water did not touch it and held his sword across his shoulders. Rowan did the same with his bow and quiver.

They moved slowly through the murk. They worried about sudden drop-offs and did not want to disturb anything that might be lurking under the surface. They would occasionally comment on the weather or how tall the grass was for the time of year in a joking manner, attempting to make their plight seem less lowly.

In the reeds ahead of them they heard one of the thunderous croaks and they stopped. Alder peered through the grass and turned back to whisper to Rowan.

"They are vodyanoy."

Rowan ventured to look, too. He had heard of vodyanoy when he was a child. They were huge frog-like creatures with fins down their backs and tails like fish. They were generally harmless and had once lived in the moors surrounding Kingsford, but had been killed because they would eat sheep, goats, and small children.

The one that sat with its back toward Rowan was huge. It was larger than anything he had heard about in the stories and would surely pose a threat for them.

"What shall we do?" Rowan asked.

"We may have to fight. Aim your arrows for the throat, chest, or back of the head. The throat and chest will be soft, the head, not so much. Watch for the tongue."

Alder crept onto the land behind the vodyanoy and, with a swift roll, plunged his sword into the great frog's chest before it could croak.

"Alder! Look out!" Rowan screamed.

Alder turned as he slid his sword out of the first vodyanoy, but he was not fast enough. A giant tongue had slipped around him and snatched him off his feet, pulling him toward a larger vodyanoy a few feet away. Alder dropped his sword as the large black tongue jerked him toward the monster.

Rowan scrambled up the bank but slipped on the slimy water and blood that now soaked the grass. He regained his footing and grabbed Alder's sword. The vodyanoy was trying to open its mouth large enough to fit Alder inside and Alder was being folded and wrapped up in several feet of tongue. Rowan could not risk firing an arrow.

He charged forward with Alder's sword and slid into the belly of the frog, shoving the sword in up to the hilt. The frog writhed and jumped into the water, taking Alder with him. Rowan fired an arrow at the back of the frog's head where Alder had told him and the creature stopped moving, but Alder was still flailing, stuck and tangled in the creature's tongue. Rowan jumped into the black water but was suddenly pushed under by what felt like a boulder.

Another vodyanoy had jumped on top of him and was pushing him under. The mass kicked off him with its powerful legs, knocking the wind out of him. Rowan choked on the black water and tried to swim to the surface for air. He spat and spluttered and the water tasted like it smelled. Rowan tried to swim toward Alder, but the third vodyanoy was moving in that direction at a much faster rate. He saw Alder's head pop out of the water for a few seconds and he coughed out the horrid swamp water before being jerked back down. Then the third vodyanoy was underneath Rowan. Rowan plunged the sword into the creature's back and it stopped moving.

He took a deep breath and dove into the water.

The water was as dark as soot, and it burned his eyes. Rowan pushed through the murk as hard as he could until he ran into a jerking mass. He felt along the way and found what he presumed to be the mouth of the vodyanoy that had Alder in its mouth. He felt the sticky tongue and reached the sword deep into the monster's mouth and cut out the tongue. Rowan felt the mass being drug away toward whatever else had drug Alder back in. Rowan reached out and grabbed ahold of the moving mass and held on as it moved through the water.

The mass stopped moving and Rowan could make out the shape of a different beast. It was an alp-luachra. A big one. Twice the size of the alp-luachra that had stolen their food.

The gulping noise started and with every gulp came a rush of swamp water as the water was spat back out. The monster was able to swallow Alder in three gulps and Rowan was forced away from it. He swam to the surface for air.

He coughed out the swamp water and did the best he could to rub it out of his eyes. His breathing was becoming labored and the burning in his eyes had intensified. His vision was blurred, but he could not give up on Alder.

Rowan could see the alp-luachra swimming toward one of the small pads of grass that jutted up out of the swamp. No doubt it was going to digest its meal. Rowan took a deep breath and plunged back into the water. He had an idea, but time would be everything. He felt that he could not fight the creature on land and his best chance would be in the water.

The alp-luachra was slow. It did not swim but pushed itself along the bottom of the swamp. Rowan caught up to it and pierced the creature's giant tail with the sword. The creature let out a roar and a rush of water came from the opposite side. Rowan removed the sword and held onto it with all his might. The creature spun on him and began gulping the water, pulling him in like a whirlpool. Rowan did not fight but positioned himself to go in feet first. He felt his waist move past the monster's mouth. Then his head. He stabbed the sword upward through the alp-luachra's mouth and into its skull.

Water, mingled with blood, rushed past Rowan from the creature's mouth for a few moments. Everything became still.

Rowan swam out of its mouth and pulled himself down to where its stomach drug in the mud. He pushed the sword in, trying not to stab too deeply. He found the stomach, Alder was still squirming inside, and cut it open. He grabbed ahold of the mass and pulled it upward toward the grassy spot. Rowan pulled them both onto the grass and he could hear Alder breathing deeply.

But he could not see.

"Alder?" he sputtered, still coughing out the water. All he could hear were deep breaths between heavy coughs.

"I need the sword to cut this thing off of me," Alder finally stammered.

Rowan crawled over and felt Alder's hand. He slid the hilt into Alder's hand and heard the heavy thuds of the tongue falling to the ground. Alder was still breathing heavily, but his breathing did not sound as shallow as it had.

"Are you okay Alder?" Rowan asked.

"Well, I have never been eaten before, but beyond that, I am all right. I would like to leave this place as soon as possible and find a way to burn this forest to the ground when we are well away from it."

Rowan smiled but said nothing.

"Rowan? Why are you still lying there? Are you all right?"

"I cannot see. I had to keep my eyes open under the water to fight and there must be some sort of poison in the water. I am sorry Alder. I cannot see." Rowan dropped his head to the ground and wept.

He felt that this must be the end. He was to die the same dishonored death that his father had died. Alder would leave him here and he would be eaten or would starve to death, his body never to be found. He was glad he had never married and had never had children. Rowan had never wanted his children to have the same life he was forced to live. Rowan wept heavily in the grass all the frustrated tears he had not been able to shed for many years.

Rowan felt Alder's hands on his face and Alder lifted it from the ground. He knew Alder was staring into his face, but he didn't know what Alder was looking for. Then Alder pulled him into and embrace and wept over his head.

"You did not have to sacrifice so much for me, my friend," Alder cried.

Rowan pushed away from him. "You would have done it for me and neither of us would have let the other die."

Alder sat back for a moment and wiped his face. "You are right," he choked.

"I would like to leave this place, but you must guide me." Rowan sighed, realizing that Alder was the same as him. Alder would not leave him to die here if it could be helped.

Alder lifted Rowan to his feet and wrapped an arm around Rowan's. They began to walk very slowly. Alder sniffled but quickly regained his wits in an attempt to get Rowan out of the swamp safely. They had a very long way to go to get out of the forest and would be spending another night inside.

Alder led Rowan as diligently as he could, but the way was rough. They were on a small island in the middle of the swamps and were forced to swim through the water to get to where the banks finally rose above the black water. The banks were covered in large, thick, knots of roots from the massive trees that were at least two-hundred years old.

Alder did his best to lead Rowan through the maze, but they were slow. They were both exhausted from the battle and felt their muscles starting to slow down. They both coughed up a mixture of blood and black swamp water.

They reached the top of the banks and went a little further through the thick brush. Rowan tripped frequently, but Alder kept a firm grip on him so that he would not fall. After several hours of wading through the brush, Alder was forced to admit defeat for the day.

"We cannot go farther today. It will be dark soon and I think that it is best that we find a place to sleep. I will try to find us a safe place. I fear that I will not be able to stay awake to keep watch through the night."

"Do the best you can for us and we will be in the hands of the gods," Rowan patted gently.

"I do not believe that the gods wield any power in this place," Alder murmured.

A large tree stood at the base of the hill and a small hole had washed out from around its roots. Alder crawled inside with sword drawn ready for a fight but found nothing. He helped Rowan climb down into the roots.

It was the most pleasant place they had found in the forest. It smelled like fresh earth and fresh wood. It was cool and dark and they felt somewhat safe within the roots. Alder could see through the roots to the outside world, but nothing would be able to see them at the back without coming into the hole. Nothing large would be able to climb through the web of roots without breaking them and Alder felt that he would be able to slay anything should it begin work.

Rowan was sitting at the back of the tree, staring blankly forward. Alder looked at him sorrowfully. Rowan was completely covered in the black residue from the swamp water. His dirty blond hair was stained black and matted against his head. He was naked and shivered slightly, but Alder did not believe that it was from the cold. His bow and quiver still hung around his shoulders, but they looked almost useless with weeds and mud hanging from them. Small lines of clean skin ran down Rowan's face away from his eyes, showing where Rowan had been crying silently throughout the day. Now he sat silently staring forward with unseeing eyes looking like a shadow.

"You should lie down and try to sleep. Maybe rest will help your sight," Alder offered.

"I do not believe that my sight will come back. That water was some form of poison, I am sure. Perhaps it is because I am only human that I am affected. But I will try to sleep so that I am not as much of a burden to you in the morning. Wake me if you hear anything, not that I will be of much use."

"We will be safe here. I will wake you in the morning," Alder whispered.

Alder began to cry again but attempted to be as quiet as possible. He looked out of the small window of roots and wondered what they were to do. They had no food or water, and it was unlikely that they would be able to find any within the forest that could be trusted. Rowan was unable to fight and none of the paths through the forest allowed for an easy journey for anyone, especially not a blind man. He tried not to think of what other monsters were lurking in the woods, waiting for them to fall into their laps. Alder had only heard stories of the things they had seen and could hardly believe that they were true. Now he had fought them and had almost been killed by them.

Alder woke to the leaves and trees swaying like a great storm had come. A booming sound like distant thunder sounded, but the earth shook with every rumble. The sounds were growing nearer. Alder pushed himself closer to the back of the tree between the entrance and Rowan. Rowan appeared to be sleeping.

The tree was creaking and swaying above them and strange glows were flashing across the ground outside. The smell of burning wood filled the alcove and small embers drifted through the night air. The sounds were getting closer and Alder hoped that the creatures creating the sounds would be far too large to notice them, especially with them being under the tree.

Darkness covered the entrance. "Thig a-mach feadhainn bheaga. Cha dèan sinn dochann ort. Cuidichidh sinn thu."

The creatures were speaking Elvish, but Alder did not trust them. They said they would help, but would they really? Alder could not risk getting himself killed and leaving Rowan to starve to death. The creatures repeated the call and still, Alder did not move.

"What are they saying, Alder?" Rowan murmured.

"They say for us to come out, that they will not hurt us, and that they wish to help us."

"Is it a trick?"

"I do not know."

"Can you see them?"

"No. All I can see is darkness and embers raining down."

"I thought I smelled smoke. Is the forest on fire?"

"No. There is no light except the strange lights we have seen before."

Alder sat and stared at the entrance. The creatures were still there, but they did not repeat their offer.

Suddenly, Rowan charged past Alder and scrambled out the entrance before Alder could tackle him. Alder clambered out of the tree to see Rowan in the hands of a great tree-like creature. The creature was smaller than the trees and its well-defined head was pointed with small sticks coming out at the top like hair. Fire burst from two holes that served as eyes and smoke escaped out of its mouth. Its hands were like roots, its arms and legs were great tree limbs, and its body was narrow. It was almost completely covered in moss except where the internal fire burned around its mouth and eyes.

Rowan was completely wrapped in its hands, but he did not fight the tree. His legs dangled limply and his head seemed to be laid back on the tree's fingers.

Alder screamed with rage and charged forward, but felt a root wrap around his leg and then encircle him completely. He was lifted into the air and another tree faced him, burning with a blue flame. Flowers bloomed around his face and pollen burst from within them. He felt his body going limp and he slipped from consciousness.

Chapter 8

"Dùisg."

Alder heard the rumbling word in what seemed to be a distant world.

"Dùisg," came the rumbling again with gentle shaking.

Alder felt his head roll back onto something and he strained to open his eyes. They flickered open, but a great weight kept them closed. His head rolled forward and scraped against tree-bark. His memories came flooding back and he forced his eyes open.

He was wrapped in the tight grip of the tree's fingers. He struggled for a second and the fingers squeezed him tighter.

"You are awake," the tree creaked.

"What did you do with Rowan?" Alder demanded.

"The man is with the others. He has many wounds and he has been poisoned by the swamp water. Black as death it is and stronger than any man. He is very near death. You Elvish types are strong, but you are not unable to die from the evils of dark magic."

"What are you?" Alder asked.

"We are the coisiche teine to the elves. In the common tongue, we are fire walkers. We prefer Elvish for they have always respected us. Man has only ever tried to hurt the forest and slay us. Long have we been, longer shall we remain. We were woken by the gods and saw the first Elvish children born among the trees. We raised the first Elvish children, and they were meant to raise the man-children, but children can hate their fathers and part from their teachings," the fire walker trailed off.

"Take me to Rowan," Alder demanded.

"He will not be awake for several days. Much poison did he drink."

"I care not! Take me to him!" Alder shouted.

The fingers squeezed tighter around him and he felt as though his bones were about to snap.

"We do not take orders from elves or men."

"Why are you doing this? Why not kill us and be done with it?"

"Kill you? We do not mean to kill you. You are not so worthy as Rowan as you call him, but you both slew many monsters in the swamp. Those dark creatures were brought by the dark elf. They do not belong in this forest, but we cannot venture to the swamps to kill them."

"Why can't you go to the swamps?"

"The swamp water will douse our fire. Evil poison it is. The swamp was once a beautiful pond with many beautiful birds and fish of unimaginable sizes and colors. Now it is only full of evil creatures with poison in their veins."

"What keeps you burning?" Alder stared into the blue light flickering in the tree's eyes and mouth.

"The universe," it hissed.

Alder did not say anything for a while. The fire walker stared off somewhere in the distance. "It is your turn now," it rumbled.

They were off quickly and nimbly through the forest. The fire walker knew every tree and bush and passed through the openings in the forest like a blur. Alder noticed the trees were becoming taller and thicker. Clear water was now running past the fire walker's feet.

The water grew deeper and soon the fire walker was up to its waist. Every so often it would dunk Alder down into the water and then pull Alder out after a short time, coughing and gasping for air. The fire walker would smile and keep moving forward.

They came to the deepest spot in the water and stopped. Downed trees stuck out of the water, and, in their places, larger trees had grown up, covering the whole area in a pale shadow.

"Your friend is here," hissed the tree.

Alder scanned the trees, but could not see Rowan. He began to panic and looked into the water.

Rowan was several feet under the water on a fallen tree. A root was sticking out of his mouth and he appeared to have been pierced by many smaller roots. Clouds of red blood drifted lazily around where the roots were penetrating him.

"You're killing him!" screamed Alder, again fighting at the fingers. The fingers wrapped tighter, and his arm snapped. He screamed in pain.

The fire walker plunged Alder into the water and pinned him to one of the trees. Alder kicked and fought and the fire walker pushed harder. Alder felt his ribs snap and he gasped. A root slid into his mouth and down his throat. He felt smaller roots penetrating his skin and begin anchoring him to the tree. He writhed, but he could not move or scream out. Purple flowers bloomed in front of him, and he fell asleep.

Alder woke to the sun shining on his face. Soft grass rose from around him. A faint breeze moved across him. He started but felt slightly light-headed.

"There, there, elf master," came the hissing of the fire walker.

"What has happened to me?" he managed to ask.

"You have been cured of your ailments. The poisons are gone from you and your bones have been repaired."

Alder managed to sit up and look around him. He was on the soft rolling banks of the magic pond. He could see everything that had fallen into the clear water for several feet before the banks sloped into a white, sandy bottom. The trees that grew out of the water were larger than those at the edge of the forest and they seemed to stretch several hundred feet above Alder's head. The fragrant plants were green and soft as in spring, not showing any of the decay that was rampant in the rest of the forest.

The vines and mosses and evil-looking mushrooms had all vanished from this part of the forest. Nothing, not even a leaf, floated in the water. The grass was green from its tips down to the dark brown soil it grew out of. Alder dug his fingers down into it and felt the cool, soft soil. "What is this place?" Alder asked.

"This is the birthplace. This is where the trees were first born and this is where the elves were first born. We raised the first elf children here. Everything here is as fresh as the day the world was made. Often do we come here, searching for the gods, but they do not return," said the fire walker.

"Do you have a name that you are called?" Alder asked.

"Azure," he hissed.

"Where is Rowan?"

"The man has been taken to the mother. He was near death and needed more than what the water could provide."

"You must take me to him," Alder begged.

A spurt of smoke escaped the tree's mouth as it smiled. It reached out a hand and grabbed Alder.

"Wait! My bag!" Alder panicked.

"Your bag is lost. It perished in the swamps," the tree hissed, beginning to move through the glen.

"Then all is lost. We will never gain admittance to see the elves without it," he mourned. He was naked, without food, water, a horse, a weapon, or the book. The book was the only thing that he felt could have saved them. It was true that he had not found anything important in it, but he was hoping that the elves had forgotten its contents and that he and Rowan would have at least been permitted to speak with the Elvish leaders. Now they had nothing to barter with and no way to enter the Elvish cities.

"You have an Elvish medallion of great value," said Azure.

Alder felt at his neck. The medallion had somehow stayed around his neck after all their misadventures. "Do you know anything about it?" Alder asked.

"No, but I sense great magic around it. That is how we found you and your companion. That is why we saved you."

"I cannot feel any enchantments on it."

"We are more sensitive to these things than elves or men."

They moved onward in silence. The glen was beautiful, the most beautiful place Alder had ever seen, but all he could think about was Rowan, the loss of the bag, and the strange medallion.

The trees opened into a meadow with a huge apple tree at the center. Despite it being summer, the tree was still covered in blossoms, but bore fruit, despite being in flower. Petals drifted down into the low grass of the meadow. Rowan slept at the base of the tree.

Tears came to Alder's eyes. He could not believe that Rowan was there, safe and alive. Rowan was clean and was no longer covered in the black water. His golden hair and beard looked as though they had been washed and combed. He no longer had cuts or gashes on his skin.

"If you could know one truth, what would you learn?" Azure asked.

"What?" Alder asked, unprepared for such a question.

"If the mother favors an elf or man that eats from her tree, she may share a truth with them. What would you wish to learn?"

Alder was aghast. He did not know that such things were possible. Even in the fairy stories he heard as a child, nothing of this kind had ever existed. He could think of a million different things he wanted to know, things that could turn the tide of the war, but what should he ask? He could ask where the stone was. He could ask who their enemy was. He could ask about the medallion. He could ask about his mother.

"But she does not always give an answer, or sometimes she will lead you to it if you are patient," Azure added.

Azure set Alder down a few feet from where Rowan was sleeping. Alder scrambled to Rowan's side and looked over him. Rowan was completely cured. Alder gently shook him.

Rowan's eyes flitted open and he scanned the world above him. His eyes rested on Alder, and he jumped. "Alder!" he pulled Alder into a hug, and they held each other for some time.

Alder sobbed and held onto Rowan with all his might. "I am sorry, Rowan. I have always endeavored to protect you and lately I have failed. I was unable to protect us from any of the evil creatures that have haunted us these past days. I do not know that I will be able to protect us as the days grow darker."

Rowan pushed away from him. "Am I not a man?" Rowan asked with a smile. Alder only looked at him. "Have I not led us most of my adult life? I am the one that took us to the Pass of Handuin the day we saved the royal party. I am the one that insisted that we help Bacach. I was the one that said that we should go south to help the villagers. I am the one that got us here, not you, Alder. You have nothing to apologize for. You are my brother. We will fight together until the end."

Azure knelt in the meadow by the apple tree. Another fire walker emerged from the forest carrying a handful of mushrooms and wild onions.

"I bring more food for you, Master Rowan. It is not good to eat more than a few apples from this tree in one's lifetime," the tree hissed. The fire burning within it was gold.

"Thank you, Amber," Rowan said, turning to the tree. The tree placed the bounty in front of Rowan and Alder. Many of the mushrooms Rowan and Alder had never seen before, but they trusted the fire walkers. They devoured everything that had been set in front of them.

"Have you thought of what you are going to ask the mother when you eat the apple?" Rowan asked.

"I wanted to ask you what you asked and if you received an answer. It would be a shame if we asked the same question and we received the same answer," Alder said.

"I asked where the stone was hidden, but the mother has not answered me. I was not expecting her to tell me where it would be, but Amber told me to be patient. She may one day show me the way."

"I wished to ask about my mother if you had already asked about the stone," Alder sighed.

Rowan nodded. "I thought about asking how my father had truly died, but I know that finding the stone is more important. However it happened, it does not bring him back. Your mother could still be alive."

Alder stared at the tree. He could learn why she had left him and where she had gone. Maybe she was still alive and was living in one of the Elvish cities. He did not know which of the Elven races she had been from but had recently assumed it to be Tuigseach after reading Eachdraiche's book.

Alder stood and picked a beautiful red apple from the tree. He took a bite.

It was the most amazing thing he had ever tasted in his life. He felt as though he were weightless. His head spun. His entire body felt warm and tingly. But nothing appeared within his head. He took another bite, and another until the apple was gone. Nothing appeared.

"Well?" Rowan asked.

"Nothing. She has not answered me."

"Time will show if she will answer, elf," hissed Azure. "The mother does not bestow gifts upon the unworthy, but she does not always show the worthy the easy way."

Alder sat next to Rowan with his back against the tree. "What are we to do, my fearless leader?" he asked.

"The only thing I can think to do is to carry on with our plan. Perhaps we can beg clothing of the farmers. They may take pity on us if we are fresh from the forest."

"Or they may think we are demons, coming from the forest unscathed without weapons, clothing, or food."

"If we had clothing, we could beg work, but I am afraid that you are right about us appearing out of the forest without a shred on us. The madmen that leave the forest and wander to the inns may be in tatters, but they are not naked."

Azure chuckled at this. A crackling chuckle like when a fresh log is thrown on the fire. Wisps of smoke slipped out the corners of his eyes and mouth. "Perhaps you would like to meet the man in the tower? He may take pity on you. There have been others that he has taken pity on."

"If you believe that he will help us and not harm us, we will go to him," Rowan decided.

"It is a long way to travel. You will be very hungry when you reach the tower, but you will be able to pass through the forest. The mother has protected you," Amber bowed.

"How do we find the tower?" Rowan asked.

"The forest will guide you." Azure waved toward the edge of the trees. A small path no bigger than a deer trail wound away from the meadows and into the forest.

Rowan looked to Alder. "Are you ready?"

"It is that or die here," Alder laughed.

They thanked the fire walkers for saving them and entered the forest. The forest felt much lighter, and it was noticeable that the fire walkers kept the evil creatures out of the sacred areas. Alder could still feel the magic of the place, but it was not the heavy burden of dark magic as it had been before.

They wound through the woods all day and when darkness fell, they found a small rock outcropping and hid amongst the boulders. "Sleep now, Rowan. I will keep watch," Alder whispered as he pushed his way between the mouth of the rocks and Rowan.

"You must sleep, too," Rowan argued.

"I am unable to sleep, therefore you must," Alder smiled.

Rowan stared at him and saw that arguing would be of no use. He laid his head against the rocks and slept. Alder listened to Rowan's steady breathing and backed himself closer to Rowan. The rocks would protect them, but Alder was weary to close his eyes. Too much had happened to them and despite Rowan's words, Alder felt responsible.

Rowan was in his twenties. He was still a boy. Alder did not know his age. Time had blurred together for most of his life. Mercenary work had kept him busy and he had never had a reason to count the days, months, or years that he would be gone on a job. But everything had changed when he had found a newly orphaned Rowan in the woods.

Chapter 9

Alder roamed across the moors. It was a crisp winter morning and everything was still. Ice had formed over the stagnant water of the moors and icy frost coated the grasses and bushes. All the birds had flown south and the sun shone palely on the still world. Alder could smell the wood smoke from the city. He had just come from the inn. He was warm and his stomach was full.

The last few jobs had been easy. A few goblin chiefs were getting rowdy up north, a wildman had been attacking merchants. Easy kills that had only taken a few days each. The jobs had paid well, and he would have plenty to live on. His new wool cloak would last years. His new sword would last until the next major battle.

He would not be able to find vegetables on the moors at this time of year, but he hoped to find some rabbits in the forest. Their coats would be white now and they would be easy to catch. As he approached the forest, he heard the weak sobbing of a child. None of the city children would be out this early.

Hesitant of a trap, Alder circled the area he thought the noise was coming from. He saw no signs of a band of thieves. Alder softly stepped into a clearing in the trees and saw a boy curled up on the frozen ground in front of what had been an attempt at a fire.

The boy had long blond hair that had not been cut in months. His clothes were nothing more than rags and he did not have a cloak or shoes. The boy appeared to be about six years old and was starving.

Alder approached the boy, and the boy lifted his head. He let out a gasp and tried to scramble back into the trees, but he was too cold and tired to get very far.

"Do not be afraid," Alder soothed. "Are you alone here?"

"I am. My father has been gone for nine days. He said to wait here, but he has not come back. We are not allowed in the city, but I do not know where else he could have gone," the boy cried.

"Hush now. Do you have a mother?"

"Mother died during the sickness. It was just me and Father, but now Father is gone." The boy began to bawl.

Alder took his cloak off and wrapped the boy in it. The boy was too small and shivered violently. Alder took him in his arms and held him to try to keep him warm. The Great Wailing had been five years ago, which meant that this boy had narrowly escaped death himself and had never known his mother.

"Do you know where your father went? Maybe I could help you look for him."

"Soldiers came with a message for Father. Everyone was angry and Father sent me away. I could hear them shouting, but I don't know why they fought. Father came and found me and told me to stay here while he was gone."

Alder thought for a while. Soldiers from the king never meant anything good. The boy was surely an orphan by now. But what was he to do with a small boy?

"What is your name, boy?" Alder asked.

"Rowan, son of Lionn," the boy whimpered from inside Alder's cloak.

"Well Rowan, son of Lionn, I wish to take you into the city. Would you like to come with me? We can find you some food there."

The boy looked up at Alder and Alder smiled at him. The boy wiped his nose on Alder's new cloak and nodded.

Rowan was light in Alder's arms as Alder carried him into the city. Alder wondered if the boy had eaten since his father had left. *Even then, they could not have been eating well. The boy is so small and light. He has had a hard life,* Alder thought.

The townsfolk stared at Alder as he walked through the streets toward the Grey Goat. Alder was used to the staring, but now they were curious about the small child he carried. He entered the inn and set the boy down at the table in the corner by the fire.

"Stay here and keep warm. I will get you some food," Alder smiled as he set him down in the chair. The boy looked slightly frightened but nodded.

Alder found Margo, the innkeeper's wife, and waved at the now two-year-old Margie. "Who was that you brought in with you, Master Alder?" Margo asked.

"His name is Rowan. I found him in the woods this morning. He is orphaned," Alder explained.

Margo patted Alder's hand. "There are too many in the world." She frowned softly.

"Have you heard of a man named Lionn? The boy says that is the name of his father and that his father came to the city nine days ago with guards from the castle."

Margo thought for a moment. "Lionn used to be a good customer of ours. A gypsy girl used to dance here and the two married a while back now, I suppose. I remember they got into some trouble, but I don't remember what it was all about, and I haven't seen either since."

"Thanks, Margo," Alder nodded.

Alder purchased a bowl of stew and a small slice of bread. He did not want the boy to have too much food too soon if he had been starving. As he approached the corner table, his heart stopped. The boy was gone. He set down the food and looked about the room. It was crowded, but he did not see the boy anywhere. He looked at the men that sat eating porridge at the next table.

"Did you see the boy that was at the table here?" Alder asked.

"Is he yours? Another man just took him out the door!" The man stared at Alder in horror.

Alder dashed out of the inn. Snow had begun to fall, but not enough for someone to create footprints. The usually muddy street was frozen solid. Only two paths lead away from the inn, meaning the man had gone left or straight. If he was kidnapping the boy, he would be taking him out of the city. Alder tried to think like a criminal, but for every moment he spent thinking, he was losing precious time.

What reasons would a man have to kidnap a boy? The man must have thought Rowan would be worth something on the market. Alder cursed himself. He had wrapped the boy in a very expensive cloak and left him alone. The man had probably thought the boy was from a wealthy family and thought he could get a good price for him. Then the man would be taking Rowan south to New Market.

Alder ran as fast as he could to the top of the city walls. He peered out as far as he could see. He could make out a man with a bundle riding quickly toward the south. Alder had been right, but he knew he could not catch up with a horse no matter how quickly he ran.

He ran towards the second section of the city and bought the first war horse he found for whatever price the man had demanded, which was surely more than the beast was worth, but Alder did not hear the amount. He was now out of money. He kicked the horse and charged down the streets and out of the city. Alder knew that he had to catch the man before he got to New Market. Rowan would be sold quickly and there could be buyers from any region there.

"I want to catch him where there are no witnesses," Alder thought sourly.

Alder pushed the horse, and he could see that he was gaining on the man. When Alder was only a short distance the man looked over his shoulder. He saw Alder and cried out. He kicked his horse as hard as he could, and the horse sped forward.

Alder kicked his own horse and stood in the stirrups. He could almost jump onto the man's horse. A few seconds passed and Alder was ready. He pulled his dagger and climbed onto the saddle. He jumped and cut the other horse's leg. The horse crashed to the ground, throwing the man and Rowan.

Alder sprang to his feet and charged the man. He got his sword to the man's throat.

"Why did you take the boy?" he snarled through gritted teeth.

"I saw you carry him in. I thought he was an elfchild. I wanted to sell him to Bargol the Chieftain."

Alder pierced the man's shoulder with his sword. "You would dare sell a child to Bargol? Do you know what he does to children? Do you know what he would do to an elfchild?" Alder raged.

"Everyone knows! But the money!" the man writhed.

"For a few hundred bonns you would sell a soul?" Alder leaned over the man to whisper in his ear. "I have done worse things to better men than you."

With a rage Alder had never known, he killed the man. He had left his sword piercing the man to the ground and had stabbed him repeatedly with his dagger. When little was left of the man, Alder began hurling the pieces into the sea.

Finally, Alder returned to Rowan. The boy was unresponsive. Alder shook him, but nothing happened. Alder panicked. He was too late. He knew the poor thing did not have much time left in him. *"I should have killed the man quickly and been done with it. Now the boy is dead and it is my fault. All because of my anger,"* Alder writhed.

He listened to the boy's chest. A faint little heartbeat could be heard. Alder squeezed the boy to his chest and rushed to his horse. They returned to the city as quickly as the horse could run.

Margo was much more attentive to Rowan once the morning rush had ended. She saw that he was well-fed on broth and a little watered milk. She poured a bath for him and cut his hair. She forced coins into Alder's hand and shoved him out the door to go find cloth for new clothes for the child.

Alder was thankful. He had raised himself but somehow couldn't find the instincts within him to raise this other child. Margo, having buried one child and now raising young Margie, knew exactly what to do and how to do it. She would see that Alder was set on the right foot when it came to child-rearing.

The biggest shocks to Alder came from the susceptibility of human children to ailments and wounds. Alder could never recall injuries or ailments as a child. But Rowan was constantly covered in mucus and coughed and was hot to the touch. Rowan would run with the other children, fall, and would return to him in tears, sporting a bloody knee or hand.

At first, Alder was terrified to let Rowan out of his sight due to these gory wounds. But Margo quickly laughed Alder into submission. Rowan was a child, the scrapes would heal, and Rowan would be tougher because of them.

Alder watched as Rowan grew stronger and healthier. The boys that used to bully Rowan would now find themselves running home with bloody noses or black eyes. It was when Rowan turned from waif to strapping lad that Alder decided to begin Rowan's education, in fighting, language, and letters.

Dawn was upon them. Alder stared at Rowan affectionately as the light shone across his face. Rowan had been so much trouble and so little at the same time. Alder had been surprised at his instinct to protect Rowan from the moment he saw him. It was an instinct that had never gone away.

Rowan began to stir. "Why didn't you wake me so I could keep watch?" Rowan asked angrily.

"I did not sleep," Alder lied. He wondered if Rowan remembered that first day.

They carried on down the trail. They were unable to find food and they were hungry, as the fire walkers had told them they would be.

After many hours of walking, they came upon a grove with a large, twisted stone tower in the center. Strange vegetables were growing around the base of the tower and birds came and went as they pleased. Purple clouds of smoke curled out of several places in the metal chimney. The roof was pale blue and as they approached, the door was painted bright green.

Alder knocked on the door. No sound came from within, but the door slowly opened to reveal a young girl in pink silks that flowed around her figure. Her raven-black hair fell around her tan face in dark curls. Rowan thought that she was beautiful, but she was quite young. The girl said nothing but stared at them with big brown eyes. She moved slightly to allow them to pass and shut the door firmly behind them.

The bottom floor of the tower was the kitchen, or something close to it. Multiple cauldrons of different sizes and colors were bubbling furiously in the huge fireplace. A massive wood table with strange carvings was in the center of the room with many different chairs around it as if they had been fashioned at different times through history. A spiral staircase wound around the other side of the room. A thick red rug filled up almost the entirety of the floor. Curved bookshelves, overflowing with books, lined the space that was not covered by the fireplace and stairs. The only door was the one they had just entered through.

"Melati! My sweet bud! Who was at the door?" Came a nasally voice from the stairs. The girl said nothing. Two more girls, slightly older than Melati, appeared wearing scarlet silk gowns of the same fashion. One girl was pale and had black curls similar to Melati's and the other girl had blonde hair twisted around her head with a red ribbon.

They were both beautiful. None of the girls spoke but only looked curiously at the new arrivals.

Finally, the warlock appeared. He wore a patched robe that at one time had been purple velvet. The patches were of many different colors, shapes, and sizes and appeared to have been sewn on by the warlock himself. The robe was loosely tied around him with a gold cord and, as he stepped down the stairs, bare legs with purple slippers would appear.

The warlock was tall and lank with a wispy white beard. His white skin had the appearance of not having seen the sun in many years and dark beady eyes peered out from his long, white wispy beard. He wore a long purple hat that dropped down over his long white hair. Rowan wondered if the hat had stood up at one point or if it had always been limp.

The warlock reached the bottom of the stairs before looking at Alder and Rowan, who stood naked in his home. He stopped and stared at them for a few moments before saying anything.

"Had a rough go in the forest, did ye? I say, the fire walkers sent you here, I can see the auras clear as day. I suppose they sent you here to beg for help. Well, I ought to say no, but I need some work done around the house. How do ye feel about a trade? Ye work for me for a bit and I will send ye on your way with what ye need. Sound like a deal, lads?"

Alder and Rowan looked at each other, taken aback. They had expected a powerful and slightly terrifying man.

Now they found a decrepit old man who knew their needs without them having to say a word.

"All you need is housework? Nothing unnatural?" Alder asked.

"Just some manual labor my girls can't do themselves," the warlock said with a nod.

"Are there terms?"

The warlock thought for a moment.

"Ye cannot leave this place until the deal is complete. Ye will be sworn to my service until I release ye."

Alder hesitated and Rowan stared at Alder. "So we are slaves and must rely on you to keep your word and release us," Alder stated pointedly.

"The way I see it, lads, ye don't have much of an option."

Alder and Rowan did not have any other options and accepted the warlock's conditions.

They were escorted upstairs by the warlock and followed by the three girls. The first floor was a sort of hay loft, but they continued climbing the stairs. The second floor was a library with a divan in the center, a desk by a large round window, and floor-to-ceiling bookshelves around the entire room. The third floor was where they stopped.

The third floor had no windows. It was completely dark, besides a faint glow coming from a purple fluid bubbling inside a giant cauldron in the center of the floor. Strange markings in red surrounded the cauldron on the floor. Plants, unlike anything Rowan and Alder had ever seen hung from the ceiling in bunches. A table at one side of the room was covered in books. A bookshelf next to the table contained no books, but jars of different colors and sizes. Rowan felt in his stomach that he did not want to know what was in these jars. Somewhat out of place, was a large, black wardrobe.

"This way lads. Over to the cauldron," the warlock waved.

Rowan and Alder approached the cauldron wearily.

The warlock took each of them by the arm and shoved their arms into the bubbling liquid. When they removed their arms, a gold shackle appeared on their wrists. The girls, who Rowan and Alder had not seen leave the room, reappeared with loincloths for them to wear.

"Now lads, let's have some grub."

The warlock sat in the largest chair and immediately put his feet on the table.

Alder and Rowan sat down at the table. The girls buzzed around the cauldrons and began procuring items that could not possibly have been within them. Melati removed a whole roast chicken, the blonde girl removed several loaves of bread, and the black-haired girl began removing several roasted and mashed vegetables. All of these items were placed on the huge table.

The girls placed a stack of wooden plates and gold goblets on the table. Magically, the items began to arrange themselves about the table for each seat.

"Ye see, lads, ye won't want for anything while yer here. I will take care of ye well. The fire walkers wouldn't have it no other way," he smiled with a strange grin that was barely perceptible under his beard.

Rowan and Alder ate heartily. The goblets filled themselves with cider, but they expected that the other goblets were filled with wine. The girls ate daintily and sipped from their goblets. The warlock ate bits of things and drank heavily from his goblet until his cheeks were rosy and his eyes were shining. No one spoke at the table, but the warlock frequently belched and looked at Melati.

"Well if ye have had yer fill lads, ye should be off to bed. Ye will have yer work cut out for ye in the morning."

The girls rose from the table and collected all the items. All the food went back into the cauldrons and the dishes went into a washtub. They then went obediently up the stairs. Alder, Rowan, and the warlock rose and, supporting the warlock, went up the stairs.

When Rowan and Alder reached the second floor with the warlock, the girls were already laying out blankets for them on the thick bedding of straw.

"This is yer home now, lads. The girls will wake ye up in the morning and take care of the beds. Breakfast will be downstairs and then it will be off to work for ye until evening. I expect ye to wash daily. I will see about a washtub for ye. Unless ye are ordered, ye are to never go above this floor. Well, goodnight lads." The warlock, escorted by the girls, was led up the stairs to the upper floors.

Alder moved his blankets to be closer to Rowan. They lay down in their beds and found it to be very comfortable in the fresh straw. The torches that were attached to the walls flickered out almost immediately.

"What do you think of this?" Alder asked.

"I am frightened. We have never entered servitude and we have always endeavored not to enter any bond that may prevent us from leaving as we would like. The warlock speaks very rapidly and he seems to know everything, but that only serves to put us at a disadvantage."

"I agree with you. I just pray that the fire walkers knew what they were sending us into."

Rowan woke to the gentle touch of the girls. He opened his eyes and found the black-haired girl kneeling next to him and shaking his arm gently. She stared into his face and then rose and walked away. The blonde girl had woken Alder and the girls disappeared down the stairs. Alder and Rowan left their blankets and went downstairs, as they had been told to do.

The girls were already laying out breakfast when they sat in the seats they had sat in the night before. Melati was not there. The girls still did not speak, but their faces showed some grief that they had not shown the night before.

Alder and Rowan did not question them, but ate their breakfast and then went outside. The door seemed to seal itself as they shut it. On the outside of the door was a scroll with a to-do list on it. The first item: weed the garden.

The garden was a great expanse that circled around the tower. They set to work.

The sun was hot, and they had no protection from its rays. The weeds, unlike anything Alder and Rowan had encountered before, took all their strength to remove. They were huge, fierce plants with thorns and giant root systems that required digging to remove. Large, unusual bugs flocked around the garden, crawling all over Rowan and Alder, biting and harassing them.

The garden seemed to consist overwhelmingly of gourds and squashes of many different varieties. Some of the pumpkins, green, purple, orange, yellow, and white, were bigger than Rowan. Rowan wondered what the purpose of growing them so large would be. The squash he had seen sold at the markets were typically small and fragrant; with more flesh and fewer seeds. These giant pumpkins must be full of seeds and have thin walls that would be tasteless.

"Have you noticed that the girls have not said a word since we arrived? At first, I thought it could be shyness, they most likely do not get many visitors, but they do not even whisper amongst themselves," Alder talked from across the patch they were weeding.

"I think it is strange," Rowan offered, not knowing why the girls would be kept quiet.

"Only the older girls were present this morning and they seemed upset about something," Alder added.

"Maybe the younger girl is ill."

"How old do you think they are?"

"The youngest seems about fourteen. The oldest may be nineteen. The middle I would think would be around seventeen or so. None can be in their twenties."

"I agree. They are all different in appearance, so they cannot be related. What is the warlock playing at I wonder?" Alder trailed off.

They kept working. Their hands bled and their backs ached. Their feet hurt from the rocks and sticks they were forced to stand on. Sweat drenched their dismal loincloths.

The sun was setting, and it became hard to see so they decided to try the door. The door opened and then sealed shut behind them. The two older girls were at the cauldrons, adding bottles of strange liquids, and preparing the meal. Melati was still missing.

Rowan and Alder went up the stairs to their floor and found two washtubs with fresh water. They removed their loincloths and sat down in the tubs. They sank down in the tubs up to their shoulders. The tubs had only been a foot deep from outside appearances and they both gasped as they sank down. The water was scented like roses and they both scrubbed themselves until they were spotless. Fresh loincloths had been provided for them.

They returned downstairs and found the warlock at the table, despite him not having gone down the stairs while they were bathing. Melati, now wearing a red gown exactly like the other girls', was serving the warlock. She looked haggard and she winced as she moved.

"Fine work ye lads have done, fine work," the warlock said as they sat down at the table. "None have worked as hard as ye have done on this day."

Rowan and Alder quietly ate the exotic foods. Rowan did not know what most of it was and found that most of it was too spicy for his liking. The warlock ate his food contentedly but stared at the girls hungrily. He drank wine from his refilling glass, and the glassy look soon appeared in his eyes.

"I think that'll be about enough," he slurred. Rowan and Alder nodded and stood. The girls quickly removed the dishes from the table and went to their master to help him up to his chambers. Rowan and Alder followed the slow procession until they reached their floor and then nestled into their spots in the straw.

Rowan found that he was exhausted, but couldn't fall asleep. "Alder?" he whispered.

"Yes?" came the reply in the dark.

"How long do you think we have been gone?"

"I cannot say. I have lost track."

"Do you think anyone misses us?"

"I am sure Margie does, but I do not believe anyone else would."

"Do you think Bacach might?"

Alder did not speak for a moment.

"I am not sure."

Alder's voice was pointed. Alder had always been mistrustful of Bacach, and the image of their last meeting was still imprinted on his mind. It was quiet now.

The days seemed to blend together. Rowan and Alder toiled continuously. They saw little of the warlock and they had never heard the girls utter a word. The garden flourished under their hands. The crops grew larger and more vibrant in color. It seemed that autumn was approaching and the warlock had not said anything about their freedom.

"The harvest is approaching, lads," the warlock said one evening after they had finished eating.

Rowan and Alder stared at him, waiting for him to continue. The warlock sipped his wine and did not say anything for a few minutes.

"When the crop is harvested, we will take it, among other things, to be traded."

"Where is the market?" Alder asked.

"Ah, nowhere ye ever heard of lad. It is a place just for my kind. Now off to bed with ye."

They rose and went to the hayloft.

The next day the scroll on the door told them to harvest.

Rowan and Alder stood mystified as they stared at the largest pumpkin, which was the size of a cottage.

"What are we to do?" Rowan asked.

"I know not. Perhaps we can remove everything from the vines and stems and then worry about piling everything. I do not know how he intends to get this crop anywhere," Alder murmured.

"How do we remove the vines? We have no tools," Rowan asked.

Alder stared at the ground. Rowan got an idea.

"I suppose we existed for quite some time without tools." Rowan picked up two rocks and smashed them together, creating sharp splinters of rocks. He handed one shard to Alder and took another. It took some time to cut through even the smallest stems, but they made slow progress. They were exhausted at the end of the day from the constant climbing and sawing.

Alder and Rowan discovered the next morning that all of the produce they had harvested the previous morning had shrunk in size. A plain wooden cart had appeared in the center of the field. Although the product had shrunk in size it seemed to not have diminished in weight. It took Alder and Rowan's combined strength to lift a single golden yellow pumpkin onto the cart. The cart groaned under the weight but showed no sign of weakness. They had only managed a dozen gourds at the end of the day. They collapsed into the straw that night.

Rowan felt his strength returning. He had felt so weak and unsure after his time in the forest. With the large meals and back-breaking toiling, Rowan felt like he could face any challenge in the future. He thought often of his freedom and what would happen once they were allowed to leave the tower. They would go to the city and find work. Once they had enough money for supplies, they could go into the south to fight the wildmen.

Rowan thought of the city and wondered if the people were all right. He wondered if any other evil had befallen it since their disappearance. He thought of Bacach and his strange behavior. He wondered if Bacach regretted his actions.

The warlock, not the girls, came to wake Rowan and Alder in the middle of the night. "Wake, ye lads. Get moving this instant. Imps or goblins or some creature has broken through and is having at the vegetables! Get out to the field now!" he raged.

Rowan and Alder took off running but hesitated at the door.

"We have no weapons," Alder called before they rushed out of the tower.

"What do you need weapons for?" the warlock called angrily.

"To rid the garden of whatever creatures are in it," Alder retorted sourly.

"If you must have something, take them sticks next to the fireplace."

Alder and Rowan took up the large sticks the girls used to mix the cauldrons.

They stared at each other for a moment, worried about what was outside and their ability to fight it with sticks.

They opened the door and stepped out into the night.

The full moon shone across the garden, reflecting on the withering leaves and tangles of vines. The cart, which was full of the produce they had been harvesting for a week, was swarming with imps, their high-pitched cackling cutting through the otherwise silent night.

The imps seemed unaware of Rowan and Alder, being more interested in raiding the cart.

With a mighty yell that sent the imps shrinking and gasping, Rowan and Alder charged, sticks held high. The first imps were sent sprawling as Rowan and Alder hit them with the sticks with all their might. Quickly regaining their composure, the imps realized it was two men with sticks and not some fierce group of warlocks after them. They retaliated.

With wings buzzing wildly, and their sharp pointed tails poised, they flew toward Rowan and Alder. They bit scratched and stabbed. Several of them tried to wrestle the stick from Rowan and he was forced to beat the stick, with the imps attached, against the cart, smashing the imps unconscious against the wood.

Alder managed to get the imps away from him and began to hurl rocks at them with such precise aim Rowan wondered why Alder did not carry a bow.

The battle seemed to be in Rowan and Alder's favor after a time, the imps that were not unconscious or dead on the ground, were now retreating out of the barrier and into the forest.

"Well lads, ye have done mighty fine work," the warlock mumbled through a full mouth of food at breakfast.

Alder and Rowan sat quietly. They were in the habit of waiting for the warlock to finish his thoughts over the course of their meals.

"Tomorrow we will travel to market. Those imps you killed will make fine editions to the stall. Ground imp is fetching a nice price right now. I want ye to make sure everything is washed and ready for the market. Then I suppose ye can have the afternoon, but I want ye to make sure ye get a good night's rest. Ye will need to pull the cart for me lads."

Rowan and Alder did as they were told. With their magically refilling buckets, they washed all the gourds on the cart and discarded the vegetables the imps had ruined. They rinsed the blood off the cart and made sure everything would be acceptable to the warlock.

They were very familiar with the garden, having been over every stone and stick in their long servitude, so they decided to lounge in the cool shade of the tower. Alder was able to nap, but Rowan looked out across the dying fields. He didn't like how much time he had to think in this place.

When they were in the outside world, they constantly had to be making decisions, observing, and processing information. It wasn't like that here. Their days were filled with mindless tasks that required very little mental effort, although the physical effort required was enormous. They were able to sing songs and chat as they worked, but the songs had all been of the old days and of the outside world. They were living in an unknown time and place in the world. They could guess what the next day would bring within the tower, but they did not know what was happening in the outside world. He frequently wondered what was happening to his friends. If the city was safe. If anyone in Kingsford was still alive.

A new thought occurred to Rowan that he hadn't thought of before.

What side was the warlock on? All the warlocks were supposed to be evil, but the fire walkers had sent them here and promised them safety. This man did not seem like someone the fire walkers would endorse, yet they had. Imps attacked, but imps were lesser monsters that would raid goblins if the opportunity presented itself.

A faint idea began to form in Rowan's head.

He stood up quietly, trying not to wake Alder. As when he had hunted in the woods, Rowan picked his way through the field and crouched low as he approached the barrier. He selected a long, but thin stick and poked at the barrier. The stick went in and out with no effort, the barrier forming around it like water. But the stick was a neutral item.

Rowan crept closer, now crouched lower than the dying leaves of the plants. He reached out gingerly, not knowing what to expect. Perhaps there would be a shock or it would strike him dead where he stood. But he wanted to know what would happen.

Slowly, he touched the barrier. It was firm. It was as solid as stone to him. He could not leave through the barrier. With the feeling of being watched, he quickly looked back over his shoulder. None of the windows on the upper floor faced his direction, but he had a strange feeling, regardless. Rowan crept back to where Alder slept.

At supper, Rowan and Alder ate their food and drank the water in the goblets in silence, but Rowan thought his water tasted somewhat strange. It tasted as though it had been taken straight from the stream, whereas it had usually tasted like fresh spring water. The food seemed more humble tonight, with delicate floral cakes for their dessert. After they were finished, Alder and Rowan went upstairs to bed, leaving the warlock and girls downstairs.

Chapter 10

Rowan woke feeling strange. He found that he was not in the tower, but out in the garden. His head swam and his eyes seemed to roll about his head. He tried to stand up, but something was wrong. His muscles, his body, they were not his own.

He looked around. His head felt heavy and it crashed into something next to him. Next to him in a harness was a silky black horse. He tried to move away but found that he was in the yoke alongside the other horse. He looked down and saw hooves. He had been turned into a golden horse.

He tried to say something, anything, but all that came out was a loud whinny. His tail flicked and swished uncontrollably. He fought against the harness and then felt a whip across his back. He whinnied again and felt the whip bite him a second time.

"That'll be enough out of ye boy," came the warlock's rebuke. "Now, if both of ye are awake and used to yer situation, let's be off."

The whip cracked over their heads. Rowan looked at the horse next to him. He could see in its eyes that it was Alder. That brought him comfort, but he wasn't sure how much. The whip cracked once and Alder snorted then it hit Rowan the third time and he tossed his head.

They pulled against the harness, slowly bringing the cart into motion. They both struggled against the weight of the cart, but they knew that they had no option except to pull. Once they got the cart moving at a fair speed, the dome around the tower became misty. They reached the mist and kept going, traveling through thick fog for a long time.

With a pop and a burst of light, they appeared out of the mist and in the desert on the outskirts of a city.

It was night, wherever they were, but the city shone like gold as if it had been day. Everything was cylindrical and wound away from a central, massive domed building that towered over the rest of the city. The walls of the city were made of sandstone and all the roofs were lined with gold. Torches and lamps burned almost everywhere, casting off enormous amounts of light that was then reflected from the domed roofs. The streets were paved with the same yellow sandstone the walls were made of, making it somewhat easier for Rowan and Alder to pull the cart.

"Welcome, lads, to Gleansach, home of the magic folk."

The streets were crowded, despite the late hour. Humans and all sorts of other creatures were dressed in shimmering robes, all buying and selling goods along the street. Rowan and Alder found that it was easy to push through the crowd. No one wanted to get in the way of the two massive horses.

After moving through the sea of thousands of people, the warlock called them to a stop. They stopped at a small, empty market stall with a table, canopy, and large tent. The warlock unhitched Alder and Rowan from the cart and took them around the backside of the tent where a trough full of a strange orange liquid waited.

"Drink up, lads," the warlock said, swatting them on the rumps before leaving the tent.

Rowan and Alder looked at each other hesitantly. Alder finally snorted and began to drink from the trough. As he drank, the horse's body began to melt like wax onto the ground, before oozing away between the stones. Rowan drank from the trough and felt his bones and muscles shrinking and snapping back into place. He was finally in his right shape again. They were naked again.

Alder smiled at Rowan. "I did not enjoy that even a little."

Rowan looked into Alder's eyes and saw the same look he had seen the day Bacach had chased them to the Pass of Handuin.

The warlock returned after a few minutes sporting a silver robe and what appeared to be a silver nightcap. He gave them new, gold-colored loin cloths and blew strange dust on them. Gold swirling patterns marched across Alder's skin and blue appeared on Rowan. The warlock stared at them curiously for a moment.

"Go unload the cart lads. When ye are finished, bring the cart around back here."

Rowan and Alder did as they were told. The vegetables took the same amount of strength to unload as they had to load. The cart was then moved to the back of the tent. When they were finished, they sat at the corner of the market stall on one of the largest pumpkins and watched the people and creatures that were moving through.

Everyone appeared to be dressed in their finest robes with their finest jewelry. Many creatures wore elaborate headdresses adorned with feathers, jewels, beads, and metalwork. A group of women wore hats of white lace that was shaped in many different styles. They spoke in hissing noises.

The warlock greeted everyone that passed, beckoning them to investigate his stall. A lot of customers seemed extremely interested in the gourds and vegetables, but mostly in the ground imp. Customers did not pay with bonns or any other form of money when they made a purchase. The currency appeared to be jewels. Occasionally, there would be a patron attempting to trade an artifact of some kind and the warlock and patron would haggle for some time. The patron's slaves would then appear and carry off the agreed on amount of vegetables and the warlock would lock the artifact in a chest with a smug grin, as though he had swindled the patron out of a great fortune.

Hours went by and the crowds did not seem to grow or shrink in size. Every so often a cart full of goods would break up the crowd as it was pulled deeper into the city by a team of colored horses or oxen. Men would walk past, sometimes freely, other times being marched in shackles or ropes with the same loin cloths and markings Rowan and Alder now sported. A few other men had blue markings similar to Rowan's. Other men sported green, purple, or red markings, but no one else had gold markings like Alder's. Rowan wondered if any of the magical beings did their own work or if all of it was done by slaves. He wondered if the slaves were servants like Alder and him or if they would work for their master until they died.

The night did not fade, even after Rowan was sure a full day had passed. The sky was always dark, and the lamps were always burning intensely. An unceasing flood of people passed the tent and the dull roar of voices sounded from all around them. The warlock would come and go from the stall. Sometimes he would return with a sack of goods that he would greedily add to the chest and other times he would come back with nothing, muttering and looking stormy. He would occasionally bring Alder and Rowan food or drink.

The food was like nothing Rowan could imagine. Fruit that was shaped like stars and had spikes, a vegetable soup filled with a soft white vegetable that made Rowan feel like he was home beside a fire, and rice served inside a bowl with white flesh and a hard exterior. The preferred drink was a hot brown liquid that was made from milk and beans and was very thick and sweet.

Rowan and Alder had not been permitted to speak. They were slaves and had to look like slaves. They sat quietly and watched all that happened around them.

The sound of distant horns blared from somewhere on the outskirts of the city and a small rush of people pushed past the tent.

"You will not want to miss this one, lads," the warlock grinned, beckoning them up to the table.

The river of people stopped and the center of the street cleared. People hung out the windows of the buildings and crushed into every available space. Rowan and Alder were protected behind the table from the jostling of the crowd.

Music could be heard from the entrance of the city. People laughed and smiled and seemed to hold their breath in anticipation. Rowan and Alder looked down the curving street, but nothing had appeared yet.

The cheers and music grew closer. The sound vibrated the building and the market stall. A burst of flame came from just around the corner. The first groups of performers appeared.

Acrobats, wearing bright red and gold, cartwheeled and flipped down the street. They threw fireworks as they flipped, creating flashes and bangs around them as the acrobats flew through the air. Some would breathe fire, and others sprayed embers from their hands that danced around the crowd.

Next came dancing girls that were dressed in only laces and sheer fabrics. The men jeered and called to them, including the warlock. Rowan was ashamed for them, but the girls looked happy enough to dance and catch the jewels the men would throw at them.

The musicians that followed were dressed in green, purple, and gold and played instruments, unlike anything Rowan had ever seen.

"Have you ever seen anything like this?" Rowan whispered to Alder.

"No. I did not know things like this existed," he murmured back. Clearly in awe, but weary of everything around them.

Exotic animals and creatures came next. Their riders wore bright colors to match the beasts they were riding. The animals had been painted, studded with piercings, and now sported decorative bridles and saddled. Strange, colorful birds larger than a man fluttered past, some with riders dressed in colored silks, others without. A giant, white oxlike animal with six horns bellowed out as it plodded past. The rider, dressed in blue and silver, had painted the ox decoratively with blue paint.

Animals that were clearly carnivorous were in cages pulled by the oxlike animals. A pale-green tiger prowled around a cage, reaching out to swipe at the observers with massive claws. It roared in outrage at everyone, wanting to sink its teeth into whoever it could get its claws into.

Black elephants with gold paint and gold houdahs on top walked stately with their trunks in the air. Their drivers were dressed in gold, shimmering clothes and had painted black zigzags across their faces and necks.

The final animal was that of the warlock that owned the strange menagerie. He rode upon a gold, winged lion with a tail like a scorpion. The lion pranced about and would occasionally jump into the air, beat its wings, swoop over the crowd, and land in the procession. The warlock would raise his hands in the air to tumultuous applause. He wore a large gold robe that was embroidered and beaded with jewels.

Another band section that wore bright orange and black tunics with black tights marched past, playing strange instruments. They played the same tune as the previous band section, which Rowan assumed must be the theme of the parade, though he did not know what that could be.

The warlock tensed as the following group rounded the corner.

Giant bears roared, but not angrily, as they pulled huge golden carts. The bears were many shades of blue and had dark blue horns coming from their heads.

Rowan couldn't control himself. He had never seen animals as magnificent as the bears.

"Master Warlock, what are those bears?"

"They are uisge bears. Now leave me be. I am trying to watch," he grumbled.

The ground shook as the bears stomped past, pulling their heavy carts. The carts were fashioned like cages. Crimson velvet curtains hung on the outside of the cage, pulled back with a gold cord. Human faces stared out of the cage.

Alder stiffened.

"Those are girls," he murmured.

After the cages rattled past, came floating bubbles containing mermaids. The bubbles would bounce off the street, hover, then fall to the ground again. All the while the mermaids sang melodies and swam in circles around their bubbles. A giant clamshell with a squid woman followed, being pulled by giant red octopi. The squid woman's tentacles hung over the clamshell and merrily tapped the rhythm of the song the woman was conducting. The woman smiled and waved and was rather pretty with white flowing hair grazing her pale blue skin as if she were still underwater.

The woman seemed to see Alder among the crowd and stared at him curiously. Their eyes met for an instant. She smiled and bobbed her head back into the music.

The parade seemed to go on indefinitely. More acrobats performed, more creatures ambled and bellowed, and more rattling carts of humans and other creatures bounced past, all without end. Just when Rowan thought his legs would give out from standing for what must have been a full day, the last group appeared around the corner.

Giant drums being pulled by giant green stags appeared. The drummers, hulking men covered in tattoos, beat on the drums to create a low rumble like distant thunder. A call sounded like that of a falcon and the men sprang into action, drumming with their entire bodies.

Soldiers appeared in black and white armor with red feathers bouncing out of their helmets. They wore no insignia and did not have a flagbearer.

Groans and cheers rose from among the crowd as the creature rounded the corner. A high-pitched roar rang out above the sound of the drums. A bright red drake appeared, blowing purple flames into the sky. The huge monster scurried forward like a lizard before stopping to shoot out another burst of flame or let out a roar. The monster was harnessed to a solid gold carriage. The carriage glittered with jewels in the firelight. Two massive windows on both sides of the carriage allowed a glimpse inside and a silver forcefield pulsed within the window, showing obviously to all that whatever it was, it was well-protected. On top of a red velvet cushion was a solid gold box that was covered in black and red jewels.

Another set of soldiers and drummers followed the carriage. They rounded the next corner and the parade was over.

The warlock muttered under his breath with his brow knit. He paced for a few moments as the flood of people crushed back together and proceeded up the road behind the parade. Rowan and Alder watched him as he paced. Then, with a shrug of his shoulders, he walked off.

"What do you think was in that box?" Rowan asked.

"Nothing good. Strong spells surrounded that carriage, not just the windows. That is why whoever it belonged to was forced to use the drake to pull it. Drakes are extremely powerful magical creatures. I did not know that any still existed. That drake looked like a young adult, as well. It hardly had any horns. Whatever was in that box was very valuable to have such heavy magical spells surrounding it. I doubt our master could have lifted even one of them," Alder smiled.

Rowan had a sinking feeling in his stomach and did not know why. Something about that box gave him the chills.

The warlock reappeared through the crowd with a triumphant look on his face.

"Alder, lad, ye will be coming with me for a while," he said cheerfully.

Alder and Rowan looked at each other. Alder did not move.

The warlock frowned slightly. "Come here now, lad."

Alder moved to the warlock. The warlock slapped golden shackles on his wrist.

"What are you doing?" Alder raged.

"Stop fussing. You'll be back," the warlock ordered.

"Alder?" Rowan panicked.

The warlock shoved Alder forward into the crowd and they were swept away.

Rowan climbed up on the table, trying to see Alder's black hair in the crowd, but he was gone. Rowan jumped down and debated taking off after them. He then thought better of it. The chances that he would be able to find Alder in the city were slim. The warlock could step into any building and Rowan would keep walking past.

He would have to hope that the warlock would keep his word.

Rowan counted the number of people that flowed past him in a minute. He could then multiply that to find out how many people passed in an hour. Now he was able to calculate the passage of time within the city that never felt the sun's rays.

Four hours had gone past since the warlock had left with Alder.

Rowan wondered if the warlock really could be trusted or if this had all been an elaborate ruse to sell the farm's produce and two working men. Only Alder wasn't a man. He was an elf. Rowan did not doubt that the warlock could get a good price for Alder.

Rowan was sitting in thought when a man appeared at the counter. He was shrunken and wore dingy blue robes. Rowan wondered if the man was a beggar in this city of wealth where people embroidered their robes with gold and jewels.

"I apologize sir, but my master is not here right now and I am not permitted to do business," Rowan told the man softly, afraid someone would report that Rowan was speaking to customers.

"Have you any idea when your *master* will return?" the man said with a half-smile.

"No, sir. He has been gone with my companion for some hours."

"Do you know what he is doing with your companion at this moment?" the man asked with the same grin.

"No, sir, I do not," Rowan murmured, slightly taken aback.

The man leaned in to whisper to Rowan. "He is trying to sell him to the sea queen."

Rowan felt dizzy. "What? What sea queen?" he stammered.

"You saw her in the parade, lad. The squid woman with the mermaids. Haven't you heard the stories of the sea queen?"

Rowan shook his head, dazed and scared.

"You see, lad, the mermaids used to be elves. But when the great battles were to be fought, the elves that lived by the sea refused to join the battle, for they were safe in their sea haven. Talamh, goddess of the earth, cursed them so that they could never leave the sea to walk upon the land they refused to defend. Undying are the elves, so they were forced to live in the sea. Their bodies changed to that of sea creatures and they were forever cursed in the depths. None came to see them after the battle and they grew angry that no other clan rebuked the gods. That is why the other elf clans do not venture upon the sea. They are afraid of the mermaids that will drag them to the depths. But, as you know, elves can only mate with elves. In order to reproduce, the mermaids need elf-men and they are hard to come by, even in a place such as this. The sea queen wants your friend to be her king. She will buy him from your *master* and she will take your friend to the depths at the end of the market."

Rowan stared at the shrunken old man in his dingy robes. His head was spinning. He felt like he was going to vomit. Alder was probably already in the hands of that woman. The warlock, probably on his way back with a sack full of jewels.

"Is there anything we can do?" Rowan asked.

"I have a proposition for you, lad," the man said with a gleam.

"What is your name?" Rowan asked, hesitantly.

"Keniferous of the Fae Forest."

Chapter 11

Another slave man had been procured, thanks to the jewels in the warlock's chest. He had purple markings across him and could not speak. Keniferous brought forth a potion, and gave some first to Rowan, and then to the other man. Within a moment or two, the other man looked exactly like Rowan, colored markings included.

"That's that. This man will watch the stall and you will come with me," Keniferous bobbed.

Keniferous took Rowan's arm and dragged him into the stream of people. They were propelled forward by the river of moving bodies. Rowan stayed with the old man, thanks to their arms being interlocked, but he could no longer see the outside edge of the moving mass, as they had been pushed toward the center by people joining the crowd.

"It does not matter, lad. We are going all the way to the top. The sea queen is in the palace," Keniferous patted.

"Do you promise to tell me what all this means in the end?" Rowan asked, remembering the fragmented story he had just heard, and not knowing if he believed.

"I promise you, lad. If we make it out of this all in one piece, I will tell you the whole story from the start."

They continued toward the palace, which was the hulking cylindrical building Rowan had seen on the outskirts of the city. The emperor was throwing a grand party at the palace and everyone that had been in the parade was invited, partially to enjoy the party, but mainly to provide the emperor with the first choice of goods.

People started to leave the crowd as they approached the final spiral leading up to the palace. Most people had no reason to venture closer. Keniferous pulled Rowan to the side of the thinning crowd.

They stopped at a stall that was covered in bright red fabric and gold fringe. A ghastly grey woman with thick red hair pulled up under a black hat in the shape of a cube stood over her table with a small smile on her face that revealed two giant tusks.

"Madame Gorum, I wish to buy a new robe," Keniferous bowed.

The woman smiled wider, revealing jagged teeth inside her mouth.

"Payment up front, sir," she grunted with a smile.

Keniferous reached inside his robes and pulled out a handful of gems, all from the warlock's chest, and placed them on the table.

"That ought to be enough?" he asked with a glint in his eyes.

Madame Gorum chuckled and opened the curtain to the tent. The tent stretched out farther than it should have and was filled with hundreds of robes that ran the length of the tent walls.

Keniferous began rooting through the many splendid robes and Rowan sat on one of the plush cushions in the center of the walkway.

"What sort of creature is Madame Gorum?" Rowan asked.

"She is an orc shaman," Keniferous said absent-mindedly.

"I thought orcs all lived in tribes and were fierce creatures?" Rowan gasped, having heard the stories from the Plains of Hutuloth.

"Oh they are, lad, there is no mistaking that. But Madame Gorum is a businesswoman. She lives here in the city. She abandoned her tribe almost fifty years ago to start her new life. She sells robes to us magic folks during the market and lives off the money the rest of the year. She does quite well for herself. But I pity the fool that thinks of crossing her. She was born in the tribal lands and is quite knowledgeable when it comes to axe-wielding."

Rowan imagined Madame Gorum in animal skins, with her hair down and the bones and feathers in her hair like in the stories. She would be a terrifying and formidable opponent, being a full foot taller than Rowan and quite a bit bigger in the shoulders.

Keniferous finally picked out a robe. The robe was black with silver trimmings and tiny black jewels across the bottom. He slid the new robe on, placed the matching hat on his head, and they left Madame Gorum's tent with a bow.

They rejoined the flow toward the palace. Those that continued into the final spiral were more richly adorned than Rowan had seen outside of those that participated in the parade.

"Now, once we are inside, lad, you are my servant. You do exactly as I say and keep your head down. If we are forced into conversation with others, you must bow to them like a slave. That old bastard is prone to drink, so he may still be enjoying the libations if we are lucky. If they are already in a separate room, we will have to find a way to draw them out."

Rowan nodded as they flowed into the massive palace.

The main room was bigger than the castle at Kingsford. Rowan could not see the walls, but the colossal, domed ceiling was covered in gold and all the pillars surrounding the room were white marble. Carvings of all sorts of magical creatures and plants circled around the pillars. Cream lanterns with gold scrollwork hung in the air above the crowd. Music thundered through the room and forced everyone to yell to be heard by the people next to them.

As they pushed through the crowd toward the opposite side of the room, Rowan's arm firmly interlocked with Keniferous's, Rowan could hear the mermaids singing as they had done in the parade. He could see them swimming around their bubbles alluringly as they hoovered slightly above the crowd and then fell back down to the ground.

When they reached the mermaids, Rowan was amazed at what he saw.

A serpent was carved into the wall with only its head sticking out from the wall. Clean, clear water jetted from its mouth and into a pool that had been built into the floor. A few mermaids swam in this pool, splashing and enticing the men that were standing around the edge.

"They have fresh water inside?" Rowan asked quietly, unable to contain himself.

"Most magic folk have water indoors, lad. We can't be bothered to go fetch it at all hours of the day and night. Didn't you notice how clean the city was?"

Rowan had not noticed. Now, he couldn't believe that he had overlooked it. There had to be a million people within this city and the streets were clean. They were not covered in the mounds of waste that surely would have been present in a human city had that many people been present.

He wanted to taste some of that water coming from the wall, but he did not want to venture any closer to the mermaids.

He recognized a loud chortle from somewhere in the crowd. He turned his head in the direction the laugh had come from, but he could not see the warlock.

"Aye, lad, I heard it. He seems deep in his drink. That could be good or bad for us. Let us hope it is good and the deed has not yet taken place."

A gilded servant appeared with a tray of different colored drinks and offered them to Keniferous.

"How about a drink for yourself, lad?" Keniferous asked the servant.

The man shook his head, unable to speak.

Keniferous produced the vial, grabbed the man by the wrist, and poured a bit into his mouth, laughing as if it had all been a good joke.

"That'll have you feeling better!" he chortled, pretending to be drunk. The servant quickly disappeared into the crowd.

"Now you take a sip, lad."

Rowan took a sip from the vial and felt a strange tingling throughout his body. In a moment, he had become the servant.

"Now to get the warlock and your friend to change places requires a bit more work. You need each person to drink twice, taking turns after each swing. Your friend will be the easy part. Get him to drink from the glass first, then the warlock drinks from his own, then replace it with the glass your friend drank from. Then a bit of this other draught." Keniferous produced a small blue vial.

"What will that do?" Rowan asked.

"It'll seal the deal." Keniferous winked.

Rowan took the vials and pushed through the crowd, trying to get behind the warlock if he could. He had to find Alder first.

He spotted the warlock, but Alder was nowhere to be seen. Rowan felt his stomach drop. The sale had already taken place.

Rowan spotted a table with different foods and drinks on it and took up one of the trays. He approached the warlock with the tray and offered one of the bright pink drinks to the warlock in the same way the servant had offered them to Keniferous.

The warlock looked at the tray with a drunken roll of his eyes and took one of the glasses. He threw it back in a few seconds.

"Why don't you be a good bug and take one of these to the fine lady in the next room? She has much to be celebrating and I say she'll love a nice Acadia juice."

Rowan pointed towards a small hallway that ran off the main room.

The warlock grew irritable.

"First room, ye idiot. Go!"

Rowan scurried off like a dogged servant. The passage was the same cream marble the great hall had been made of, but it was significantly darker. A few glass lanterns were along the walls, but long shadows were cast down the corridor. The floor gently sloped downwards, giving Rowan the impression of some dungeon.

A cream-colored door appeared on the right. Rowan hesitated outside of it for a moment, listening for any sort of noise. He could not hear anything coming from inside.

Rowan opened the door slowly, afraid that the sea queen would be there. The room was completely empty. Rowan shut the door and walked more quickly down the passage. The passage turned and a set of stairs plunged Rowan down much more quickly.

Slipping on the stone stairs, Rowan found that they were covered in some sort of mucus.

She is a squid, Rowan thought nervously.

He quickened his pace. He was getting closer, but he needed to hurry.

The sound of trickling water echoed down the darkening hallway. As he continued on, the sound grew louder and louder.

"The water from the fountains must empty out down here into a large pool," Rowan thought.

He came upon a heavy, dark door. He opened this slowly. The door opened into a dark room. A stone walkway surrounded a large pool of water with a waterfall emptying into it from a carving of Uisgeachan. A small stone island rose out of the center of the pool.

Alder was chained to this island. He looked up as Rowan closed the door. Alder had an expression of horror as he looked at Rowan, only seeing the servant carrying potions on a tray.

The sea queen appeared out of the water with her tentacles rolling about the walkway.

"Thank you, boy. Are these the potions I sent for?" she asked with a musical voice.

Rowan shook his head yes.

The sea queen smiled, and a tentacle wrapped around one of the glasses. She carried this to Alder, pried open his mouth with two other tentacles, and dumped it down his throat. One of the tentacles wrapped itself around his mouth, forcing him to swallow it.

The sea queen began to sing. Rowan had never heard anything like it. He felt haunted. Like he would never be able to get that enchanting voice out of his head. Rowan began to step forward toward the pool.

She beckoned to him and smiled at him while she sang. Rowan continued walking until he plunged into the water, tray and all. A tentacle wrapped around Rowan's waist and pulled him toward the sea queen.

A part of his senses seemed to return as he saw the mute horror on Alder's face. He still held the vial.

The sea queen pulled Rowan to her, her tentacles now fully wrapped around him. She sang quietly and sweetly to him. As she lifted him to her, Rowan jammed the vial into her mouth.

The thin glass broke inside her mouth, the contents pouring down her throat with the mixture of blood and glass.

Her shriek was earsplitting. Her tentacles thrashed about the water, whipping at Rowan and Alder.

The fight did not last long.

The sea queen's head rolled and all that escaped her lips was an agonized moan. Rowan, treading water and watching the sea queen's every movement noticed a key on a thin chain around her neck. He swam to her and tore the key from her.

Rowan swam as quickly as he could to the island where Alder sat. He climbed up and unchained Alder with a smile.

Alder looked at this strange man that had saved him.

"Who are you?" was all Alder asked.

"I'll explain everything, but first let's get out of here. I think that potion only put her to sleep," Rowan smiled.

They hurried out into the corridor and ran straight into a servant carrying a vile, black, bubbling drink on a gold tray. The servant was shocked at the sight of the two men. Perceiving that it was a jail break, he dropped the tray to run, but Alder seized him and, with a vehemence that shocked Rowan, snapped the man's neck. The body crumpled to the ground.

Alder said nothing, but they ran as quickly as they could back to the party. Rowan took Alder's arm and led him toward the rendezvous location in the center of the crowd. Keniferous was there, chatting with some other magic folk. Rowan guided Alder slowly to his side and bowed when Keniferous acknowledged them.

Keniferous chatted for a few more moments and then took his leave of the magic folk.

They sauntered out of the party.

Keniferous led them down the winding road to a dingy little apartment on a side street. The apartment did not have a door, only a blanket of sorts. A window, which Rowan was not sure if had been made on purpose or if a hole had been blown in the wall by some accident, was the only source of light in the one room. The wood floors felt solid under Rowan's feet and Rowan was thankful they were not rotten. A few cushions were thrown about. The only thing out of the ordinary in the room was the table covered in books, magical creature parts, and the cabinet full of jars of strange substances.

"Now, let's get you back to rights, lad," Keniferous said, mixing liquids into a vial.

He handed Rowan the vial and Rowan drank it without hesitation. He felt the strange tingling sensation for a few seconds and felt that he had returned to himself. Alder stared at Rowan and then crushed him madly in a hug. Alder sobbed weakly and Rowan held him tightly.

"I thought I was done for, a fate worse than death, and you came for me," he cried.

Rowan hugged Alder for as long as Alder needed.

Alder finally sat back, looking weak and tired.

"Why don't you lads get some rest? I'll keep a lookout. There will be much to do when we get ourselves out of here."

Rowan and Alder moved the cushions into a pile and slept.

Rowan was not sure how long he had slept. The sky was always the same shade of darkness. He could have slept for several days and wouldn't have known the difference. Alder was still sleeping when he woke. He knew Alder had barely been sleeping for a long time and knew in his heart that Alder was not well.

Keniferous was standing at the door, looking out through the open curtain.

"You lads slept like the dead, you did," he remarked upon seeing Rowan's movements.

"I do not know how long we have been here and we have not slept since our coming to this place."

"Well, the festival has been going on for two weeks now, so I'd say you lads needed your rest."

"Two weeks?" Rowan stammered.

"Aye, the festival lasts a month. The parade is in the middle of the month. The party at the palace will last one week while the emperor picks the items he wishes to buy. Then the trading opens to the rest of the folks here."

"But people have been buying our gourds since we got here," Rowan questioned.

"That is the small, petty, trading. The big trades. The stuff you saw in the parade. It's all illegal goods. Illegal to take from the outside world, and illegal to have, but those folks make a great fortune off the selling of them. Especially the beasts. The beasts are captured out of the Elven lands across the world. The Elvish gamekeepers will kill any of the poachers on sight, but it's a risk worth taking for old Grimish, that's the owner of the menagerie. He uses his slaves to capture the creatures, anyhow. No risk to his neck."

"The elves know about this place?" Rowan asked.

"Of course, they know of it, but they don't know how to get here. Nor would they want to. One or two magic folks against the elves wouldn't stand a chance. But an army of elves versus the whole city of magic folk, there's a difference. The elves would be slaughtered and what ones weren't slaughtered would be captured and sold off.

Elves are worth a lot as slaves. They don't die like men do."

"Then what are the girls used for? Surely there isn't that much housework that the warlock would need three girls for it. They are all young, too."

"The warlock has three girls at the tower?" Keniferous asked angrily, staring directly at Rowan now.

"Yes. A blonde girl of about nineteen, a black-haired girl of maybe seventeen, and Melati who is about fourteen."

"Have these girls spoken to you?"

"No, they don't speak at all."

"What color are their dresses?"

"The older girls' dresses are red. When we first arrived at the tower, Melati's dress was pink, but now it is red, too. She must have spent a long time dying it for we did not see her for a few days after our arrival."

Keniferous raised his hand for Rowan to stop talking. Rowan felt nervous. Something had angered Keniferous, but he wasn't sure what he had said.

"How did you lads come to the tower?"

"The fire walkers told us to go there. They said a warlock lived there and would help us, but I no longer believe that he had any intentions of helping us."

"So the fire walkers did not know what happened and have been continuing to send men there…" Keniferous trailed off.

"Do not know what?" came Alder's voice. Rowan looked behind him at Alder. His face appeared shallow, but he had been awake for a while.

"Keniferous, you promised you would tell us the meaning of all this once we rescued Alder," Rowan implored hesitantly.

"That is my tower you lads have been in. Joyong took it from me with the help of another warlock. You see, lads, there aren't many established areas for us magic folk anymore. We try to keep away from the cities of men, except for those that prey on humans, like the witches. My realm has been established since the beginning of men. I inherited it from my master, and he from his master. Well, not all can be so fortunate. One day Joyong appeared inside the barrier. I still don't know how he managed it to this day, but little good it will do now. He appeared with another I don't know the name of. Never saw his face to be honest. We made battle and I lost, not being much against two warlocks. With nowhere else to go, I came here and took up this apartment.

"The fire walkers were right to send you to the tower. In my time, and my master's, we would always help the weary traveler the fire walkers thought worthy enough to send to the tower. They were provided with food, drink, shelter, and whatever else we could spare them. I fear that Joyong has been selling these men as slaves or trading them for the girls."

"But what of the girls? Why does he have them?" Rowan asked.

"Why would a man want girls, lad?" Keniferous retorted, staring at Rowan as if he was a child.

A wave of anger filled Rowan.

He had to free them.

"What can we do to help?" Alder asked, his voice hard and his face grave.

"Why, lads, we are going to take the tower back," Keniferous smiled.

Chapter 12

Rowan, now dressed in a long, smoke-colored robe, passed up and down the winding street with his hood pulled up. The masses of creatures would keep him hidden from the market stall, as well as Alder and Keniferous.

The slave that had taken on Rowan's appearance still tended the stall and shooed people away, pointing to his mouth to show that he could not speak.

No one had been sure when Joyong would return to the stall. He wasn't really allowed at the emperor's party, said Keniferous, and would wear out his welcome probably sooner rather than later.

They must wait for Joyong to return. Alder must not be seen under any circumstances. The murder of the sea queen would be a death sentence for all of them, whereas a property dispute between magic folk was frequent and most turned blind eyes to the complaints, or deaths, of the party.

Rowan was to keep tabs on the stall and watch for Joyong to return. Once he had returned from the party he would most likely try to sell 'Rowan' to the highest bidder. This would be the perfect time for them to stow themselves inside Joyong's chest and return with him to the tower without him noticing.

Now it was waiting.

After Rowan felt too tired to continue the pacing, he returned to Keniferous's apartment where he and Alder waited. Keniferous then took his turn and allowed Rowan to rest.

A bowl of fruit, cheese, and flattened bread was laid out for Rowan. It was a strange purple fruit with red flesh on the inside. Alder assured him that everything was quite good eaten together.

"Do you believe this man?" Alder asked quietly.

"His story about the tower? I believe he is telling the truth. He seemed to know many things without me having told him anything. Even if he is lying, I do not see that it could make much difference. Surely, we will not be worse off with him than Joyong."

"I want to kill him myself," Alder said idly.

Rowan patted Alder's arm. "I do not feel that you will be the one to do it. If Keniferous fails, then we will be killed."

"Then I shall take him with me." Alder lay back and stared at the stone ceiling.

Rowan began to wonder if Joyong would ever return to his stall after several days of pacing. At the end of the week, however, Joyong did return. The market was about to open for the sale of the major goods and Joyong would need all the money he had gained to this point.

Joyong did not leave the stall for a few days, endeavoring to sell all the gourds before he counted his jewels to know what he could purchase. To everyone's relief, he paid little attention to 'Rowan' who sat on the cart most of the day, quietly out of the way. The next day, Joyong took 'Rowan' into the crowd of people.

Suddenly, a great commotion began to take place in the city. Where everyone had once tried to get deeper into the city, everyone turned and was now trying to get out. So much noise came from outside that Keniferous was forced to see what it was about.

He was gone for a short while. When he returned, he was out of breath and looked scared.

"We must go now, lads. It's now or never. Someone has stolen from the emperor. No one is saying what was stolen, but the soldiers are working their way down through the city. Folks are being searched and put in jail. They are saying the city is going to be shut down and no one will be able to leave."

"Can they do that?" Rowan stammered.

"He can do as he likes. He is the emperor. Same way barriers work to keep people out, they can be used to keep people in."

Rowan thought about the day he had touched the barrier at the tower. Keniferous was right. They could be stuck here indefinitely if the city was closed off and it was now only a matter of time before the sea queen's body was found. There hadn't been any news of her waking and telling the emperor that she had been poisoned by one of his servants, so it must be the worst.

Alder wrapped himself in a black robe and threw the hood up, obscuring his face completely. Rowan and

Keniferous raised their hoods. Before leaving the apartment, Keniferous handed each of them a small vial.

"It'll be a little bit of a strain lads, but you need to jump into the chest and drink this at the same time. It'll shrink you down as you fall into the chest. There are enchantments that won't let you in otherwise."

They were out the door and into the crowd. It was easy making their way toward the stall now. They no longer had to fight against the crowd to move down the street. Within a few minutes, they were at the stall. Joyong had not returned, but they knew it would only be a matter of time.

Alder was to go first. Keniferous instructed him again. Alder jumped toward the chest and drank the potion. He disappeared mid-air.

Rowan looked at Keniferous in surprise.

"It worked, lad. Now you."

Rowan copied Alder. He didn't feel any different. He just suddenly felt the terror of the foot he had jumped off the ground turning into what seemed like hundreds of feet. He, however, landed softly on the pile of jewels. Keniferous came right behind him.

"Not so bad, was it lads?" he asked with a grin.

"How did we not die during the fall?" Rowan asked.

"Have you ever seen a bug fall off a tree?"

"Yes," Rowan said hesitantly, waiting for more.

"Well, lad, we are about the size of an ant now and ants don't die when they fall off trees, so neither did we."

This made sense to Rowan in its vagueness, but he now questioned why it was that ants did not die when they fell from trees.

It was only a matter of waiting now. They sat on the pile of jewels and waited for Joyong to return. They knew he would be in a hurry, not being anyone's favorite citizen.

The moment came. Joyong's grave face appeared over the open chest. He frowned, scanned his jewels and artifacts, and shut the lid with such force it shook them all. They felt the chest being lifted and the jewels shifted. They held on as tightly as they could as they rocked about inside the chest.

They felt themselves being thrown on the cart. A loud, mournful groan roared outside the chest. Joyong had bought a beast to pull the cart.

They rattled on down the road at what they imagined was the fastest pace they could push through the crowd. It was a rough ride for those in the chest. With every bump, the jewels shifted along with Rowan, Alder, and Keniferous.

To their relief, they did not stop. Keniferous had been afraid of the cart being stopped and searched. The chest would be searched. Each squad was accompanied by a seer that would discover them and they would all be arrested.

Mist crept into the chest from the keyhole and they knew they were passing through the barrier. Then came a pop and daylight shone through the keyhole. They had returned to the tower.

"Now lads, we must wait until the right moment for the charge. The chest will be taken up to the third floor, which will give us the advantage of the high ground. The glutton will go to supper right after he gets his affairs sorted. This is when we will take the other potions. Then we go in for the attack."

"What are we to do?" Alder asked.

Keniferous frowned. He had thought out the duel between himself and Joyong but had completely cut out Alder and Rowan from his scheme.

"Just keep out of the way, lads. It is bound to be messy."

The cart came to a stop. The chest was carried up the stairs and set down somewhere. All else was quiet. Keniferous seemed to be contemplating the time with his eyes shut.

"Now's the time lads."

Keniferous climbed to the front of the chest and took a swig of the new vial. He shot up like a bolt, throwing the lid of the chest open. He quickly stepped out of the chest.

"You next, Rowan. My bones don't break as easily as yours," Alder smiled.

Rowan did exactly as Keniferous had done, being sure he was well away from Alder.

He shot up to his normal height and stepped out of the chest. Keniferous was there but was watching the stairway.

Alder shot up next and had a deadly gleam in his eyes.

"Let's go lads," Keniferous waved.

They crept down the stairs, staying close to the wall, afraid that the old rotten wood would creak under their weight.

They passed through the second floor, where Rowan and Alder had spent countless nights.

Keniferous pulled a black vial from his robes as they continued down the stairs. The element of surprise was paramount, but the nature of the spiral stairs allowed Joyong to get a glimpse of them before they were able to see him, especially where he sat at the head of the table. They could always hope that Joyong would be drunk, and his senses would be dimmed.

Keniferous suddenly jumped down the remaining steps with a sprightliness they had not seen in him before. With a battle cry, he hurled a vial at the floor and an inky black smoke filled the room.

Rowan and Alder rushed down the stairs and into the smoke. It did not hurt their eyes, but it was impenetrable. They felt around the wall in an attempt to reach the door. They jerked at the handle. They slammed their bodies into it. It was no use. They were stuck inside until whatever end came.

The smoke began to settle to the floor. Rowan and Alder found that they were completely covered in the stuff. Keniferous stood in a stand-off with Joyong. They did not speak but glared at each other as though they were the worst enemies the world had ever seen. Blue electric light shimmered in Joyong's hands. Keniferous held a bright red vial of liquid.

Joyong's hand shot out, the electric light coursing through the air toward Keniferous. Keniferous threw the vial just below Joyong, the glass shattering at his feet. A bubbling ooze shot into the air like a geyser. The electric light from Joyong's hands never made it to Keniferous, for the ooze attacked.

Keniferous produced another vial as Joyong fought the ooze. He threw the second bottle, and a lime green smoke burst forth, enveloping Joyong. He gurgled for a moment, but then an explosion shook the tower. Joyong burst from the smoke and the ooze with his entire body engulfed in flames, but the fire did not seem to affect him. The flames roared across the room to Keniferous, catching his robes on fire. Keniferous dropped his robes, wearing only a tunic underneath.

With his other hand, Joyong spewed a black vapor into the room.

"Cover your faces, kids!" Keniferous yelled to Rowan, Alder, and the girls that were cowering in the kitchen.

They did as they were told, no longer able to see what was happening around them.

The sounds of crashing, explosions, the buzzing of electricity, and the smashing of glass came from both sides. The warlock yelled, and the alchemist screamed. It did not seem as though either team was making any headway.

Rowan looked up. Keniferous had let out a beastly groan. A metal spike was through him and he gripped it feebly before it disappeared, leaving only a hole in Keniferous's chest that gushed blood down his front and onto the floor. Joyong had won.

Rowan grabbed Alder and they pushed against the door. Joyong still had not noticed them, reveling in his victory against the alchemist.

Like a flock of harpies, the girls screamed wildly. The girls rushed at Joyong, plunging knives into him from the kitchen. Joyong tried to spin on them, but the blonde girl slashed wildly with her knife, slitting his throat.

The blood poured out of his neck. A loud crack came from above them and the whole tower began to shake. The whole thing shook like an earthquake. Rubble began to fall from the ceiling. Rowan looked across the room. The girls held each other in terror, staring at the ceiling as more cracks began to form and stones fell. A new girl Rowan had never seen before huddled with the other three.

Alder pulled Rowan against the door, putting his arm across his chest. The ceiling crumbled and dust blinded them. Rowan closed his eyes and did not open them until the crashing and shaking stopped.

He was badly bruised. He could feel that. His ears rang from the noise of the tower collapsing. He opened his eyes and saw that Alder was still standing next to him, but he held his arm tightly. A stone had hit his arm and it was already swelling.

"Are you all right?" Rowan asked. He felt as though he was shouting.

Alder nodded, slightly wide-eyed.

Rowan began to climb the pile of rubble. The door had remained intact and sealed, but the rest of the tower was now sprawled across an empty field. The garden was gone. The magic had vanished with the deaths of both magical beings.

Rowan made his way toward where he had last seen the girls.

Only the blonde girl remained.

She was collapsed on the ground, vainly trying to move stones, and weeping.

"We didn't know this would happen!" she wailed.

Rowan and Alder looked at each other in shock. They began to dig through the rubble as quickly as possible, praying that the other girls would be alive. They shouted into the rubble. No reply came. Moving some of the rubble away, they discovered parts of the girls' bodies. The other girls were gone.

They climbed down and sat down in front of the blonde girl. The only sound was her sobs.

"Why did you kill him?" Alder asked.

The girl's body shook. "He-he was a monster," she wailed.

They waited for her to speak.

"We were slaves. We were kidnapped and then sold at the market. He bought us as young girls and would keep us until we were of age. Then he forced himself upon us. When he forced himself upon Melati, we knew it would only be a short time before he wanted a new girl. Then when he went to the market and brought Clary back, we knew we had to do something before he hurt her. We couldn't bear to see him torture another girl. We hoped that the other man would be able to kill him, but he didn't. So we killed him. We didn't know all this would happen and now they are dead anyway!"

She wailed for a moment, her sobs became ragged, and then she was quiet. She was unconscious.

"What do we do?" Rowan asked.

Alder stared at the girl. "We can't leave her here, but I don't know that we can help her in any way. We are a little better than being completely naked. We could have done this much had we stayed in the woods and then we wouldn't have lost so much time."

"We will take her to town with us, but I think we should stay here for the night and leave in the morning," Rowan decided.

Rowan and Alder sifted through the rubble, looking for anything that could be useful or valuable. They managed to find some gold statues and a few jewels. They could not find clothing or weapons of any kind. Their robes would have to do.

They woke at first light. Rowan gently shook the girl. "You must wake. We must be on our way."

They carried the small treasures and began to walk toward what Rowan hoped would be town.

"What are you going to do with me when we reach a village?" the girl asked.

"We have not discussed it," Alder replied.

"Are you going to sell me?" she asked, almost casually.

"I do not believe in slave trading," came Alder's cool reply.

"We are hoping to sell these few things at the market. Alder and I need clothes and weapons. You are now a free woman to do as you choose," Rowan stated unfeelingly.

Almost telepathically, Rowan and Alder had decided to get rid of the girl as quickly as possible.

They walked for two days before reaching the first farms. A shepherd was minding his flock when they emerged from the woods. He looked in terror at the well-dressed girl with two men in dark robes appearing from the woods.

The group stopped before him. "Shepherd, we have had a hard journey. Have you any food? We have items we can trade," Alder called out.

"I'll want none of yer cursed jewels witch-slave! Begone with ye!" The man's voice quivered, and it sounded more as though he was begging them to leave than ordering them.

"We are not witches or demons. We are travelers that have been lost in the woods. We are in need of aid," Rowan implored.

They continued to approach. The shepherd fled, leaving his flock.

"Well, that went as well as we could have hoped," Alder laughed.

"We could try to reach the mill," Rowan offered.

Alder smiled. "Tomil Miller does owe us a favor. He had nothing to give us after we took care of those raiders for him."

Rowan sighed. "I feel as though we are going to be calling on quite a few of the villagers we have helped over the years."

Alder put his hand on Rowan's shoulder. "We are not begging. We have jewels and gold that we can trade."

The girl spoke up. "You mustn't trade all of it. I will need a dowry."

Rowan and Alder stared at her in shock. She stared back, unabashed.

"I have made up my mind. I do not wish to go with you. I wish to marry a man in the city, but I will need a dowry. I can use the jewels to win a husband of high class. I do not wish to be a servant."

"We are all servants in some way," Alder replied. He began walking in the direction of the mill. Rowan followed and then the girl.

"Have you thought of what you are going to call yourself?" Alder asked the girl.

"What is an aristocratic name?" she asked.

Alder pursed his lips and shook his head slightly. Rowan smirked.

"It is still fashionable to name your children Elvish names. King Amadan gave his sons Elvish names and named his daughters after flowers," Rowan offered.

"I do not wish to be named after a flower. The warlock named us after flowers of his choice."

"Then what Elvish name would you like?" Alder smirked.

"Elves are illegal. Why do royalty choose Elvish names?"

"It is a dying tradition. It shows that the family is educated and of high class. The lower classes do not know Elvish and cannot give their children Elvish names. Few people know Elvish anymore, even in the higher ranking families."

"Then pick a good Elvish name for me," she ordered.

"Annasach. You could go by Anna for short," Alder offered after thinking for a minute.

Rowan looked at him and noticed the devilish look in Alder's eye. He chuckled to himself, knowing whatever name Alder had chosen for her was not a compliment.

"I sort of like that. Annasach. Anna," she repeated, feeling the name roll off her tongue. "What will be my family name? Certainly, a wealthy man would want to know that."

"You cannot have ours, so you best think of one yourself. Surely you can remember your own family name," Alder spat.

"I can remember, but I don't want to be called Potter. My mother and father were peasants that paid more in rent for their workshop than what they made. My father was thrown in jail for his debts and me and my mother were sold off," she huffed.

"Perhaps Weaver is more suitable?" Alder proposed.

"Hardly! What sorts of people work in the castle?"

"There are plenty of cooks, servants, maids, butlers, seamstresses, weavers, and laundresses. There is the entire noble court that stands around waiting for the King's orders. Then there are the tutors, guards, nurses, mistresses, and chandlers," Rowan said coolly.

"What does a chandler do?"

"They make and light candles."

"Is that a high-ranking position?"

"No."

"Who is the highest ranking of the servants?"

"The marshal or the steward, depending on how you see things," Alder replied with some sourness.

"Anna Marshal," the girl sighed. "That does sound poetic, does it not?"

Rowan and Alder exchanged glances.

"That is what I shall be called. From this moment forward I will be called Annasach Marshal," she declared.

"You might find it prudent to think out your story up until you were forced into slavery," Alder offered.

The remainder of the walk was quiet as Anna thought out her tale.

Rowan felt his heart quicken when he saw the sails of the mill. He couldn't help smiling to see Tomil Miller outside, stacking sacks of wheat into separate piles.

"Tomil Miller!" Rowan called out. Tomil looked up from his work and appeared to be startled. He backed away slightly, then stopped. He was a short, bald man, with fringes of salt-and-pepper hair around the sides of his head. He wore a plain tunic with dark tights and leather shoes. He was all in all, a simple man.

"Who is it that calls for Tomil?" he called back gruffly.

"Rowan, son of Lionn," Rowan declared as they reached talking distance.

Tomil stared at Rowan and then at Alder.

"Why bless my soul, it is Mr. Rowan and Mr. Alder! Why the news is that you were both killed off by King Amadan after that evil business in Kingsford! But here you are, wearing strange robes, covered in soot, and starved outside my mill. Flesh and blood still attached! Come in, come in! I'll get a fire going and we can has us some porridge. Then we can has us a nice talk!"

Tomil opened the door to the house next to the mill and let the group inside. "And why you have a wee las with you now! What a pretty las! What is her name?"

"Annasach Marshal," Anna replied in a stately manner, holding out her hand.

The miller did not notice and waddled past. He stoked up a fire quickly and began stirring the pot of porridge on the stove.

"As you know, I keep little foodstuffs for myself, not needing much, but I found some chestnuts on the edge of the forest yesterday and added them to the porridge. You're lucky you came today, before I ate it all," Tomil laughed.

"How are you Tomil? How is your family?" Rowan asked, sitting on a small stool next to the fire.

Tomil's face grew gloomy.

"My wife, bless her, died last winter. Some sickness nothing could cure. I spent all the money I saved trying to cure her with some doctor out of the city, but alas, she's gone to Spioradan's Hall now."

"I am sorry Tomil. She was a good woman," Rowan soothed.

"Aye, she was a good one. The best one. I don't know that I'll ever take another. But my son is off to the military academy. He will have none of this miller's life! Wants the path to greatness and glory says he! Nothing greater than being simple folk that provides for their neighbors, says I, but you know how the young men are. They want to prove to the world that they are something. A cut of a different cloth than what they were weaved in."

"So you are here all alone?" Rowan asked sympathetically.

"Aye. I don't mind it much anymore. The winter will be hard when I am stuck indoors with nothing to keep myself busy 'cept my thoughts, but I'll manage. I was thinking of finding myself a dog…" Tomil drifted slightly. "So what has happened to you men? Everyone be saying you're dead and then you pop up here with nothing but some mightily devilish robes!" Tomil laughed.

"It is too long a story to tell, but we have come to ask for help," Rowan sighed.

"Well say no more! After all the trouble you saved me from, I owe you more than me life!"

"You will not have to trouble yourself much, Tomil. We need clothing and weapons. If you could find clothing for us, enough for us to make it into the city, then we can do the rest ourselves."

"I have just the thing for you! My boy left a few things here when he left, said he wouldn't be needing them at the academy! I suppose they would fit you just fine!" Tomil scurried away.

He returned shortly with two plain tunics and two pairs of dark tights. They were almost identical to his.

"No wonder his son left them here. A young man chasing honor and glory would not want to wear the clothes of a poor peasant", Rowan thought but was thankful the son had left for honor and glory and neglected to bring his clothing.

Rowan and Alder quickly changed into the clothes. Alder looked unamused at his clothes. He had never worn such a thing in all his life and the tights were too short, revealing Alder's ankles. For a moment, Rowan wondered if Alder would have preferred to go into the city wearing the robes.

They thanked Tomil Miller heartily and ate porridge by his fire. Rowan was thankful for some plain, wholesome, non-magical food. Simple food made from good growing things that a farmer had loved and cared for.

"Why Mr. Rowan and Mr. Alder, you look plum tired! You are welcome to sleep here tonight if it suits you. Anna, lass, you may have my son's blanket in the corner if you'd like," Tomil offered.

Anna, with some new-found pride, went to argue, but Alder shot her a bone-chilling glare. "She would be honored, Mr. Miller," Alder replied in her stead.

Anna retreated to the straw pile and quilt in the corner of the room. Rowan and Tomil embraced and Rowan thanked him again. Tomil retired to his own bed in a small side room which was separated by a curtain.

Rowan and Alder moved the stools and chairs to the side of the room and lay on the straw-covered floor by the fire.

"Things are going to get better now," Rowan whispered. Alder looked at him and smiled.

"I am glad you think so."

They took their leave from Tomil Miller, leaving two rubies on the mantle, knowing Tomil would never accept them if they had offered them openly. The road before them seemed easier. Rowan and Alder had regained some of their hope, strength, and dignity. The city of New Market was less than a day's walk and they could blend into the crowds much easier dressed as they were. Tomil had given them a grain sack that had been cut too small to carry their gold and jewels in.

"Rowan," Anna began.

Rowan inwardly groaned and Alder smirked.

"You are going to have to pretend to be my elder brother. Girls can't call upon rich households and demand that their son marries them. You will have to call upon them and do it for me. You can tell them that our parents died recently and all they left was that sack of gold and jewels and the hope that their only daughter could marry into a good household."

Rowan was speechless. He was a good deal confused, but simultaneously shocked and slightly outraged at the audacity of the girl.

Rowan could see Alder trying not to laugh.

"I will do nothing of the sort," he managed.

"You have to," Anna cried, not expecting Rowan to refuse.

"Why do I have to?" Rowan asked lightly.

"Because-because-of everything I've been through! I was a slave! The warlock forced himself upon me! You have to help me, so I never have to do any of that again!"

The smile died from Alder's face and the cold fire kindled in his eyes. He shot Rowan a glance that Rowan knew all too well. If Rowan didn't finish this now, Alder would.

"Have you any idea what we have been through?" Rowan asked.

"It can't have been worse than what I've been through!" Anna stated sourly.

"Both of us are orphans. Alder raised himself on the moors and became a mercenary when he was old enough to fight. Alder found me and raised me himself, but frequently left me in other people's care when his work was too dangerous for a boy to be brought along to. When Alder was away, I was left a servant to whichever household would take me. Often enough, I was left with

King Amadan because it was he that was sending Alder away for work. Although Prince Bacach and I became friends, every other member of the household treated me like a slave. The other children abused me. The servants abused me. But it could not be helped. Alder had to work to provide for us, but he was just as much a slave to the king's requests as you were to the warlock. If Alder had not done the king's bidding, he would have been killed. Alder once told you that we are all slaves and it is true. Do not think just because you marry a rich man that will mean that you are any less a slave."

"I won't be a slave if I marry a rich man. I will have servants! I will have slaves!"

Alder spun around and slapped her. Rowan knew it hadn't been hard but was shocked that he would do such a thing. Alder had never attacked a woman, even the bandit women. He always left them tied to a tree for the soldiers to retrieve.

Anna dropped to the ground on her own accord and began to wail like a child. That was Alder's reasoning. He was proving that Anna was ultimately a child. She had been the eldest of the slaves but locked away in the warlock's tower, she had never developed into a woman.

Alder towered over her, stormy and menacing.

"You think because you have had bad things happen to you that the world owes you riches and happiness? The world owes you absolutely nothing! There are people in this world that have had worse trials than you could ever dream of! You think the warlock was a bad master, you should ask the escaped slaves how the wildmen treated them! You had the safety of the tower where the worst thing that could happen was the warlock would force himself upon you. The women the wildmen captured had every member of the tribe force themselves upon them! The warlock never struck you. You had a tower, a bed, rich clothes, and food. The women of the wildmen have none of that. They are forced to work until they die from sickness, hunger, or exhaustion in the bitter elements with only scraps of clothing to shield them. They are forced to bear the wildmen's children and mothers are forced to watch their daughters be given away and bear more children. You had your revenge on the warlock. You held the blade in your hands. Those women aren't so lucky. If you would like to try your luck, I will find you some of the escaped slaves when we reach the city. They do not live in rich houses. Most live on the streets even now without a single person taking pity upon them. They lose their minds out there. Or worse, if they happen to hold some of their looks, they are kidnapped and sold again.

"Even if you marry a rich man, what do you suppose will happen within your household? You are his slave. As his wife, you forfeit your rights to him. He becomes your master. You gain command over the servants, but they may leave your service when they tire of your demands and your husband may override your demands at any time. You speak of slaves when you have only tasted freedom for a day. You would so readily force someone into the chains you killed to be rid of? There is evil in that and I will not be party to it. If you seek to gain the life you speak of, let us part ways now, for I do not want to see what becomes of you."

Alder took the bag of gold and jewels from Rowan and took a few things out. He tossed them at the girl who was pouting like a scolded toddler and began to walk down the road. Rowan glanced at Anna and then followed Alder.

Alder walked briskly as if he meant to put as much distance between them and Anna without running from her. Rowan did his best to keep up.

"I cannot believe that you hit her," Rowan said quietly.

"She needed it. She is a spoiled child. There is no excuse for what the warlock did to those girls. I know she tells the truth when she says he forced himself upon them. He deserved to die in more violent ways than how they chose to kill him. But she, having just experienced evil, is so quick to turn to it in order to make her own life better. It is sickening."

"Alder?" Rowan questioned, hesitantly.

"What?" he demanded coldly.

"With the sea queen—" Rowan began.

Alder spun on him. "Nothing happened."

"Is that the truth?" Rowan asked, holding onto Alder's arm firmly.

Alder looked dejectedly at the ground. "Nothing could happen. She needed that potion the servant was bringing," he said distantly.

"That's why you looked at me with such terror when I brought the tray. You thought that I had brought the potion she needed."

"Yes," Alder whispered.

"But nothing else happened?" Rowan asked again.

Alder did not answer.

Alder was saved from Rowan's questioning when Anna reappeared, carrying the jewels Alder had thrown at her in her arms. They began walking again in silence.

As the sun fell from the sky, they began to pass farmers returning from the city. Most of the men wore brightly colored tunics and the women wore pastel-colored dresses. The carts they pulled were elaborately decorated as if to demand as much attention as possible. The carts themselves were painted bright colors with exotic paints that could only be bought from the dwarven merchants in the city. The families had then further decorated the carts with growing things. Being fall, most of the carts sported tree branches with brightly colored leaves, giant gourds, and wheat dolls.

Most of the carts sold the same product to the city folk. The people that lived within the city did not have space for their own gardens, forcing them to rely on the farmers to provide them with farm goods. This left the farmers competing for business and the best way to do that in their minds was to have the most beautiful carts, and their wives felt the most beautiful clothes they could rationally, and sometimes irrationally, afford.

Rowan stopped one of the farmers who was dressed slightly more shabbily than some of his predecessors.

"Excuse me sir, but we are hungry from the road. May we buy some of your goods?"

The man looked pleased to stop, mostly to have a break from pulling the cart.

"Of course lad. Have a look and let me know if there be anything you fancy," he puffed, leaning against the cart.

Rowan picked out a few apples, a loaf of bread, and a small farm cheese. He handed the goods to Anna.

"What is your offer lad?" the man asked, mentally adding up what he thought the goods were worth.

Rowan dug around in the sack and pulled out a small sapphire. "Will this be enough?" he asked.

The farmer's eyes almost fell out of his head. He took the sapphire in his hands, and held it up to the light. Turned it over and over. Smelled it. Did everything he could think of to prove that it was real.

"Why lad, this is more than enough for what you have! Are you sure that is all you will take?"

Rowan smiled. "This will be plenty for us, good farmer. Safe travels to you on your return home."

The farmer shook Rowan's hand wildly. "And the same to you, Master whoever you are!"

The farmer took up the cart with new vigor and began to pull it down the road, humming a happy working song to himself.

They sat down on the side of the road, making sure to be out of the way of the carts. Rowan broke the bread into three equal pieces, distributed the apples, and broke the crumbly cheese the best he could into triangles. He looked at what he considered a bounty. They had certainly been worse off.

He looked to Alder who would normally have swallowed his share whole. Alder now only stared at the food in his lap.

"Alder, you must eat. You need your strength," he begged.

Alder made an attempt at a smile but did not eat.

Rowan looked at Anna who was eating heartily, then at his own food. He had no appetite, but he knew he had to eat. Their life had been so unstable. He did not know even what the next hour would bring, and they had been traveling all day. He mustered his courage and ate as quickly as possible, trying to keep the food from forming lumps in his throat.

Alder shoved the food in his mouth quickly and lay down on the ground, staring at the darkening sky.

"Everything always has to be complicated with us," he murmured.

Rowan stared up at the sky. "It will be easy someday, but until someday arrives, we should keep moving."

Alder stood up and pulled Rowan to his feet with a grin. Anna stood up slowly, looking tired.

"Can one of you carry me?" she groaned.

Rowan and Alder looked at her, wide-eyed.

"Have you broken your legs suddenly?" Alder asked, somewhat amused.

"My feet ache with every step. I want to rest!" she whined.

"We just had a rest and we are almost to the city," Rowan offered.

Anna sat on the ground with her arms crossed.

"I won't go another step!"

Alder growled and Rowan became genuinely afraid for Anna's safety.

Alder, with a wildness in his eyes, grabbed Anna by her arm and jerked her to her feet. He dragged her, her feet firm in the dirt of the road, before finally throwing her over his shoulder like a sack of onions. She complained loudly the entire time, but this had been what she wanted, in one way or another.

They walked down the road toward New Market.

Night had covered the sky by the time they reached New Market. Candlelight shone from every window, setting the city aglow. The Òrail River running through the city reflected the light of the candles and the pale light of the moon. The sea extended past the docks and ships, shining brightly in the moonlight.

The city itself was built from whatever materials the builders could get their hands on at the given time. Some buildings were made from wood and plaster, others from stone and mortar, forming a ringed pattern as the ever-expanding city radiated away from the ocean. Every so often a new section of walls had been built to protect the city, but houses were always appearing outside the walls.

Looming over the city stood the military academy that churned out hopeful soldiers for King Amadan's armies. It was a giant, cubical, stone building. The only windows were located at the top of the building and offered views in every direction. The immediate area outside the academy served as the training yards, barracks, stables, and other outbuildings for the academy. A path led to the royal navy's exclusive docking area.

Not too far away from the military academy was the Earl's castle. It was dwarfed by the academy, but the castle dwarfed the remainder of the city. It was a whitewashed building with a red roof, standing out brilliantly against the foreboding grey of the academy. Rowan had heard that the grounds could not be more different. The castle boasted huge gardens, a private waterway, and luxurious, although unnecessary, outbuildings. The academy's grounds were devoid of life.

The bridge to the city was down as they approached. The bridge was always down, but it was always guarded by a full squadron that could raise the bridge at any moment. The guards took no notice of them as they passed. It was dark and from all appearances, the group looked like every other group of peasants around the countryside.

New Market was not nearly as clean as Kingsford. Garbage and refuse littered the streets. Animal droppings from the beasts of burden pulling the carts to and from the market covered the main road. Whatever could not be burned, was simply thrown out of the windows and into the street with little account for who or what was nearby. Rowan and Alder walked down the center of the street.

They had been to New Market many times and knew the ways of the city. They headed toward the Silver Swan Inn, which was anything but a Silver Swan in appearance.

It was dicey, far worse than the Grey Goat in Kingsford had been considered, but it was cheap and the innkeepers were pleasant enough to Rowan and Alder.

The door was open when they arrived, it being warm for an autumn evening. Drunken men and loose women crowded the streets outside the inn. Rowan kept a firm hand on the sack of treasures. Alder followed, still carrying Anna and making sure that Rowan was not followed or bothered.

The inn itself was a wood building with a stone floor. It was twice the size of the Grey Goat and had a much larger staff attending to the never-ending requests of the patrons. Round tables filled the great hall and a bar lined the nearest wall. Across from them was a large stage. Giant chandeliers hung from the ceiling with candles burning brightly. A fire burned in the large stone fireplace in the corner of the room. A stairway wound around the edge of the hall and up to the rooms.

Tonight the inn was packed to the brim with sailors. A group of ships had come in from Whitecliff and would be remaining in port for some time, allowing the sailors frivolity at the inn. A group of sailors were playing songs on the stage as people danced. Many of the people sitting at the tables watched the dancers, clapping and singing along to the songs, and drinking their various pints.

A girl hung herself on Rowan as he tried to pass through the crowd. He gently pushed her away. She sidled off into the crowd. Rowan purchased a room for as many days that a very clear emerald would buy him. A young boy showed them to their room.

Alder shut the door firmly behind them. Blocking out only some of the noise from below.

"What a racket," he frowned.

"I thought it was exciting!" Anna exclaimed as Alder dumped her on her bed.

"I hate sailors and all their lot. They come in from sea, cause as much chaos as possible, and then sail blissfully into the sunset. Not one of us would be safe near the docks right now with the way that lot is carrying on down there. Their drinking is one matter, but their other habits are deplorable," Alder snarled.

"What other habits?" Anna asked, fascinated with everything.

"The consumption of moonflower for one, the second being their usage of women."

"What are moonflowers?"

"It is a poisonous flower that grows to the south. They dry the flower, grind it, and eat it. It causes hallucinations." Alder flopped onto the bed he and Rowan were to share.

"If it is poisonous, why don't they die?"

"Some do, others are more careful about how much they eat," Alder laughed.

"Have you ever tried it?"

Alder sat up and stared at Anna. "Absolutely not," he said seriously.

He stood up and went to the window, opened the shutters, and poked his head out.

"Come here," he whispered sternly.

Anna moved to the window quietly and stuck her head out with Alder.

"See those men in the alley, shaking and as pale as death? They are hooked on the stuff."

Anna moved from the window and Rowan took her place. Two men huddled in the alleyway. Both of them were almost completely naked. They were shivering violently and looked as if they had been living in the wild for years without food or shelter.

Alder closed the shutters and returned to bed.

"Let us rest now," Rowan tried, tired of the questions, the somber discussion, and the bickering.

Anna crawled into her bed and Alder undid the bed for himself and Rowan. Rowan blew out the candle and crawled into bed with Alder.

"I enjoyed our walk today, darling," Alder whispered, touching Rowan's hand.

Rowan punched him as hard as he could from his strange angle in bed and Alder yipped with pain and laughter.

Rowan couldn't remember the last time he had slept so well. He had slept peacefully through all the noise of the tavern. He woke to a knock on the door, knowing that he had overslept from his planned wake-up time.

He rolled out of bed, stumbling as he shook off the grogginess, and opened the door. A maid handed him the breakfast tray he had ordered the night before and quickly scurried off without a word.

Rowan shut the door firmly and set the tray on the small table. Alder eyed it from the bed.

"Darling, would you be so good as to bring me a fair ration of that bread and a large helping of butter"?"

"I would bring you a swift boot if I had any," Rowan retorted.

Alder dramatically flipped the blankets off himself, turned himself in the bed without sitting up, and with much effort and groaning, brought himself to his feet. Rowan only eyed him and shook his head.

Alder crossed the room, pushed Rowan out of the way, and ripped off a portion of the bread with a smile. Rowan returned the shove and ripped off another portion of the bread. Alder eyed him playfully. Rowan returned the gaze. It had been a long time since they had wrestled over food. Rowan preferred that it did not occur in such a small room, but was ready for Alder's advance.

Anna interrupted their games. "Why is there so much noise?" she whined.

"Breakfast is ready, Mistress," Alder quipped.

"It is so early though!"

"What do you mean 'it's early'?" Alder demanded. "You were up far earlier than this when you lived with the warlock and you had to prepare breakfast!"

"But I want to sleep like everyone else!" she complained.

"*No one* gets to sleep in this late except nobility and drunks," Rowan asserted, rather tired of Anna's dreams of grandeur.

"I suggest you rise and make yourself ready or you will find that there is no food until supper," Alder warned.

Anna sat up in bed and glared at Rowan and Alder. Her long, golden hair was a mess and her dress was bunched and wrinkled.

Alder stared at her for a moment in thought. "You did not do anything in the warlock's household, did you? The food came out of the cauldron which was magic and all the dishes from the meals were thrown back into the cauldron or in, what I am assuming, a magic washtub. The only thing you had to do was lie with the warlock. Before you were sold, you and your mother spent your father's money faster than he could make it. Him being a loving father and husband, never told you 'no'. Then one day you and your mother were taken and he was sent to a work camp. I bet you had a servant. What was her name?"

Anna looked shocked. She opened and closed her mouth as she tried to find an excuse. Rowan looked at each of them, not sure how Alder had come to his conclusions.

"You are on moonflowers!" she shouted furiously.

Alder's mouth had the twinges of a snarl in the corners and a flash crossed his eyes. He crossed the room, took up the sack of treasure, returned to the tray, shoved his portion of bread in his mouth whole, took Anna's portion, and left the room.

Rowan looked at Anna who was again speechless. "Do not leave this room until we return. I will leave word with the innkeeper not to let you out," Rowan ordered.

He exited the room, shutting the door and locking it with the key behind him.

Rowan preferred New Market at night; the filth of the streets was less visible and only the stench was left. The filth was exceptionally high in the mornings for it was custom for the households to dump the waste of the day out of their windows in the evenings so as not to stink the house through the night. The homeless and hungry would root through the scraps throughout the day, eating what they could, and would reduce the amount of waste decaying in the street. The diligent and ambitious men would appear at first light with their carts and shovels to scrape the animal droppings from the street to use on their fields as fertilizer or sell it for the same purpose.

Alder and Rowan knew where they needed to go and how best to avoid the waste of the city. They headed toward Old Town. Old Town was in the heart of the city and was the crossroads for the Earl's castle and the Academy.

They passed companies of soldiers marching as they came closer to the gates of Old Town. Whitewashed stone buildings presided over the streets in a noble fashion. Many of the families that resided in these homes had lived in them since the founding of the city. A small, but elaborate temple to worship the Diathans had been built at the mouth of the gates, commanding all passerby's immediate attention. Preparations were being made for the Ubhal festival that would be arriving in less than a week.

Rowan smiled at Alder. It had been many years since they had attended the Ubhal festival. The festival celebrated the harvest and tributes and sacrifices were made to the Goddess Buain in the hopes of her granting the farmer a plentiful harvest the following summer. In years when the harvest was bountiful; fruits, vegetables, wines, and cakes would be placed at the foot of her statue in the temples or the wicker effigy of her that the villagers built in most village squares for the festival. In bad years, animals would be slaughtered at her feet and the blood would be poured over her statue or thrown across the barren fields.

All in all, it was a week of merrymaking. Girls would braid autumn-colored ribbons into their hair or wear brown veils, depending on their status. Men would wear sprigs of Aduxa berries or the Aduxa leaves in their belts for health in the winter. In years when the harvest was plentiful, food was prepared in abundance. Every household baked cakes, bread, and chutneys for the occasion, and the families served the food with ciders and wines. In years when the harvest was bad, a simple bread or oat cake would have to suffice. There would be dancing, drinking, and other merrymaking. The effigy of Buain would be burned in a grand celebration at the end of the week.

Alder smiled back at Rowan. They had been in the warlock's grasp so long that they did not know what the harvest had been like that year, but they were excited for the festival, regardless.

They were on a budget. They needed clothes, weapons, and horses, but they had plenty of jewels and gold for that. Rowan knew in his heart that they had to see Anna securely stationed somewhere before they could leave her. What she did after that, was in her own hands. With the leftover money, Alder and Rowan would enjoy the festival.

They walked two blocks past the temple and turned into a small square with a fountain. The square was perfectly clean. All the buildings were perfectly whitewashed. The shutters were painted, the doors showed no scratches, the windows sported glass and not an ounce of garbage or droppings littered the streets.

Vitta Modiste was the best seamstress in all New Market. Her family had been the first clothing makers in New Market and had been prosperous no matter the tide. They had weaved their own cloth, tanned their own leather, spun their own wool, anything it had taken for them to continue their path. It had paid off.

Vitta had never married, but it was no secret that her two assistants were her daughters. She lived in the largest house on the square and the inside of her home was as perfect as the outside. She kept no maid, but a charwoman came to the house every night.

Rowan knocked on the door. A wooden sign hung above the door with *Madame Modiste's Fine Garments* written in gold paint. A young woman of about twenty with gold braids wrapped around her head opened the door.

"We are here to see Madame Modiste," Rowan stated.

The girl looked him up and down. She frowned and shut the door.

Rowan looked at Alder in confusion, but they could hear a conversation inside.

"Mama! There are beggars outside!" the girl hissed.

"Are they beggars or are they customers?" an elderly voice demanded.

"Beggars, surely! Their clothing is of peasant rags!"

"Nonsense, girl. We are a shop. We sell to those that wear rags so that they do not have to wear rags anymore! If you want to be a seamstress to Lady Hammel then you go right ahead and see where that lands you!"

The door flung open. An elderly woman dressed in dark green velvet looked down her nose at Rowan and Alder.

"Why if it isn't Rowan and Alder! You two boys got yourselves into another scrape I daresay. Haven't seen you in some time and you show up on my step in such a state! Come in, come in! Goirta! Fresh tea and biscuits! Your beggars are dear old friends!"

The woman led the way into the house. The entryway was dark with a set of stairs on the right leading up to the living quarters. The first room on the left was the showroom.

Dark red damask covered the walls of the showroom. The furniture of dark wood and cream-colored fabric accented the room well. A short table was in the center of the room with a padded stool next to it. Floor-to-ceiling windows covered the outer walls, flooding the room with light. An unfinished dress was being displayed by a milliner's mannequin off to the side. The huge dress was obviously for nobility with burnished-gold silk, pearl beading, and a dark fur neckline.

Vitta caught Rowan staring at the dress. "For Lady Hammel. The Hammels have decided to break tradition and host their own Ubhal festival at the castle on Losgadh Day. We still have quite a bit of work to do on the dress before Losgadh Day, but we will manage. My two girls are quick with a needle and Goirta is excellent at embroidery and beading! But come now, what are you two boys needing today besides sensible clothing?"

Alder laughed. "It is as you say, Madame, we are in need of sensible clothing."

"We do not know when we will be able to return to the city. We need clothing that will be able to hold through the winter upon the road," Rowan added.

Vitta eyed them both suspiciously. "What trouble have you boys gotten yourselves into?"

Rowan fidgeted and looked at Alder who was looking at him. Alder was not going to do the talking on this one, despite having known Vitta her entire life.

Vitta turned to face Rowan with her hands on her hips. She wasn't going to let this slide.

"We have been banished from Amadania. We are breaking the law by being with you right now. After the Bean Nighe appeared and killed everyone, we were blamed and we were banished by King Amadan."

"I've heard that much from rumors. What have you done since then? That was months ago!"

"We tried to cut through the forest—"

"Fools!"

"We were attacked by many of the creatures. We almost died. But we were rescued by creatures that called themselves fire walkers. They saved us. Then we were sent to work for a warlock who lived in the forest. We entered servitude under him until he was killed by one of his slaves. We met with Tomil Miller who gave us clothing and shelter. We arrived in town only yesterday evening."

Vitta shook her head at them. "You should have came straight here! Why would you ever enter the servitude of a strange man in the woods? He would have kept you forever if he hadn't been murdered! Those magic folk have been rotten ever since the evil moved into the south. Surely you have heard those stories, Alder! I've heard them and my years don't hold a candle to yours! You know what they say, don't you? The magic ones are waiting for his return! They want him to resurface. Those magic ones take us to a place that isn't on any map where they sell us normal folk and then they use us as slaves!"

Alder and Rowan looked at each other, hiding their shock. Vitta had the whole story without knowing it. Rowan felt a strange feeling in his stomach. They had narrowly escaped a lifetime of servitude.

The kettle screeching in the kitchen broke the silence.

"Ah, teatime, dears. Then we will see about some proper clothing for you. I'm thinking of a nice dark blue for Rowan and a dark emerald for Alder. Those will suit your complexions."

They followed Vitta into the kitchen, not knowing anything about complexions.

Vitta's daughters set out gingerbread, new rolls, butter, preserves, and tea.

Alder and Rowan showed restraint, despite the mound of heavenly gingerbread in front of them. Vitta was a very formal woman and monitored how much was decent for a guest to have in one sitting. She had been known to deem others 'bad guests' for what she considered greed. Although rich, Vitta was frugal and did not waste anything.

They each took a roll, some butter and preserves, and two gingerbread biscuits and forced themselves to be content.

They returned to the showroom after tea. Vitta quickly took their measurements and wrote them down on a piece of parchment. She then rustled around in her workroom until she found the fabric she intended to use. She held up a dusty blue wool to Rowan's face, stared intently at him to the point of making him nervous, and then bustled away. She returned with the green fabric for Alder, held it up to his face, then slapped him lovingly on the chin, before scurrying off.

"I should be able to have everything done in four days if you boys can stay out of trouble until then," she lectured.

They took their leave. Vitta had not questioned them about payment. She trusted them, even when they were down and out.

The next stop would be the cobbler.

The cobbler was a gruff man. He did not say much. Rowan and Alder both sat on stools as the cobbler held up lasts to their feet to see their size.

"Come back in two days," he grumbled, waving them away.

"How much do you suppose all this will cost?" Rowan asked.

Alder did some figuring in his head.

"One of those gold statues should pay for everything. We will have to trade it for bonns with one of the merchants. We cannot continue to trade full gems for scraps," Alder sighed.

They traveled to the section of the city that contained the market. A vast number of merchants, tents, and stalls were always present in New Market and were the main source of income for the kingdom thanks to the heavy tariffs and taxes King Amadan charged and Earl Hammel enforced.

It was not as interesting as the magic market they had traveled to, but Rowan was thankful for that. He never wanted to go to that place again and knew Alder wished the same. The fat merchants with their simple wares and simple snares were good enough for them.

They had never traded with the gold merchant and were not sure what to expect. Rowan handed the bag of treasure to Alder with a thought.

"You should do business with the merchant. Perhaps we have a better chance if you can convince him that you are trading elf trinkets."

"That is a very good idea," Alder smiled.

They found the gold merchant who had a tent, rather than a simple stall like the other merchants. He was a fat man and wore a bright red tunic under a thick black fur cape. He wore a puffy black hat over what Rowan assumed to be a bald head.

He eyed them suspiciously as they entered his tent. Alder bowed to him slightly and Rowan followed suit. The man was still suspicious but relaxed slightly when he saw that Alder was an elf.

"What can I do for you elf Master?" he asked hesitantly.

"I come with trinkets to trade. I have fallen on hard times and must sell the few things I have left. My manservant has come as well to seek his remaining wages before he leaves my service."

The merchant stifled a laugh and pretended to cough.

"Elven folk are outlawed. It must be hard trying to do business outside your own lands."

"Yes. I used to own many ships, but they were overseen by a man that was bought over by the pirates. They have taken my ships and all the goods I had purchased that were upon them. What is in this sack is all that remains of my great fortune."

They all sat down in the cushioned chairs. Alder set the gold statues on the covered table in front of the merchant. With every new item, they watched the greed in the merchant's eyes grow larger and larger. It seemed as though his mouth grew dry as he hunted for words to begin the transaction.

He sat back in his chair dramatically and shook his head.

"Well I say, I have not seen much Elvish work in my day, but it is not as fine as the *Dwarvish* works. I can give you twenty bonns for each statue."

Alder sneered. "You forget that I am a man of business myself. If you do not wish to partake in a fair transaction, I will find someone that will."

Alder began to put the statues back in the sack. The merchant's eyes grew panicky. A bead or sweat appeared on his forehead.

"Do not be so hasty, master elf! We can discuss this matter! Now tell me, are the statues solid gold?"

"Completely."

"What lands do they come from?"

"They come from Tuigseach, the realm of my kin. These were fashioned before Kingsford and even before the great war. They are heirlooms. I was told as a child that they had magical properties, but to this day I have not discovered how they work."

The merchant licked his lips. "Well, that changes matters completely! I will give you one hundred and twenty bonns for each."

Alder seemed to mull it over in his head.

"One-hundred and seventy-five," Alder demanded.

The merchant looked aghast.

"One-hundred and fifty."

Alder looked at Rowan who pretended to lose his patience.

"I will take one hundred and fifty for each statue," Alder declared.

The transaction was done. Alder knew that they could have gotten much more for the statues, but six statues at one-hundred and fifty bonns could buy them anything their hearts desired within the city and they still had the jewels.

"Let us save the jewels for Anna. We must try to help her before we leave," Rowan ventured.

Alder sighed but nodded.

Their last stops for the day were to the smith and to the fletcher.

The smith had a neat shop next to the yard where he worked. The smith was hammering a new sword outside as Rowan and Alder entered the shop. Inside, a pregnant woman sat on a stool behind the counter.

"Good day," she called as they entered the shop. "If I may be of service, call out for me!"

"We can manage. You rest there," Rowan smiled. The woman was very large and Rowan was fearful of her moving at all.

Alder browsed the shop and began to grumble. Alder was notoriously picky about his swords. Rowan had seen him break swords in battle and the results were hideous for whomever he was fighting.

"Madame Smith, where are your finer swords? Your husband's family has done mighty work for many generations. I know that these are not the best he has."

The woman laughed and slowly slid off the stool. "They are in the back room. My husband does not like to keep them out here. They sell for a high price, but there are too many foolish young men that buy them to never use them, and my husband only wants to sell them to those that will serve a greater purpose."

She showed them to the backroom, waddling slowly.

Alder's eyes fell upon a bright longsword with a silver cross guard, black handle, and pommel with an open circle. Silver leaves fluttered around the cross guard and the blade reflected Alder's smiling face.

He swung it about, balanced it at the cross guard, tossed it in the air, and snatched it. Rowan knew that Alder was in love. He was given the black sheath that accompanied the sword. He held onto it like a small child with a beloved toy.

They both picked out jambiya-styled daggers and paid the woman. She smiled and thanked the boys heartily.

Rowan and Alder then ventured to the fletcher. Rowan immediately asked the man for his yew bows, not willing to settle for anything less. He tried a few, found one with the best draw, and purchased it with a quiver full of arrows.

Finally, they were able to return to the inn.

They ordered supper to be brought to the room in the evening and went to their room.

Anna was asleep on the bed. They could tell by her eyes and ragged breathing that she had been sobbing.

"We really must find a suitable home for her," Rowan whispered.

"But we do not know what she is good at. She has never worked; I am certain of that. She is too old to become an apprentice. No one will hire her when they suspect that she is nobility and they will send her off the moment she shows that she cannot, or will not, work."

"Is there anyone that you can think of that may take her?'

"We have not been to New Market in at least a year, and, by all appearances, this was a bad harvest year. People will not be hiring girls like her when they can barely provide for their families."

Rowan sighed. Alder was right. Few people around the city appeared to be celebrating this year and he had seen more than a few animals being brought into the city. Farmers would be sending their children into the city to find work and those that could afford to hire servants would hire a farm girl, not Anna.

Supper was brought to their room. They woke Anna and all ate quietly.

"I would like to go downstairs this evening," Anna declared.

"We had the food brought to the room so that we would not have to go downstairs," Alder retorted.

"I have never gotten to experience a tavern and once I am married it will not be quite right for me to go to the tavern, especially without my husband."

"The sailors are too rowdy. They are not the sort you should be around, regardless of your marriage status," Rowan tried.

"I am going. You are not my master. You can't keep me locked away in this room all day. I should be learning the city for when I live here," she argued.

"Then go downstairs and see what happens," Alder said dismissively, tired of arguing.

"I will!" Anna stormed out of the room, vainly trying to slam the heavy door.

"So at what point are we going down to look after her?" Rowan asked with a smile.

"How long before she is in trouble?"

"I will give her an hour," Rowan decided.

Alder looked at him in astonishment. "I was only going to give her long enough to get down to the bar and strike up a conversation with someone."

"Shall we then?" Rowan laughed.

They stashed the jewels and bonns under the bedframe and left the room, locking the door securely behind them. They crept to the edge of the balcony and peered out, trying not to let Anna spot them.

Anna, being quite beautiful and dressed in extravagant clothing, was surrounded by a group of men. They seemed to be speaking to her all at once and she only shook her head and laughed.

Rowan and Alder moved downstairs and found a table to sit at. From their position, they could see Anna sitting at the bar.

The tavern was tumultuous. Gambling, arm wrestling, and every other sort of lowly activity was taking place throughout the hall. The music was loud and fast. Dancers swung around the front of the stage. Painted women sat in the sailors' laps. They hung over the gambling men, seeing who might win and who might share their winnings with them for the night.

Alder did not relax as he would have in the Grey Goat. He stayed on high alert, watching every movement of every person in the room. Rowan did not let his guard down, either. He tried to keep his eyes on Anna the best he could, but the group was always ebbing and flowing like the waves in a storm.

"Would you fellows care for anything?" A middle-aged woman stood at their table.

"Have you any sweets?" Alder asked.

"Nay, sir. There is no ingredients to make sweets and this lot threatens to eat us clean. We only have squash bread if you are after something sweet."

"Have you heard why there are no ingredients?" Rowan asked.

The woman fidgeted and then leaned in over the table.

"Some say it's the wildmen again, but I don't believe it. I say it has been the weather. There has been a drought, sir. The harvest was bad. I don't know that anyone has much to sell. I think the weather must be bad everywhere because we just don't have the amount of merchants coming into town and none have seen them on the road. They tell me I'm a fool because even these sailors weren't able to bring in the fish they are used to bringing in. Been out at sea for weeks and they hardly bring back a thing. I blame the weather. The weather or something strange is happening on the road."

The woman walked off with a nod.

Rowan and Alder stared at each for a long while. A bad harvest was one thing, wildmen were another. They had seen no reason to believe that wildmen were the reason for the bad year. They had not seen the fortifications or panic that coincided with the movements of the wildmen. But neither wildmen nor a drought would affect the fish hauls. Something strange was happening.

Rowan looked back to the bar. Anna was gone and so were her sailors.

"Alder! She's gone!" Rowan panicked, standing to look over the crowd. Alder stood too, peering through the crowds.

"I do not see her," Alder cursed.

"Let's sift through the crowd and meet at the door. If we do not find her, we will go outside."

They began wandering through the crowd, looking at tables, the bar, and the dance floor. Anna was gone. They left the tavern.

"They would take her toward the docks," Alder declared.

Rowan agreed. Slave trading was illegal in the city and the countryside, forcing traders outside the city or underground to conduct their business.

They hurried down the street, making sure to look in the alleyways. Several homeless men, women, and a few children slept against the walls of the buildings, but no Anna.

"Curse her," Alder swore.

"We must try to find her," Rowan begged.

Alder stopped. "We need our weapons. Even if we find her, we are defenseless."

"You are right. If they are kidnapping her, they will fight us."

They returned to the inn and leaped up the stairs to their room. Alder hesitated, staring at where they had hidden the bonns.

"There is nowhere safe in this room to hide the sack. If Anna talks, they will come into the room and tear it apart until they find the bonns and jewels and we have no rightful claim to it."

"Where should we hide it then?"

"Perhaps it would be safer divided between us," Alder proposed.

"That will have to do. I do not like the idea of leaving it in the room unguarded," Rowan agreed.

They quickly divided the bonns and jewels between them. They then took up their weapons and headed out into the night.

They had no idea how they were going to track Anna down. Their only thought was to go to the docks and hope that they could catch wind of her.

The area around the docks was dirty, and dingy, and showed the wear and tear of centuries of struggle. The pirates from the south had attempted to invade several times. Buildings had been blown up, burnt down, and rebuilt. The pirates had devised a way to build small catapults and trebuchets on their ships and had used them to fling projectiles at the city. It caused damage, but little else. There had not been fighting for some time, but the scars still showed.

The buildings were now a patchwork of different materials and styles as different sections had been destroyed at different times. Some buildings had never been repaired and now stood half-collapsed. The poor would sift through the rubble to find materials for their own home repairs. Some beggars would seek shelter in the skeletal buildings that still offered dry spaces out of the elements.

Rowan and Alder checked every decomposing building, alley, and tavern along the docks. They could not find any sign of Anna.

The hour was growing late and many of the residences were now in darkness. The taverns and inns were the only buildings that were still illuminated. The streets were dark and most of the alleyways were occupied with sleeping beggars or moonflower addicts. That left only the ships.

Many of the ships were in darkness excluding the lamps of the watchmen. Two ships, however, were fully illuminated.

Alder and Rowan dropped into the calm water next to the docks. They swam as quietly as possible to the rode and then began to climb. They climbed the rode and then found themselves aboard the ship. No one was on the deck.

They moved below deck and crept towards what they hoped would be the brig. They did not find any sailors at all, not even a drunk or watchman. The vessel appeared to be deserted.

"What shall we do?" Rowan whispered.

"We can try the other ship," Alder offered.

They looked around for a little while longer and found a dark corridor. A woman's voice could be heard at the end. She sounded distressed.

Rowan looked at Alder, who nodded. They were putting themselves in a bad situation. Rowan began to wonder if they could really help Anna after all.

They reached the end of the corridor and found a heavy door with light shining through the top and bottom.

Rowan pushed it open as gently as possible.

They had found the brig. It was full of civilians.

The room went on for what was a standard cargo hold. Three rows of cages extended the entire length of the room. One for men, one for women, and one for children.

Everyone appeared to be asleep, but on closer inspection, Rowan and Alder discovered that everyone had been drugged. Rowan and Alder crept down the aisle that had women on the right and children on the left. Children had been stuffed in the cages until all they could do was stand and two or three women huddled in each cage. Even while standing, the children seemed to either be asleep or in some sort of trance. The women's eyes were closed, though some continued to mumble and murmur.

Alder stopped suddenly and grabbed Rowan's arm.

"We have to get off the ship. Now," he hissed.

Alder did not release the grip on Rowan's arm but dragged him back down the aisle and into the dark hallway.

"What about Anna?" Rowan pulled.

Alder shushed him. Steps could be heard above them. Alder pulled Rowan faster through the ship. They climbed the steps to the main deck and Alder peered out. A drunk sailor was playing with the rigging and singing heartily. The man sang in an accent Rowan had never heard before and he did not recognize the song.

Alder rushed Rowan to the rode.

"You go first. Go as quickly as possible. Do not drop into the water, but follow the rode all the way down."

Rowan began to climb down and Alder quickly followed. After a few moments, they were in the water.

It was none too soon.

All the sailors were beginning to file back onto the ship, jeering loudly.

Rowan and Alder swam back to the docks and disappeared into the city.

Alder shut the door to their room and locked it. He stood listening for a moment.

Rowan could see the fierce animal instincts spiraling in Alder's eyes as he made sure the coast was clear.

"Why did we come back?" Rowan asked, irritated that they had given up looking for Anna.

"Did you not pay attention to anything you saw tonight?" Alder asked, returning the same tone of voice Rowan had thrown at him.

"I saw slaves that we should have tried to free," Rowan replied.

"Who owns those slaves?"

"No one. They are free people!"

"That is a boy's answer. They are not free anymore. Think, Rowan, who is brave enough to capture slaves in New Market right under the royal guards' nose?" Alder scolded.

Rowan thought for a minute. "That was a pirate ship we were on."

"I believe that ship was from An-Ioch, but it could have been from Neo Àbhai."

"How are pirates operating in such a manner right here in New Market?" Rowan asked, furiously.

"Did you notice how that pirate was dressed? The drunk one before the others arrived?" Alder asked, having already come to all his conclusions, but trying to make Rowan think out the answer.

"He was dressed as an ordinary fisherman," Rowan murmured.

Alder nodded sarcastically. "They are luring citizens down to the docks, drugging them, and then locking them up in those cages. They are dressed as ordinary sailors and fishermen because they would be killed on the spot if they even showed a piercing."

"So what are we going to do about Anna?" Rowan asked.

"Forget about her," Alder whispered, sitting on the bed dejectedly.

"We can't leave her as a slave!" Rowan stammered, jumping to his feet.

"What do you want to do, Rowan? Two men cannot go liberate the slaves aboard that ship. If we had any chance of freeing them, I would have done it while we were there! It is a suicide mission! These are not malnourished wildmen. These are trained soldiers and they are not going to let anyone stand in the way of the fortune they are going to make off that load of slaves!"

"Anna does not deserve that. We owe her our freedom," Rowan fumed.

"She does not. No one ever deserves to be abused in such a way. We have never deserved to be treated the way we are treated, but here we stand. Yes, she freed us from the warlock. But I was going to kill him myself. She only sped the process. We cannot go back to the docks or we risk becoming slaves again ourselves. I wish we could save her, Rowan. I truly do. But there is nothing we can do now and surely nothing we can do if we are dead with our heads cut off and dangling from the bulkhead."

"Are we just as doomed as her?" Rowan murmured.

Alder stared at him, his face softening. "Life has been cruel to us both, but someday things will change. There have been many times that I have wished to fall in battle. Bacach's betrayal was one of those times. But we will find our way."

To Rowan, the days could not go by fast enough. Rowan wanted to hold his dagger to every fisherman's throat he saw, learning to tell the difference between the locals and those he deemed pirates, but being unable to do anything about it.

They returned to the cobbler to receive their boots and Rowan was glad to not have to walk through the filthy streets barefooted any longer. He tried to be kind to the poor and be tolerant of the fact that they had no other way of disposing of their waste, but he frequently wondered what diseases he was dragging his feet through every day.

The festival began, and as they had expected, it was a dismal year. Every statue of Buain was soaked in blood.

A few families were able to hold market stalls in the square to sell treats and other goods. Rowan bought as much dried fruit and meat as he could for what he had budgeted for food.

Girls smiled and giggled at Rowan, but mostly at Alder. The pretty country girls had arrived with ribbons in their hair and their best dresses. Alder would flash his typical grin at them and send them giggling and fluttering away.

Rowan and Alder met with Vitta several times before their clothing was finally ready. Vitta took enough money to cover the materials and labor but would take no profit from them. She shoved gingerbread in their mouths and sent them away.

The festival was becoming merrier as the days progressed. People began arriving from Taigheland and the surrounding settlements. What plenty anyone was able to share had been gathered and brought to the city and now sat waiting in the cupboards of friends and family in anticipation of the grand feast on Losgadh Day.

Rowan and Alder sat in the square the night before Losgadh Day. The bonfire piles had been built and tables and chairs had been brought for the feast. Women would decorate the tables with grain, leaves, and berry sprigs in the morning before people began to bring their food. Soldiers who wore freshly cleaned tunics, shined helmets, and chest plates, patrolled the area constantly.

"In two days, we head east," Rowan acknowledged.

"I have been ready since we received our clothes. It was wise to suggest not purchasing horses until we are ready to travel. We do not have to provide them with as much food," Alder laughed.

"Our budget is rather tight," Rowan smiled.

Chapter 13

Rowan and Alder woke to the sounds of laughing and singing outside their window. People all over the city were already on the streets for the festival. Wreaths of grasses, leaves, and berries had been woven and hung on doors. They would be tossed into the bonfires at midnight.

Rowan and Alder did not order breakfast. They wanted to eat the delicacies that would be in the square. They dressed quickly, took up their weapons and what little was left of the money and jewels, and left the room.

As soon as they left the inn, they could smell the sweet smell of friogais. They walked, quickly, to the square and found families frying the sweet dough wreaths in cauldrons of fat. Children danced around the square, waiting for their families to purchase the friogais for them. Many adults were milling about, waiting for their turns.

Rowan and Alder joined the line and waited to purchase as many friogais as they thought they could stomach. Once they had completed that task, they sat at a small table and ate their bounty. Sure enough, they had bought more than they thought they could eat.

It was not hard for them to spot the orphan children, creeping around the edge of the square, hoping to taste the treat. Rowan and Alder took their leftover friogais and gave them to the children who took off into the allies like squirrels to eat their feast.

Rowan and Alder helped unload the straw that the women would weave and children would use to make dolls of Buain. They helped the farmers set up the pens to keep the animals in that would be slaughtered in the evening. They then helped set the sow pigs, the symbol of Buain, to roast for the feast. As Rowan was helping the other men, he suddenly understood why Earl Hammel was having his own feast.

It had been a poor harvest. The people were hungry and the feasts throughout the city would be light. As Earl, however, he was entitled to a portion of the production of the farms and would have far more on his table than what the city and villages would be able to offer. His feast would be large and extravagant for a few nobles and persons he deemed worthy, whereas the remaining population would content themselves with the few offerings they and their neighbors could provide.

Rowan wanted to investigate his idea.

"Would you like to go for a walk with me? I am suspicious of Lord Hammel's feast."

Alder shrugged with a smile. "You know how I feel about nobles."

They walked across town. Preparations had been made in almost every home and business for the feast. Rowan was glad to see that people were still able to enjoy the holiday. They crossed into Old Town and were immediately struck by the increase in decorations.

The streets had been cleaned again. Large wreaths hung from every door and garlands of vines hung from the windows, sporting red and orange leaves. The Temple was covered in garlands and wreaths and had multiple large tables set out for the feast. Blood still marked the statue of Buain, but other offerings graced the feet of the statue here, unlike anywhere else in the city.

As they got closer to Earl Hammel's castle, they noticed an increase in soldiers and decorations. Rowan and Alder climbed onto the roof of a building next to Earl Hammel's wall.

The grounds were bustling with servants cleaning and arranging decorations. A thick plume of smoke rose from the cookhouse and servants were already carrying food into the keep.

Rowan smiled at Alder. "This was all that I wished to see."

"Wealthy men enjoying the fruits of poorer men's labor?" Alder sneered.

"I had a thought while we were preparing the square. I only wished to see if it were true."

They sat on the roof and watched the goings-on for a while. They were prepared to leave. The festival would be the final stroke before they set off for the east. They would rest today and prepare themselves for their journey.

"It feels pleasant to be in proper clothing and have a sword at my side once again," Alder sighed, laying back on the roof and soaking in the warm sunlight.

"It does feel nice. I feel somewhat like I used to, not that I think I will ever feel quite the same again after everything we have been through," Rowan agreed.

"It was not a proper adventure if you feel the same as you did before it," Alder laughed.

The sun began to set over the city and distant farmland. Rowan and Alder climbed down from the roof after watching the nobles in their elaborate gowns and tunics arrive on their expensive white horses.

They walked back through the streets to the poor section where they would be enjoying the feast and frivolity. They purchased the sprigs of berries to keep in their belts and found a place among the simple folk at the tables laden with simple bread, apples, watered wine and beer, fish, and the sow pigs that had been roasting since the morning. Girls dressed in their best dresses with ribbons in their hair carried the pitchers of wine and beer around the table, filling everyone's cups as soon as they had finished them.

When every scrap had been eaten, the tables were cleared away, leaving the square open for the dances and bonfires.

The musicians kicked off with a jaunty tune and everyone found partners. Rowan and Alder sat on one of the tables at the edge of the square, watching the dancing.

Rowan knew how Alder behaved during these types of dances. He would watch the first few reels to see who the most athletic dancers were and then seek them out. He would then be gone for the remainder of the night.

Alder perked up. Rowan knew that he had sighted his first victim, but had to wait for her to finish dancing with her current partner.

A pretty blonde covered in freckles wearing a brown dress with gold ribbons woven into her braids appeared before Rowan.

"Would you like to dance, sire?" she blushed.

Rowan looked at Alder who smiled and waved him away.

Rowan took the girl's hands and moved into the square. As Rowan was coming around the effigy of Buain with the girl in his arms, he saw Alder standing on top of the table, looking toward the docks.

An explosion shook the city. Everyone fell to the ground and began to murmur and scream in confusion. The girl looked at Rowan. Her blue eyes filled with fear. Her lip quivered.

"Get out of the city! Go as quickly as possible. It's the pirates and they have a slave ship!" Rowan ordered.

Another explosion sounded.

The girl cast a wild glance in the direction of the docks. She scampered to her bare feet and ran towards the fields.

Rowan rushed to Alder.

"We must get higher!" Alder yelled over the turmoil.

They climbed to the top of the nearest building and had just reached the roof when another blast hit.

They stared out over the city. The area surrounding the docks was in flames. One pirate ship was already in the harbor with a second and third arriving behind it. The first ship let another projectile loose from the catapult on deck. It flew through the air and crashed into the city. Rowan could see people rushing through the gates in the walls, but the walls that had been built to protect the people were now serving as barriers and creating bottlenecks.

The academy was glowing with light. The bells along the walls were ringing, warning citizens of the danger. The soldiers were moving.

Alder swatted Rowan and pointed. Rowan looked in the direction he pointed.

The fields were on fire.

The wildmen had come.

People from the farms were flocking towards the city with the wildmen close behind them.

Everyone would be trapped between the wildmen and the pirates.

"We have to help!" Rowan yelled over the roar of the screams from below.

Alder looked around. "Run along the roofs until we reach the wall. That will connect with the outer wall. There will be archers at the gate."

They ran along the roofs as quickly as they could, being mindful not to slip on the roofs with tiles and slate. Where gaps opened for alleys between the buildings, they jumped and continued running. Rowan lifted Alder onto the wall and Alder pulled Rowan up behind him. They sped along the wall as fast as they could, eventually reaching the main gate.

The wildmen were already within arrow shot. Rowan grabbed his bow and began to fire.

Alder took a bow off a young soldier. When the soldier began to protest, Alder grabbed his pointy ears and smiled at the boy and the boy backed away sulkily. He began firing, hitting a wild man with every arrow. Too many wildmen were coming with their well-known wrath and fearlessness and the soldiers were poorly trained. They were boys protecting a sleepy market town that had not seen trouble in decades. No one had invested in or taken the time to care for or maintain real defenses or real soldiers. The captains, Rowan thought, were most likely feasting at Lord Hammel's private festival.

Rowan looked over his shoulder. The fires were growing closer. The pirates had landed and were now working their way into the city. The city would be overwhelmed.

Alder was looking in the direction of Old Town.

"Vitta," he murmured and began sprinting along the wall. Rowan followed as fast as he could but was no match for the speed of Alder.

It took less time to reach Old Town running along the walls than it did on the streets and they were content to stay high above the chaos.

As they grew closer, Rowan became disgusted. More soldiers stood in the courtyard of the earl's castle than all the rest of the city.

He carried on running. The keep would fall. They would not be able to hold off the pirates and wildmen for long.

They reached the spot on the wall above Vitta's house and lowered themselves onto her roof. They climbed off the roof and onto the ground. They began to bang on her door. No one answered. Not even the charwoman was there.

Alder and Rowan looked at each other in dismay.

"The temple!" they both exclaimed.

They ran toward the temple, praying they would make it there in time. The pirates were directing their attack toward Old Town, and the wildmen were pushing people toward the pirates.

Everyone that had been at the festival in Old Town had taken refuge inside the temple.

Rowan banged on the door, but no one opened it. He could hear the scared cries and murmurs within. He grew frustrated.

"You must flee!" he called. "They are coming and you are trapped within the temple!"

A man's voice came from the other side of the door.

"We are safe within the temple! None can risk entering this sacred place with the purpose of harming the innocent without angering the gods!"

"The gods will not save you! You must flee!" Alder shouted back.

"Blasphemers!" the voice shouted back.

The wave of chaos began to rush through the gate. People were fleeing the best they could, screaming and crying all the way. Rowan and Alder had one last hope.

"Vitta!" they screamed. "We know you are in there! You must come out! We will help you out of the city!"

A scuffle was taking place inside and they could hear the old woman's muted voice.

"I will not open this door!" came the man's voice.

Alder and Rowan slammed their bodies against the door. Other desperate citizens began doing the same, trying to get into the temple for what they thought would be safety.

With five men crushing their bodies into the door, it was opened. Wailing and screaming greeted them once they were inside.

"Vitta!" Alder screamed over the chaos as the crowds crushed, some trying to go in and others trying to leave.

Rowan lost sight of Alder but saw an old woman rise above the crowd. Alder was carrying Vitta on his back. Only one of Vitta's daughters was next to them.

Rowan forced his way through the crowd, taking hold of Vitta's daughter's arm, and began to move back towards Vitta's house.

"Vitta, I need you to hold on as tightly as you can. We have to get out of the city and there is only one way," Alder explained.

"Are you able to climb?" Rowan asked the girl. She nodded.

"Where is your other daughter?" Alder asked.

"She is at the earl's castle for the feast. She delivered the dress to Lady Hammel and was invited to the supper," Vitta groaned.

"Let us hope the soldiers are able to get them out," Rowan lied. He knew the girl would be doomed in a matter of time.

The screaming intensified. The wildmen were in the old section along with the pirates. Alder began to climb, followed by Vitta's daughter, followed by Rowan. They reached the roof just as the wildmen rounded the corners. In all the chaos, they were not spotted on the rooftop. The wildmen would look for easier targets.

Vitta groaned to see the men. They were slaughtering people in the streets. Women and children were not spared. Some men would break off from the group to raid a house, but would quickly rejoin the group with a bag of plunder.

The group on the roof could see where the pirates were making progress, burning houses as they went. There seemed to be movement in both directions on the side of the pirates. They were taking prisoners.

Rowan helped Alder onto the top of the wall. He then lifted Vitta and the girl to Alder and pulled himself up.

"I must see the castle," Vitta commanded.

Alder and Rowan knew they could not disobey.

They snuck along the wall until they reached the earl's fortifications.

All the archers in the tower and along the wall had been killed. A battle between the pirates and the soldiers was now taking place in the courtyard. The castle doors had been barred, but the soldiers were being backed up the stairs toward them. For every pirate they killed, two more took his place.

At the head of the charge, was a woman. She wore trousers, a man's tunic, and a brigandine with carved eagle heads over her shoulders. She wielded her sword high and seemed to kill a soldier with every blow. They could hear her battle cries over the roar.

"Who is she?" Rowan asked Alder.

"I have never heard of a female pirate. They have strict rules about females aboard their ships."

"It appears that they made an exception for this one."

They watched as the last soldier was killed in the courtyard. The door was broken in and the screaming began. After a few minutes, long enough for the pirates to kill the remaining soldiers, the nobility began to be brought out one by one.

Vitta groaned and dropped to her knees.

"Mother!" the girl exclaimed, rushing to her.

Rowan and Alder looked closely. In a blue dress, was Goirta. They could hear her wailing as she was dragged along by a particularly rough-looking pirate. The man in front of her began to struggle. They slit his throat and she screamed as he dropped to the ground, convulsing and clenching his throat until he stopped moving altogether.

"Where are they taking her?" the girl asked.

"To the ships. They are taking slaves back to Spùinneadair," Alder murmured.

They all sat on the wall, watching what seemed to be the end of the world beneath them. The entire city was burning. Earl Hammel's castle had been pillaged and flames now exploded from the windows. The black smoke from the city and the surrounding farms covered the sky. Rowan wondered if anyone else had survived.

Vitta and her daughter slept. Rowan and Alder sat awake the entire night, watching the fire burn. No more screams could be heard, only the roar of the fire. The wildmen had left the city as the fire had begun to consume it, not risking their lives for spoils. The smoke was too thick to see if the pirate ships had left.

Chapter 14

A pale light began to appear from the east. Rowan and Alder looked out over the scorched earth. Where farms and villages had once been, nothing remained. Tufts of smoke could still be seen on the horizon where houses still smoldered.

The fire within the city had died down, leaving smoldering piles of rubble in their place. The castle had caved in on itself in the night, creating a noise that sounded as though a mountain had collapsed. They could see the skeleton of the academy. It had been a major target during the catapult barrage and all but one and a quarter of the walls were gone.

The sun appeared and began to warm the world. It had been cold during the night, but the day was warming rapidly. A faint breeze blew in from the sea, clearing the smoke in some areas and rekindling fires in others. A break in the columns of smoke showed that the pirates were gone.

Rowan and Alder gently shook Vitta and her daughter.

They climbed off the wall and into Vitta's plaza. Miraculously, the small section along the wall had been spared as the pirates and wildmen had turned toward the castle.

Vitta shakily opened the door and went inside, followed by her daughter.

"We are going to go look for survivors," Rowan called. "We will be back in a short while. Keep the door barred and do not open it for anyone. Even good friends can become desperate."

The girl nodded and shut the door.

Rowan and Alder began a cautious tour of the city. They went to the temple first.

The doors had been torn off their hinges. The pews had been overturned. Blood covered everything. The floor was littered with bodies and a pile was stacked in the corner where the people had cowered away from the wildmen. The foolish manach was beheaded in front of the statue of Cruthadair, the father-god. No one that had hidden within the temple had survived.

They kept searching. A few people wandered the streets. Some looking for loved ones, others because that was the only thing that could be done.

Rowan and Alder found no one else alive. People that had taken refuge in their homes had been burnt alive. Those that had been on the streets had been slain or taken prisoner. Some had been able to hide in strange places and had survived.

They passed the smithy. He lay dead in the street, a sword had most likely been in his right hand and now he only wielded his hammer in his left. The shop had been burned and was now caved in. The wife had most likely perished inside.

After seeing all they could bear, Rowan and Alder returned to Vitta's house.

Vitta sat in a chair by a small fire with a shawl wrapped around her.

The daughter was making tea in the kitchen, but her red face and puffy eyes gave away that she had been crying for her sister.

Alder went to the kitchen. Rowan stood by the door. He could hear Alder start a hushed conversation with the girl.

"Is there anywhere outside the city you can go? Any relatives anywhere else?" he asked.

"No. All my mother's relations have been dead for some time and I am sure you've heard the rumors about us," she murmured.

"I care not about rumors. No man is good enough to make your mother his wife. But beyond that, it is going to be very dangerous for you to stay here. There are survivors wandering the city like the undead. Once they come to terms with what happened, they are going to seek what they need to survive. A roof, food, and clothing. Winter is coming and there are not enough homes left standing to hold everyone and there is less food than that."

"We have nowhere else to go. I have never been outside the city. We speak to no others besides those that come to us for clothes or the fabric merchants that bring us supplies. There are a few women that weave and knit lace for us, but they all live in Taigheland. We have enough food preserved for about a month. We have no choice but to stay here," the girl argued.

"Fighe," Vitta croaked.

"Coming mother," the girl called, bringing her mother a cup of tea.

Alder returned to Rowan.

"They will not leave. I do not know what to do with them." Alder's face grew cloudy. "We cannot stay. I have a bad feeling about the siege. This would not have happened if Kingsford was safe. Something has happened and I feel that we must go."

Rowan held his breath. He had not thought about the big picture. The wildmen had never attacked Taigheland before and they had certainly never come close to New Market. Something bad had happened or was going to happen. Beyond that, even if something hadn't happened, none of the soldiers had escaped. There would be no one to bring the message to King Amadan that New Market had fallen. They must leave immediately.

Alder knelt by Vitta's side. "It is going to be tough here, you old badger," he said, affectionately patting her hand. "We have to go warn the king. There is no one else that will be able to do it and we have little time."

Rowan squatted in front of her.

"It is going to be hard here. If you can, find weapons and defend the house. Refugees will come to the city from the countryside. Rebuilding may not happen for a long time, but you are strong. Weather the storm the best you can. We will return if we can."

She stared distantly at them. "Fighe, go into the workroom and fetch two men's cloaks. I have forgotten to make them for you boys."

"We did not ask you to make them," Rowan soothed.

"I should have made them anyway," she trailed off.

Fighe appeared with two dark grey cloaks and handed one to each of them. They slipped them on and kissed Vitta's cheek.

Alder looked to Fighe. "Find weapons at the castle, but otherwise do not go out unless you have to. It is going to be very dangerous out there, especially for a young lady of status. There may still be wildmen and pirates lurking. Ordinary citizens may try to ransom you. If you find a weapon, practice with it. Learn to use it. Your life and your mother's will depend on it."

They took their leave and headed toward the academy. They needed horses. It would take two days for them to travel on foot compared to a day on good war horses.

The ruined academy stood ominously above the city of ashes. Beyond the academy's destruction, little damage had occurred to the surrounding grounds. The courtyard was empty. The soldiers had all died in the earl's castle.

Alder and Rowan were hopeful that no one had gone to the backside of the academy where the stables and outbuildings were.

It was their first stroke of luck in a long while. All the other buildings were intact, including the stables. The doors to the large building were shut and not barred. No one had come here during the attack; all had gone on foot.

They picked the first two horses they found that were saddled and ready. They kicked them hard and the horses sped off.

The horses sped through the ruined city and down toward the military's private docks. The military's ships stuck out of the water in all directions. The waves lapped against them gently and seagulls squabbled on the railings. Rowan and Alder could see the sky through the massive holes that had been blown in their hulls. The bloated bodies of the sailors lay upon the sand.

A small road connected to the main road towards Kingsford from the docks. Rowan and Alder turned their horses onto it. It would take them four hours to reach Kingsford if they kept the horses at their current pace. Rowan knew that they risked killing the horses if they tried. They would have to stop and allow the horses to rest.

They slowed the horses to a gallop and carried on. The sky was growing dark with clouds as if a storm was coming and the wind began to pick up.

When the horses began to foam, they stopped and allowed the horses to rest.

"What is our plan when we return to Kingsford?" Alder asked.

"We have to see King Amadan without interference, but I do not know how beyond rushing into the throne room and yelling everything we know as the guards run us through," Rowan sighed.

"We will certainly have to reach the castle as quickly as possible. If we keep the horses at full speed, we will be able to at least reach the keep. Gaining entrance will be slightly harder," Alder added.

Rowan laughed. "Gaining entrance will be easy if we show our faces. Getting King Amadan to listen to what we have to say before cutting off our heads will be the hard part."

"So we get ourselves arrested one way or another. Upon our arrest we are granted an audience with the king, perhaps we will be in the throne room before they manage to arrest us. How do we get him to listen to us? We have no proof of what happened, beyond the smoke column that can be seen from the castle," Alder thought aloud.

Alder snickered. Rowan thought it sounded similar to Alder's evil snickers.

"We don't get off our horses. Not until we reach the great hall. Once we reach the hall, we run as fast as we can to the throne room, barring the doors behind us. Then all we will need to do is subdue the guards in the throne room. That will give us a few minutes alone with the king before our heads are cut off."

After the horses were rested, they remounted and carried on. Rowan estimated that they would need one more break before reaching the city. Alder and Rowan could prepare themselves at that stage.

When they stopped, they ate some of the rations they had purchased, not knowing when they would be allowed to eat, since they would surely be arrested, if not killed by the end of the day. They made sure their weapons were sharp and ready. They tightened the saddles on the horses and were once again riding.

Kingsford appeared before them, glowing white against the dark background of the sky and mountains. Lightning flashed across the sea and the wind remained steady.

They pulled up their hoods and slowed the horses to a canter as they passed through the gates. The guards kept their heads down in the wind and paid no attention to what appeared to them as nobles from New Market.

They passed through the city unnoticed. Most of the people that were out on the streets had the hoods of their own cloaks pulled up and only noticed them enough to stay out of the way of the horses.

As they entered the castle courtyard, they kicked their horses into a full gallop. The guards noticed immediately but could do nothing. The horses plowed through the castle doors and they charged through the great hall. Rowan and Alder jumped from the horses, threw open the door to the throne room, and shut it behind them. They barred it and piled the immediate furniture in front of it. They hurried up the stairs and through the next door. Alder wrestled with the guards to the shouts of King Amadan while Rowan barricaded the door.

The guards were subdued and Alder held the king at the point of his sword.

King Amadan swelled in anger and Rowan had never seen a brighter shade of red.

"Your heads will be mounted on my throne, assassins! No one threatens my life! No one!" he sputtered.

Alder chuckled and threw back his hood. Rowan did as well. The guards pounding on the lower door echoed into the chamber.

"You two! You were banished! Banished! I will make you wish you were never born!"

Rowan fixed an arrow in his bow and aimed it at King Amadan.

"You will listen to what we have to say," he demanded.

"Me, listen to you! I am King!"

"New Market has been destroyed. The pirates from the south and the wildmen attacked together. The attack was planned. They killed most of the citizens and took the rest as slaves. The farms have been burned. The military academy, destroyed. Earl Hammel is dead and his castle has been burned."

"That is not possible! You lie! You wish to usurp me!"

Alder sneered. "If I wanted to usurp you I could have done it when you were a baby or when I stayed in the castle for weeks. I would not have waited until this moment to do so. Your legs have been cut off. New Market has fallen. Your armies have been destroyed and your people have been captured. Earl Hammel's head swings from the bowsprit of the pirate ships."

The pounding of the guards had reached the throne room door. Alder sheathed his sword and Rowan hung his bow and returned the arrow to its quiver.

"King Amadan, we are trying to warn you. Take the people and flee Kingsford. Do not forget that this doom was foretold by the necromancer," Alder plead.

"King, we have only ever served you and the people of Kingsford. Please protect your people. They love you and rely on you. Do not let them be slaughtered in the streets. You must warn them."

The door burst open. The guards climbed over the barricade. Alder and Rowan held their arms out, palms upturned. The guards slammed into them, knocking them to the ground.

"Get them out of my sight!" King Amadan roared.

Rowan and Alder were carried from the throne room and down to the dungeons. Rowan was thrown against the wall of a cell and shackled.

Alder was not taken to a cell immediately.

Alder's cloak and tunic were removed and he was chained to a pole in the center of the room. They began whipping him.

"Stop!" Rowan cried. "Please stop! We meant to warn everyone! New Market has been destroyed! You must get the people out!"

They were not listening. They were enjoying whipping Alder.

Alder did not cry out. He winced at every bite of the whip, but would not give them the satisfaction of crying out.

When they tired of whipping him, they drug him into a different cell. Rowan could hear the dull thud of them beating him.

"Quick! Get the club!" a soldier laughed.

Rowan heard footsteps cross the room and then return to the cell. Heavier thuds commenced.

"No!" Rowan screamed.

The heavy thuds continued. Alder finally cried out.

"No!" Rowan screamed louder, rattling his chains.

The soldiers laughed and kept going.

"That's enough, boys," one finally said. "We can't kill him. The king reserves those honors."

Rowan heard the smack of Alder's body being thrown against the wall and the rattle of the chains.

"Chain 'em up good now. We don't want any elf tricks."

Chains rattled and then the gate was closed.

The guards locked both gates. Rowan could hear them jeering at Alder. "Elf swine. They ain't so tough. Flesh and blood like the rest of us. We will find out soon enough how hard it is to break them elf bones."

Rowan could hear their laughing as they climbed up the stairs.

"Alder?" he called out, his voice trembling.

He did not respond.

"Alder?" he yelled.

"I'm all right," came a garbled response.

"I can't get to you!" Rowan struggled against the shackles.

"I'm all right," Alder trailed off.

Rowan wept and continued to fight the shackles. He had to get to Alder.

The sound of steps echoed down the stairwell.

Bacach opened the gate to Rowan's cell.

"Bacach!" Rowan cried.

"Hello, Rowan," Bacach smiled faintly. "I heard that a group of assassins had made an attempt on my father's life. I could hardly believe that it was you that was in charge of it. After all this time, I could not believe that you were behind it, that you were truly a traitor, but here we are."

"Bacach, we did not try to kill your father. New Market has been destroyed by pirates and wildmen. The entire city was burned, the soldiers were killed, and the people have been kidnapped by the pirates. We came to warn your father."

"How do you know this?" Bacach asked.

"We were there! We fought the wildmen, but we escaped. You must convince your father to evacuate the city!" Rowan pulled against the shackles.

"Why were you in New Market? You were banished from the realm," Bacach said absentmindedly. He was acting peculiar. He seemed to be unconcerned with the fact that New Market was destroyed.

"We had to resupply and then we stayed for the festival. What does it matter? Kingsford is going to be attacked, just like the necromancer said! We are allies with Midland, take the people there!"

"Alder seems to be incapacitated. What has happened to the book?"

Rowan was shocked. "We lost it in the forest."

Bacach grew angry. "What were you *thinking*?"

"We were thinking of not trusting the people of Midland," Rowan scowled.

"But you just told me I should take the people of Kingsford there," Bacach smiled.

"Alder and I were not safe there, just as we were not safe here," Rowan growled.

"It would have been safe here!" Bacach fumed. "Now we shall never know what it says about the stone."

"It says nothing of the stone. Just as Alder told you months ago."

"Alder lied. It must say something."

"Alder does not lie," Rowan snarled.

Bacach smiled. "Ever the boy, Rowan, never the man." Bacach stood. "There is nothing I can do to stop your execution. My father means to make an example of both of you, especially Alder. Expect pain."

Bacach left the cell, locking the door behind him. Rowan listened to him climbing the stairs.

All was silent. Rowan was not sure if Alder was even conscious, let alone able to speak.

Rowan began to cry again. Bacach had truly betrayed them. The quest for the stone had tainted his mind and turned him to greed so quickly. He sold his soul to the very idea of power.

Through a tiny window at the top of the ceiling, which was ground level to the outside world, Rowan could see the day fading.

He began to feel uneasy as the sky darkened. They had not seen the pirates along the shore but Kingsford would take heavy casualties even at the hands of the wildmen.

Rowan thought about Margie. She was in the first section of the city. She would be one of the first casualties. He had to find a way to warn her.

After some time, a guard came down to check on them. He was a younger man.

"I have jewels in my purse if you help me," Rowan called.

The man peered into the cell, intrigued at the very least.

"There is a girl at The Grey Goat Inn in the first section. She is the daughter of the innkeeper. Do you know the place and of whom I speak?"

"Aye," the man said questioningly.

"You can have all the jewels in my purse if you bring her a message."

"What's to stop me from taking all the jewels in your purse now?" he asked with a sneer.

"I believe you are better than that and this is my last wish before I am killed," Rowan begged.

The sneer faded and the boyish look returned to the man's face. "What should I tell her?"

"Find Margie. Tell her that New Market has been destroyed by pirates and wildmen. The only survivors were taken for slaves. Tell her that she must leave the city as soon as possible. If she cannot leave, she must hide in a place that will be safe from fire. Tell her the message is from Rowan."

"Is there anything else?" asked the young soldier, sounding slightly dumbfounded.

"Tell her we miss her and love her and to not come near our execution if everything else should turn out all right. You can take the jewels now. They are yours and I shall not be needing them," Rowan murmured.

The solder looked for signs of a trap, and finding none, entered the cell and took Rowan's purse. He left the cell, locking the door once again.

"Alder, I do not know if you are awake and can hear me. The soldier is going to warn Margie. She will listen. I pray that there is time for her to get to safety."

The dungeon was black once the sun set. The guards, having no reason to, had not lit the torches when they had left and the dungeon was on the backside of the castle, not allowing any of the torchlight from the entrance to circle around to this side. Rowan lost track of the time.

Exhaustion finally took him.

His hair stood on the back of his neck. Every nerve in his body was screaming to run. The castle was still. No noise could be heard inside or outside the keep. He looked to where the window was. A purple light shone outside the window. Every so often, he heard a distant moan.

Then the screaming started.

He could hear movement all around the castle, inside and outside. Ghostly wails could be heard and human screams. A battle was taking place outside the walls.

Alder began to groan.

"Alder! What is happening?" Rowan screamed, pulling at the chains.

"The voice," he groaned.

Rowan listened.

The necromancer was chanting in a low voice. The voice did not come from within or without. It almost sounded to Rowan as if it was inside his own head, speaking words he did not know and could barely catch.

Alder groaned louder.

"What is it Alder?" Rowan called out.

"It is the speech of Olcdonas. The cursed speech. All that utter it are damned and it pains the elves that remained true to hear it," he muttered.

The floor began to glow purple.

Rowan looked around him. The entire dungeon was glowing purple.

The light materialized into shapes. The dead were rising and the dungeon under the castle had seen thousands of souls killed over the centuries.

They wore all different styles of clothing, headdresses, and carried different weapons. Some held only books, others carried full battle axes. The spirits of men, women, and children appeared. Some were human, some were elves. They began to march up the stairs to the never-ending chanting of the necromancer.

The screaming from within the castle echoed down into the dungeon.

"Alder?" Rowan called out.

Alder did not respond.

"Alder?" he cried.

He still did not answer.

Rowan struggled against his chains, but he knew it was useless.

A purple light appeared in the stairway and then pushed itself through the doorway to the dungeon. The glow approached Rowan's cell. It was the most beautiful woman he had ever seen in his life. She was tall, fair skinned, and had light eyes and hair. Her dress was that of a queen, but she wore no crown. A long cut ran across her throat. She passed through the cell doors and knelt before Rowan. She was an elf.

"Who are you?" Rowan murmured in bewilderment.

She glanced toward Alder's cell, then reached up to Rowan's shackled wrists.

Rowan's hands grew painfully cold, but then he heard a loud crack and the shackles fell off him.

Rowan looked at the wall where Alder would be.

"You-you're Alder's mother!" Rowan exclaimed.

The woman smiled sweetly, but with more grief than Rowan had ever seen.

"Can you go to him? He would do anything to see you!" Rowan implored.

Her face became more grieved. She rose and then turned away, opening the cell door as she left, and headed up the stairs.

Rowan wasted no time. He jumped to his feet and began searching for the keys to Alder's cell. He found a set on a peg by the door and went to Alder's cage.

Alder was hanging from the ceiling by his arms and he was covered in blood. His face was swollen. Dried blood caked his nose and mouth. His hair was matted with blood where his head had been slammed against the stone wall. He was still shirtless, the guards not having bothered to redress him. His abdomen was already bruised and swelling and his back was still a web of open wounds from the whip. He coughed, spluttering blood.

Rowan found the stool the soldiers had used to hang him and unshackled him from the ceiling. Rowan almost fell off the stool, trying to hold onto Alder's body as he dropped down.

Rowan sat on the cold floor with Alder and held him closely. Alder was unconscious and breathing shallowly. Rowan wept. Alder was going to die, regardless of whether they were able to escape.

Rowan had an idea.

He picked Alder up and slung him across his shoulders.

He climbed the stairs of the dungeon, slowly under the weight of Alder.

He was cautious to avoid people, alive or dead.

He carried Alder into the great hall and encountered the battle.

The guards were attempting to fight the undead horde and were losing. No torches in the room had been lit but it glowed purple with the quantity of undead within it. The soldiers, a tiny lot in comparison, were being killed throughout. As their bodies hit the ground, they began to glow, and another spirit would join the horde.

Rowan attempted to stay close to the wall. He hoped that he would go unnoticed, but he was wrong.

As a soldier fell directly in front of him, the spirit saw him and moved in. Rowan did not have time to draw his dagger. The spirit thrust its spear through Rowan's side and then removed it with a grin.

Rowan dropped to his knees, unable to breathe.

The spirit left to rejoin the horde.

The pain shot through his entire body. The weapon had been of shadow like the spirit, but the blade had felt real inside him. Rowan could feel the blood. He could feel the wet, warm spot growing on his tunic.

All he could think of was Alder.

He lifted himself to his hands and knees and crawled with Alder on his back.

He reached the doorway that led to the bath and managed to open it.

His vision was growing blurry, but he kept crawling blindly.

They fell down the stairs.

He lay at the bottom for a moment, knowing that it was over. He began to drag Alder. Closer and closer, until they reached the edge of the water. Rowan's head grew dizzy, but he was able to push Alder into the water.

The world spun around him and he fell in, the blood pooling around his body.

Chapter 15

"Rowan, wake up," Alder whispered.

He had no idea how long he had been in the water. It must have been hours, if not days.

He opened his eyes and the world seemed to spin. He shut his eyes again.

When he reopened them, the world was clear. Shafts of light shown through the windows and new openings in the walls. Birds could be heard chirping outside.

Everything else was still.

Rowan was still in the water, but he sat on one of the benches that had been built into the pool.

Alder was before him. His face was no longer swollen or covered in blood.

The water had worked. They were both healed and alive.

Alder hugged him tightly. "You are brilliant, my friend," he gushed.

"All is well?" Rowan asked, mystified.

Alder laughed. "Nothing is well. We are alive, which is well, but the city is destroyed. I doubt that anyone is still alive within the castle."

"Is there word of the stone?" Rowan whispered.

Alder smiled. "I have had a thought about that, but I will need your help."

Alder dove down into the pool and Rowan followed. They swam down to a small, elaborate grate where the water flowed into the pool.

As Rowan looked closer, he saw that the decoration was Elvish words, written in such a way to appear as only decorative marks.

Alder read the scrawl and then they surfaced.

"It is a riddle," he gasped. "It is a riddle written in Elvish. I grow strong when tended to and weaker when neglected. I undo hurts, but cannot heal ailments. I am felt, but not seen. I can be given and received. I am within and without. What am I?"

"Perhaps some kind of plant?" Rowan ventured.

"I do not think it as an object," Alder returned.

Rowan stared at Alder. "Love," he offered.

Alder looked at Rowan and smiled.

"Let's see if you are correct."

They dove down again. Alder gripped the grate.

"Ghaoil!" he garbled with bubbles blowing out of his mouth.

A blue light burst from around the grate and it fell off. Alder reached his arm into the hole as far as he could reach. He pulled his arm out and held an ornate chest. They resurfaced.

The chest was small and Alder could hold it in one hand. It was white, but shimmered similarly to mother-of-pearl. The edges were trimmed with gold and gold scrollwork danced across the mother-of-pearl.

The water changed immediately. The water turned cold and stagnant and it no longer smelled of flowers, but more closely to the sulphureous smell of the moors.

"All that magic was from the stone," Alder grinned.

"We must hide it quickly in case anyone is around. The necromancer could be within the castle and it is only a matter of time before they check down here," Rowan recommended, growing nervous.

They snuck to the dungeon without seeing anyone. Alder retrieved his shirt and weapons.

"I do not know how to hide it," Alder admitted.

Rowan looked around the room. He couldn't see much that could be used to conceal the small chest.

"Should we open it?" Rowan hesitated. "The stone would be much easier to conceal by itself."

Alder held his hand over the gold scrollwork that was in the shape of a keyhole. He closed his eyes and took deep breaths.

"Fosgailte!" he called out in his clearest voice.

The scrollwork glowed for a few seconds and a small click came from the clasp of the box.

Alder opened the box.

In white silk lay the stone.

It dazzled more brilliantly than any diamond. It seemed to sparkle like fresh snow on the mountain tops. It was the most beautiful thing they had ever seen.

The small stone showed the rough edges where it had been severed.

Alder closed his eyes and murmured something in Elvish.

He then cut out the silk and wrapped the stone in it. He handed it to Rowan.

"You must bear it. I feel that I cannot."

Rowan took the bundle and pushed it into the only pocket he had that featured a button.

They took care to hide the box somewhere no one would ever find it. They then left the dungeon and returned to the great hall.

The great hall was covered in dried blood and littered with guards. They had never stood a chance. Rowan and Alder crossed the room, stepping over the bodies. By the door, Rowan noticed the young soldier that had taken his purse. Rowan's purse was tied to the man's belt.

Rowan knelt down and closed the soldier's gaping eyes and mouth. He then retrieved his purse. The soldier would not be needing it.

From above the doors hung the bodies of King Amadan and his two remaining daughters. The bodies of Bacach and Magadh were missing.

They passed around the dangling bodies and stepped lightly down the stone steps. The courtyard was much the same as the great hall. The bodies of horses, soldiers, and servants were strewn about the yard as if a storm had spat them wherever it liked. The gates had been shut and a heap of civilians were piled at the gate.

Alder took the keys from the guard nearest and unlocked the gate. The bodies gruesomely toppled over as Alder opened the gate. They climbed the bodies, ignoring their expressions of fear and pain, and crossed over onto the street.

Fewer bodies littered the streets than at the castle. Many of the residents of the city had been taken unaware while they slept. Most were dead inside their homes or right in the doorways.

As they neared the temple, Rowan noticed movement in the observatory.

"Someone is alive up there," Rowan pointed. Alder looked and his eyes narrowed.

"I may be wrong, but I believe that it is Bacach," he murmured.

Rowan felt uneasy. He did not want the stone anywhere near Bacach, but he wanted to know how Bacach had survived when everyone else had perished. "Do you think it is safe to go up there with the stone?" Rowan whispered to Alder.

"I cannot think of any way that he could know that we have found it," Alder waved.

They entered the temple yard and noticed that a few other people were moving about their duties, unaffected. One of the manach in his black robe and tall hat with seven stars, representing the first seven Diathans, approached them.

"Ah, my sons, I am pleased to see you on this day. We welcome all the survivors to the temple for prayer."

"Why are you alive?" Alder asked, skipping the formalities.

The manach was taken aback.

"This is sacred ground. The undead cannot walk inside the temple."

"You survived by hiding in the temple while everyone else was killed? No one went to try to wake or convince the people to run to the temple rather than the pile we climbed over at the castle?" Alder fumed.

"We would not have risked ourselves to go out on the streets—"

"You have manachs in your observatory at all times, surely one of them saw the hordes appear. They could not have rung the bells to warn the citizens?" Alder interrupted.

"Our manachs are deep in thought in the observatory, they cannot break their trances with the heavens to observe the trials of those below them, but even so, Prince Bacach had ordered the manach out for his own trance."

"May Spioradan take you. The city's blood is on your hands," Alder hissed.

Alder pushed past the manach who looked shaken and terrified. Rowan followed.

They entered the tower with no interference by the manach and they climbed the seven stories to the observatory.

They opened the door and Alder gasped.

Bacach was there and was staring into a strange mirror.

"Bacach! Get away from there!" Alder commanded.

Bacach jumped in surprise, broken out of his trance with whatever was happening in the mirror.

"How are you alive?" he questioned.

Alder crossed the room, unsheathed his sword, and smashed it into the mirror.

"Briseadh!" he roared.

The mirror shattered and the glass seemed to turn to dust.

"What have you done!" Bacach cried, dropping to his knees and covering his face.

Alder would have none of it.

"Have you any idea what that is Bacach? Have you any idea how much danger you put yourself and the city in? How long have you had it?" Alder demanded, circling around the alter, sword still unsheathed.

"What was that thing?" Rowan asked fearfully.

"It was a sgàthan. It is a mirror, but instead of showing you your reflection, it shows you the reflection of an event. The event may be the past, present, or future. It may be truth or it may be lies. The high elves used to use them until Torradh was said to have corrupted them." He pointed the sword at Bacach. "Everyone is dead Bacach. No one will come to save you. I suggest that you start explaining what you have done."

Bacach looked up from where he had been weeping. His expression had changed. His eyes had softened. He once again resembled the Bacach Rowan had once loved.

"Rowan, Alder, my friends!" he reached, climbing to his feet.

Alder kept his sword pointed.

"I have been under an enchantment! You broke it once you broke the mirror, Alder!"

"Don't move, Bacach," Alder commanded. "Tell us what has happened."

Bacach became fearful.

"I had been looking for the stone while you were away. Everyone had said I had gone mad. I had no authority over the staff. I was at my wits end. I had not been permitted to search the treasury, but I knew that I had to discover a way.

"I snuck into the treasure room one night when my father was unconscious with alcohol, the way being a secret chamber running away from his bedchamber.

"I searched through everything. All the gold and jewels my family has hoarded for centuries. I found a few Elvish and Dwarvish goods, but no stone. As I was giving up hope, I found the sgàthan. I had been told about them in fairy stories as a boy, but had never found mention of them in actual histories. In the stories, the governess had always tried to include a moral about the price of looking into the mirror, but nothing ever seemed to make sense.

"So I took the mirror and brought it here, telling the manachs that it would allow them to see into the past to view the creation. They allowed me to leave it in the tower so that only the elders could view it.

"I began coming here as often as I could, trying to see what had happened to the stone.

"The mirror never showed me anything! All it ever showed me were images of Alder. That is why I came to suspect that Alder had known something. When he refused to give me the book, I believed that to be proof that he knew something.

"Whenever I attempted to view the past or the future, everything revolved around him! I have wasted days in this tower, looking in the sgàthan, but all I have seen is Alder. You are the key to all this, but I have not discovered why.

"I have seen other images, as well. Every time I would try to look away, I would find that my face was inches from the mirror. When I am away, I only want to be here. I cannot sleep. I lie awake, thinking of the mirror.

"I have seen *him*," Bacach whispered.

Rowan was afraid of Bacach. He had been pacing the floor, shaking, wide-eyed, and jittery. Sometimes he would stop, to look at the sgàthan as if it was still there and then begin pacing again. Bacach resembled the addicts he had seen in the allies of New Market.

"What do you mean you have seen *him*?" Alder asked.

"Torradh," Bacach hissed. "I have seen him in his dark castle of spires. He sits in a throne of bones. Sometimes he sings Elvish songs that sound so sweet, other times he laughs like a madman when no one else is around. Do you want to hear one? I can sing them well."

Alder glanced nervously at Rowan. Bacach had gone mad.

"Well, you are King now Bacach, I suggest you begin cleaning your city. Disease sets in quickly."

"What do you mean?" Bacach asked.

"Everyone is dead, Bacach. Your father, your brother, your sisters. Everyone is gone. We are going to look for survivors in the poor quarter and we are then heading east for the Elvish lands. The western cities have been destroyed. All that remains is Whitecliff, but even they might have been destroyed."

"You cannot leave me!" Bacach whined.

Alder sheathed his sword. "And we cannot take you."

"You must! I have no guards, there are no servants, there are no peasants! What shall I do for food? How will I dress? Who will make the fires?" he cried.

Alder sneered and Rowan felt disgusted.

"You will have to learn to fend for yourself, King."

Alder turned and crossed the room to Rowan.

"I order you to take me with you!" Bacach stamped.

"We are not your subjects; we are banished by the orders of your late father. And to put it plainly, Mr. Bacach, you no longer have a kingdom," Alder chuckled.

They began their descent down the stairs with Bacach close behind.

They exited the tower and a group of manach were standing in the yard with arms crossed. They did not say anything or try to stop them, only watched.

"Rowan, please. We are friends!" Bacach begged.

"You have left us for dead, twice, Bacach," Rowan returned, following Alder's quick pace.

They exited the temple yard and began walking down the street. They were hoping that they would be able to find horses alive within the city, their warhorses having been slain.

"I was bewitched! I knew neither friend nor foe!"

Bacach stopped behind them. "Please! I will die without you!"

Rowan and Alder looked at each other. They had a silent conversation, which ended in Alder's eyes rolling and him frowning.

"You may come with us, Bacach," Rowan called back.

"But you are no King of ours. We will not follow orders. If you wish to stay alive, you listen to us."

"Thank you, friends! Thank you!"

They continued walking. They went toward the earl's mansion. Most of the nobles along the street kept horses, including the earl, but none of the horses had been left alive.

They quickly decided that it would not be worth their time looking for any other living creature. The only living creatures were the manach and people that had made it out of the city. A few shepherd boys sat on their doorsteps, crying or staring into the distance.

When they saw Bacach, they stood and began following Rowan, Alder, and Bacach. They soon had a small gathering of boys, elderly men and women, and refugees from New Market that had only just arrived. They were passing the road to the Grey Goat when Alder stopped.

Rowan and Alder both looked at the desolate inn.

Rowan turned to Bacach. "Address your loyal subjects. We will escort you and the people to Kingsland. Tell them to gather any provisions they will need for the road. It will take us almost two days to travel, given that there are so many elderly and children. Tell them not to bring any treasures, only food, warm clothing, and weapons if they have them."

Bacach nodded. He had never addressed a group.

Rowan and Alder took off toward the inn while Bacach turned hesitantly toward his people.

The bodies were strewn across the street. Òsta lay face down in the doorway.

"Margie!" Alder screamed. "Margie!"

Alder charged into the inn.

Rowan followed closely behind him.

They searched the kitchen, the rooms, the brewery. They checked everywhere and could not find Margie.

"Margie!" they screamed together.

A soft thud and creaking came from beneath them. Alder drew his sword and Rowan drew his dagger.

A door in the floor opened behind the bar with a loud creak.

Margie's head appeared through the floor.

"Heaven's above!" she cried. She finished climbing out of the cellar and ran to Alder and Rowan. She grabbed both and pulled them into one of her bone-crushing hugs. She wept big soggy tears that were unlike her.

"It was horrid Mr. Alder, Mr. Rowan! Them ghouls appeared just as we was clearing out the men. I hid just like you told me, Mr. Rowan! Father-father-thought he could fight them off, but they killed everyone!" she wailed.

"There, there Margie," Alder soothed, patting her back.

"There are other survivors. We are going to escort everyone to Kingsland. Please come with us. We will look after you," Rowan whispered.

"I never thought I'd see you two again!" she wailed, not ready to release them.

They both hugged her tight.

Finally, she found the resolve Margie was renowned for. She took a deep breath, wiped her eyes on her apron, and stood back from the boys.

"What do I need?"

"Bring provisions for yourself for two days. If there is extra, bring it. I worry that there will not be enough, but we will make do. Hunger is the least of our worries," Rowan instructed.

Margie nodded. She clanged around in the kitchen for a few minutes. Margie then appeared with a large sack of food and a large rolling pin.

"This should be enough to get us by," she declared. They left the inn and returned to Bacach.

A few more survivors had joined the group. Most everyone now had a sack on their backs, whether they had stolen it from other homes or raided their own larders, it no longer mattered.

"Have you instructed them?" Rowan asked.

Bacach looked perplexed. "I said everything you told me to say, but they seem unconvinced."

Rowan looked across the crowd. They were scared and scarred. They were not following Bacach because they viewed him as their king, they were following him because he was something familiar.

Alder now turned to the people, seeing that Bacach had failed.

"Citizens of Kingsford and New Market! Our cities have been attacked! Our land has been burned! We are refugees! The road is long and all we can do is hope that Midland still stands. Our dear princess, Princess Azalea recently married Prince Aineolach and is now Queen! We will appear before her and seek refuge! We face dangers along the road, but Rowan and I will protect you. Let us go!"

The crowd murmured. It wasn't fighting talk, but it would do.

"Bacach, you lead. We will take the rear. We will ensure no one is left behind," Alder ordered.

Bacach nodded.

They moved out. Their army of old couples, children, and New Market refugees were too shell-shocked to speak. The most fearsome member of the party was Margie, with her giant sack of baked goods, rolling pin, and the set determination on her face.

The going was slow. Most of the people within the group had never traveled outside the city and had never walked any great distance. They were now being herded along by Alder and Rowan on an unusually hot autumn day.

They crossed the moors for what would be the first and last time. Many were too old to see the rebuilding of the city. The young people would have little reason to return by the time they were grown. As this realization hit them, many began to weep and look back at the city their families had called home for hundreds of years.

"We must keep moving forward," Rowan would remind them softly.

Rowan and Alder tensed as they entered the Pass of Handuin.

"All that have weapons, be ready for an attack," Alder called out.

Everyone murmured and more cries of woe came from the older members.

Rowan could see Bacach look over his shoulder toward them. He then allowed the group to pass him and fell back to Rowan and Alder.

"I do not believe that I should be at the front of the group. I should be at the center or towards the back," he fidgeted nervously.

"Why do you believe that?" Rowan asked.

"If there is an attack, I shall be the first killed. I am King of Kingsford. If I fall, all is lost. I would be safer in the center or by you."

"You are wrong on both accounts. Goblins never attack the first member of a party. That allows the group to turn around and retreat. They attack the center so as to create confusion and pick off as many as they can. As for your kingship, Kingsford is already lost, you being king makes no difference. Your place is at the front, leading your people. Do you wish your people to see you now as a coward when they look to you for strength and courage?" Alder sneered.

Bacach flushed and returned to the front.

"They were once such a great line. When King Taighe led the race of men to victory in the great war and then led his men over the great mountains to build Kingsford in the middle of a moor, there seemed to be no end to his courage and strength. Now Bacach is the last son in the line and would rather his people die in order to save his own skin. My father used to tell me King Taighe was the first horseman in the line that led the charge against Torradh's goblin kings. My father was the second, for he would not allow King Taighe to be alone. King Taighe would have given his life for any man, woman, or child," Alder grumbled.

"Their line was broken long ago. We both know Magadh received the lion's share of the courage, but he received the same amount of lust, greed, and foolishness," Rowan laughed.

"I never thought Bacach a fool, but something is off about him. He is changed. Even changed from the last time we saw him."

"He seems almost emotionless. I have known him to be deep in thought, but this is different. It seems as though his very soul is somewhere else. His expression is vacant, but you can see something in his eyes. His presence makes me uneasy."

"I am glad that I am not the only one to feel so," Alder laughed.

The Pass of Handuin was hot in the afternoon sun. The few plants that had managed to find footholds in the rocky terrain now drooped in the drought. The bushes that once afforded protection to the goblins were barren and thorny. Rowan was dismayed to see the plants in such a state. He had always enjoyed the vegetation that could triumph over the stones.

Rowan and Alder scanned the sides of the cliffs and mountainsides unceasingly. An attack now would be devastating to the group. Many would surely die.

The tell-tale sign came. A grouse was flushed out and a crow scrambled to the sky, cawing angrily.

"Goblins!" Rowan screamed.

People cried out as they looked for places to hide. A few arrows began to fly overhead.

Rowan and Alder pushed through the group of panicking citizens. A few of the brave lads and elderly men pulled their swords and bows and stood by Alder and Rowan.

Rowan readied his bow and Alder pulled his sword.

Margie was there, standing firm with her rolling pin.

A goblin's head appeared over the top of a rock and Rowan shot. A screech sounded in the hills that was echoed by many more.

It was an entire host and they were coming now.

Rowan shot arrows as quickly and accurately as he could. He could not afford to miss. Alder gathered those that had weapons into ranks and kept the boys with bows firing arrows.

Rowan saw what he had dreaded. A goblin's arrow lodged itself in one of the boys. The boy fell and the other children began to break ranks. It was all Alder could do to keep them together. They had no chance to retreat, their only option was to fight.

The goblins made it to the road, jumping and screeching at the boys. But Alder was there to lead them.

Alder let out a battle cry that shook the goblins and heartened the boys and old men. The vagabond army of old men and children let out their own battle-cries and followed Alder into the fray.

Rowan pulled his dagger. His arrows were gone. He would fight the goblins until the end.

He ran into the host and did his best to divide the goblins. After slaying one, he took its cruel, twisted sword and turned it on the other goblins. For every agonized cry of a boy, he rushed the goblins with a renewed fury. He felt himself covered in their dark blood.

A goblin leaped into the air, aiming for a small boy that stood next to Rowan. He pushed the boy out of the way and raised his sword, piercing the goblin with the sword. Rowan turned, only to see the boy shot by another goblin that had killed his former opponent.

Rowan felt the fire and fought with a dagger and sword in both hands. He roared with anger and the goblins shrank back.

No goblin was left alive.

Rowan and Alder looked about the blood-soaked road once they finished the final goblins.

Margie was there, her rolling pin broken and bloody, looking over the battlefield.

Only two of the lads were still standing.

Rowan dropped to his knees and cried out. Those that had not fought now returned to Rowan and Alder, including Bacach. The elderly wept to see the dead children that had given their lives to defend them. A few of the women bawled over their dead husbands. Bacach remained emotionless and said nothing.

A whimper came from a few feet away.

Rowan looked up. The boy he had pushed was alive. Rowan crawled to him, holding the boy in his arms.

Blood soaked through his thin wool tunic and trickled from his mouth. He looked at Rowan with scared eyes.

He tried to speak but only gurgled and sputtered.

Rowan held him tight, knowing that nothing could be done.

The boy choked and coughed on his blood for too long, but Rowan would not leave him.

He could not.

The boy's sky-blue eyes stared at Rowan and Alder's faces. He gripped Rowan's tunic with his small hand. He could not have been older than eleven. He was a beautiful child.

His body tensed for one more cough and then relaxed. The light left his eyes. He was gone. Rowan wept over his small body and Alder comforted him.

Alder looked at the child and only saw Rowan. He felt a pain in his chest that he had only felt once before when he thought Rowan was dead in the forest.

"We cannot linger," Alder finally whispered.

Rowan nodded, closed the boy's staring eyes, and softly laid his body on the ground. They did not have time to arrange the bodies.

They began walking in silence, leading the people from the pass.

When they reached the Watchtower of Faire, Rowan knew that they could go no further. The sun had set behind the mountains and the mountains cast shadows over the entire valley. It would soon be dark and Rowan and Alder were still afraid of the open fields.

A snort surprised them.

Grazing between the forest and the watchtower were their horses. They had fled the forest and returned to the safety of the tower, waiting for their master's return.

They couldn't help feeling overjoyed.

Alder whistled and the horses both looked up. They whinnied and trotted over to their masters. Rowan and Alder greeted them and petted their noses. Alder spoke soft words to his horse in Elvish and Rowan held his head against Fior's.

"We will make camp in the watchtower," Alder called out, leading the people into the ruins. It was cramped with so many inside, but they were safer than in the open. Many fell asleep almost instantly with exhaustion from the day. Some remained watchful, untrusting of the ruins.

Rowan and Alder huddled together on the outside of the tower.

One of the boys that had fought with them sat next to him.

"That was Chiontach, the boy you saved," he whispered.

"I did not save him. He is dead," Rowan murmured.

"You saved him first. Then he was killed. Then you didn't let him die alone," the boy explained.

"Whose son was he?" Rowan asked.

"Son of Chion, but his mother died recently so he wasn't really son of anyone anymore," the boy rambled.

"How did his parents die?"

"His father was killed by the king a long time ago and his mother died of hunger a few weeks ago. Nothing could be found on the moors and they had no bow for hunting. His mother had no work since there is no wool for spinning and weaving right now. She went hungry. Chiontach went hungry too."

"How do you know so much?"

"We were neighbors. We used to play together when we were little, but we weren't allowed to play together when his father was put to death."

Rowan flushed but said nothing. This child's family had allowed their neighbor to starve to death because the husband had been put to death by the king, most likely for no reason at all other than some trivial offense to the king.

"Run off and find a good spot for sleep before they are all gone. Stay away from the woods," Alder ordered softly.

The boy stood, but before he walked away, he turned. "We are glad you are here Master Elf. You aren't at all like the stories about elves."

Once the boy had left, Alder turned to Rowan.

"What an outspoken lad," he chuckled.

"He speaks as if he is a young man and not just a boy," Rowan wondered.

"Perhaps he is taught at the temple," Alder offered.

"I only wish his parents were better acquainted with charity and forgiveness, so the boy's mother had not needed to starve. To think people were starving to death in Kingsford."

Rowan and Alder took turns keeping watch through the night. When dawn's pale light began to appear over the fields, they became dismayed.

Smoke towered over the horizon.

Cries and murmurs moved through the crowd as they all became aware of their plight.

Rowan and Alder exchanged glances, knowing that they must stem the unrest quickly. People were staring at

Bacach, searching for answers, but Bacach only shifted uneasily under their stares.

Bacach, at last, approached Rowan and Alder.

"What shall we do? Surely the city burns!" Bacach hissed.

"We do not know that. Houses burn on their own without wildmen and monsters. We should keep going," Rowan whispered.

Bacach's eyes flared, but he retained his scared look.

"We must go to the elves. That is the only safe place! Alder, you must take us there! It is your duty!"

Rowan held his breath and stared wide-eyed at the two. He half expected Alder, whose fuse had grown so short in recent days, to behead Bacach where he stood.

Alder's eyes burned their bright fire, but his face was expressionless except for the tight line of his mouth.

"What leads you to believe that I know the location of the hidden cities?" he asked curtly.

"Is that not where you went when you were exiled?" Bacach asked, slightly surprised.

"No. We went into the forest and then arrived in New Market only just in time for the sacking by the wildmen and pirates, as was told to you previously."

"You do not know where the Elven lands are?" Bacach asked in dismay.

"No. Even if we were able to find their realms, there is no guarantee that they would permit us entrance. Just as your people have hunted them for hundreds of years, so have they defended their borders from your people."

"We must carry on, Bacach. Even if the city has been sacked, we may find resources there until we are able to seek help. The people may rest there and even take residence there while we go on," Rowan stated firmly.

Bacach was dismayed. As they had suspected, it seemed as though Bacach was still searching for the stone.

Alder approached the group of villagers.

"We travel onward. We do not know the state of Kingsland. We may seek shelter there, even now. We cannot turn back."

The people murmured and many seemed to nod, others looked back at the Pass of Handuin, wistfully.

Alder and Rowan took possession of their horses, and after denying Bacach a ride, offered their services to the most infirm.

They proceeded down the road.

The fields appeared scorched and the grass was pale with dehydration. The sun was hot as they walked along the dusty road. They had very little to drink and Rowan constantly urged them to conserve what they had. After some time, Rowan and Alder swapped out the riders in order to prevent exhaustion in some and laziness in others.

At midday, they rested. They were perilously low on resources and Rowan allowed them small drinks and portions of food, only enough to quiet the gnawing hunger they all felt.

Only one member of the party kept their head raised and marched without complaint.

Margie.

Margie did not cry during their halts. She did not complain about the limited comforts. She quietly divided the food she had packed and distributed it as equally as possible. She did not speak to anyone, including Alder and Rowan.

Alder and Rowan did not go to her but allowed her to deal with her grief in her own way. Margie had lost her past and her future and she now stomped down the road in mute resolution. She had become a battle-hardened warrior.

Rowan looked to the mountains behind them and the smoke column in front of them and wondered if they would make it into the city before nightfall. He was loath to spend a night in the fields, given their history, but he was worried about entering the city at night. They could be walking into a trap and it would be harder to see their enemies in the dark.

They started the group moving again, unable to allow them to rest any longer, regardless of if they were to stop for the night or continue marching until they reached the city.

"Do you believe we are walking into a trap?" Rowan asked.

"I have a sort of uneasy feeling, but I know not why," Alder replied.

"I am anxious because of the bugbear, but almost more anxious for what awaits us in the Kingsland."

"I would not permit us to sleep on the open road. We were safer in the watchtower, but the dark creatures of the world have been emboldened. I do not wish to tarry long in any place. It may be safer for us to attempt to find a farm that will suffer us for the evening."

"What do you think of the city?" Rowan asked.

"I do not think any city is safe under the kingship of Aineolach and Azalea," Alder chuckled.

Rowan smiled. It was true that they would not be welcome there on any account. But surely, they had not yet had tidings of the fate of Kingsford or Azalea's family. Aineolach would be interested in that news. He could claim the realm if he had the manpower and, although New Market was a pile of rubble, the foundation was there and would be a worthy prize.

An elderly woman collapsed.

Rowan and Alder rushed to her.

She was one of the women that had lost her husband in the pass. She had been alone and quiet since. She had occasionally murmured to herself and she had frequently looked back upon the road. She had asked for nothing, including food or water, claiming to have plenty in the small sack she carried with her. Alder looked through the bag to find only treasures.

Her breathing was shallow. Rowan listened to her chest and recognized a faint heartbeat.

Margie appeared at their side with a small canteen of beer. She poured a small amount into the woman's mouth. Rowan held her up and watched.

The woman died.

Rowan carried her off the road and laid her on top of a small hill. He laid her belongings next to her, aware that they would be stolen the moment someone stumbled upon her body.

Rowan returned to the group who stared at him in silence.

He changed out the riders upon the horses, wondering if the woman would have survived if he had changed riders more frequently.

"Your back is going to hurt with all that weight, Mr. Rowan," Margie said as they plodded along.

"What do you mean?" Rowan asked, confused. He was carrying no more than what was required of him.

"You're blaming yourself for all them deaths. You couldn't have changed them. The lads died with honor, although they were too young. They should've never been in the pass, but neither should the rest of us. That old woman could've asked for help at any time, but she didn't, Mr. Rowan. She was only marching because that was the only thing left to do. She would've died whether she was at home sitting by the hearth with her husband or out here with our lot. Ain't a one of us would have been able to find enough food to last the winter in Kingsford.

"My father always used to tell me something, Mr. Rowan. He said, 'Margie, life is like a river. When you're born, you're thrown in a boat and pushed off the bank. Some folks' rivers are full of rocks and rapids and others' rivers are wide and smooth. But all we're given is an oar to steer with. When there is a fork, we can change rivers, if that be our will. But the water will take us where it will and we can't change that. We all reach the sea in the end'. Now you just think on that Mr. Rowan. All our rivers brought us here and I'm not seeing any forks. Those lads, old men, and that woman only reached the sea before us and the rest of us just have to keep on rowing."

Rowan thought over Margie's words. His river was turbulent, full of rocks and downed trees like the high-mountain streams. He felt as though he had lost his oar and all he had left to do was allow the river to take him where it will.

They rested again around supper and the band was allowed some more food and water. They were almost completely out of food. The portions were getting smaller and the dismay was increasing.

"We must get to Kingsland," Rowan thought.

As the sun began to duck behind the mountains, Alder set out on his horse to look for a barn. Alder and Rowan had agreed that someone should go and someone should stay with the group. As Rowan and Bacach were more friendly with each other, they determined that Alder should be the one to go.

Rowan felt uneasy to see Alder ride off over the hill alone. They did not know what sort of men or creatures were in the fields, but they had no other options. Rowan must stay with the group.

After an hour, and after Rowan's nerves were shaken, Alder returned.

"There is a barn about two miles from here. The house appears to have been abandoned for a few days. We may take refuge there."

Alder dismounted his horse and allowed an elderly man to climb up whose pride had finally been vanquished by the women's pleading. A look of relief washed over his face as he settled into the saddle.

It took them an hour to reach the barn at their slow pace and all were overcome with happiness to have reached the shelter. The straw was somewhat fresh and the animals, that should have been inside the barn, were missing. No one ventured into the privacy of the individual stalls that were meant for the horses and birthing goats. Everyone seemed to prefer to be huddled on the main floor of the barn.

Rowan and Alder made a search of the house.

It was indeed abandoned. They saw no signs of a struggle or a hurried departure. The furniture was neat and the table was set as if for a meal. The hearth was long-cold and the farm porridge had turned to a substance as thick as mortar in the pot. They would not be able to eat it.

The owners of the farm had not intended to be gone long, by the state of the cupboards. Within the cupboard was half of a wheel of cheese, bread freshly baked for the evening meal with a cloth wrapped around it, some random vegetables that had already been scrubbed, and a bowl of eggs.

Rowan and Alder collected all the food that was edible without preparation and returned to the barn.

"There must be a storehouse," Rowan whispered to Alder as they sat against the now-closed doors of the barn.

"I thought the same when we were inside. It is almost winter and although the harvest was bad, we did not find enough food to provide for even a single person during the winter. Perhaps we should make a search in the morning?" Alder offered.

"I am wary to take too much. Although the scene is familiar, I do not wish to take everything. The owners may return, or another group of refugees may need to take shelter. I only wish to take enough to get us to the city and provide everyone with enough strength to bare whatever we may find there."

"I agree," Alder nodded after some thought.

They slept in turns as usual. Neither of them trusting the current situation they found themselves in.

Strange noises could be heard all through the night. More than once Rowan was startled out of sleep by what sounded like a bugbear. He would look to Alder who would be alert and watchful with the lines of his lips tight and his sword pulled.

During Rowan's watch, he could see a distant light through the window of the barn and hear what sounded like a goblin song along the road, but he couldn't imagine a horde of goblins marching openly along the road.

Men we hate and women we ate,
Bones we crushed and lives we snuffed.
Blood ran cold because goblins are bold,

How we hate and ate the men!
Liver, spleen, and hearts were smashed,
Ground and chomped and hashed.
Meat stew and men brews,
How we hate and ate the men!

Chapter 16

The pale morning light filtered through the gaps in the wood paneling. Rowan and Alder had hardly slept, unable to sleep fully through their turns. But they were accustomed to that sort of life. Rowan looked to the pale sky and thanked the gods that they had not slept along the road. There had been beasts roaming the fields all night and they would have been easily found and slain.

Rowan and Alder passed out the food to the group and everyone was thankful for the hearty portions. They would reach Kingsland in a few hours and did not have to conserve as much. While everyone made preparations for the day, Rowan and Alder hunted through the house for more food. They took as much food as they thought was right and then departed, leading the group back to the road.

It was now obvious that goblins had passed through during the night. In the dust of the road were the footprints of the bigfooted, clawed creatures. Cracked bones and other forms of garbage littered the way. Rowan tried not to think about the ghastly song they had been singing when he saw the fresh bones that still had bits of meat hanging from them and the gnaw marks of the goblins.

The smoke still rose beyond the horizon and it cast a shadow over their hopes. The city had been sacked, that was for sure. Nothing else could produce such smoke. But Rowan and Alder pressed the group onward.

When the first of the group crested a small hill, a wave of dismay rippled through the group. The groaning and weeping began afresh. Rowan and Alder walked to the front of the group. The shoddy houses made of wood and straw had been burned and the walls of the city had been reduced to a heap of smoldering logs.

Untouched, however, stood the hall of the king.

"There is hope still, friends. The hall still stands. The king and queen may live still and after such ruin, they may be glad to see us," Rowan implored.

The group was hesitant to continue the march, but after a few minutes, they saw that they had no other alternative and they continued.

The town was empty. The bodies that should have littered the streets, which had been the case in New Market and Kingsford, were missing. The lack of obvious death somehow made the ruins eerier.

Rowan and Alder both felt as though something horrible had happened to the citizens. Even the bodies of the soldiers, which should be numerous, were gone. The smoking, burning, remnants of the buildings was all that remained.

As they marched up the dusty road toward the hall they began feeling as though they were entering a trap. They did not see an escape route other than the way they had come in. The ruins created a barricade alongside the roads that cut off any likely escape routes.

"I don't like this," Rowan whispered to Alder, fighting the urge to ready his bow, for fear of scaring the group.

Alder only nodded, his hand resting on the hilt of his sword.

They stopped dead.

Standing between the impaled corpses of the king and queen by the closed doors of the hall was Princess Uiall. The long, black, webbed dress that clung to her figure was a sharp contrast to the skin that was as pale as death.

She stared at them, as though they had been expected, but were late for a dinner party. She was not surprised that they were there. She was not surprised that only a handful of children and elderly men and women were the only people alive. She was not surprised that Bacach was leading the group. She was only mildly surprised that Alder and Rowan were trailing behind the rest.

"You're late," she called out loudly.

Rowan and Alder said nothing. No one said anything at all. Most of the group did not know who this woman was. Margie put a hand on her hip.

"I was beginning to suspect that you really had succumbed to the goblins. They rarely do as they are told, not that they were told anything in particular, I was only beginning to wonder," she laughed coldly.

"What has happened here?" Rowan called out.

"You dare address me in such a manner, son of Lionn?"

Rowan reddened but did not avert his eyes from the woman.

"He asked you a question," Alder retorted.

Uiall looked from one to the other. The group began to disperse to the sides, feeling uneasy between the glares of these higher people. Only one person did not move.

Bacach stood beneath Uiall, staring up at her.

"Why don't you ask Bacach what happened here," she laughed cruelly.

Bacach slowly turned to face Rowan and Alder who looked at him with horror.

He smiled the same cruel grin as Uiall.

"I find it amusing that you had not suspected me in the destruction of Kingsford," he laughed.

Horror-stricken, they made no reply.

"Her Majesty." He closed the distance to Princess Uiall and took her hand, pressing it to his lips with a bow. "Queen Uiall is the necromancer. She called Bean Nigh and the banshee. She organized the attack on New Market and summoned the spirits in the fall of Kingsford. All in the name of Torradh!"

Bacach lifted his hands to the sky as if taunting the gods to do something about this new-found power.

"It is easy to see what she gets out of the bargain, but what do you get Bacach?" Alder asked coolly.

Bacach chuckled and Rowan saw a strange flicker within him. Bacach was feigning strength. He was a puppet. Uiall had made promises to him and now he was only praying that she would keep them. Bacach was strong because Uiall was strong beside him. He knew he was walking on the blade of a knife.

"Why Uiall cannot rule both Baccia and Uiallia alone. We will be two states under one country! Torradha we shall name it!" Bacach declared.

It took Rowan and Alder a moment to understand what Bacach had just said. He had renamed the realms and placed the stewardship under himself and Uiall, but retained that Torradh would be the king. He had murdered his entire family only to change who held the keys to his chains. He was already King of Kingsford. Why continue on this quest?

Bacach and Uiall whispered to each other excitedly. Uiall, her face calm and poised, smiled her unfeeling smile, and Bacach's eyes grew wider and wider.

Finally, Bacach turned to address Rowan and Alder. "Do not be afraid, son of Lionn and son of Adder. Every great kingdom needs servants. I will take you, son of Lionn, and Uiall will take you, son of Adder, as our manservants."

Rowan and Alder stared at him in disbelief.

"Come forward now," Bacach smiled with his arms open.

They did not move.

Uiall and Bacach frowned.

"Such insolence," she hissed.

"Stand before us now!" Bacach ordered, shifting his weight between his feet.

Alder and Rowan looked at each other and Alder shrugged his shoulders. Uiall being a necromancer was inherently dangerous, but where was the danger in disobeying Bacach? They had done it many times before and were failing to see the gravity of the situation now.

"If you shall not obey commands, then we have no use for you," Uiall stated whimsically.

She raised her hands and with dozens of screeches, the goblins burst from the ruins and took up the remaining civilians.

An arrow struck the wood door behind Uiall, narrowly missing her head.

"Traitor!" a voice rang out behind Rowan and Alder.

They turned to look.

Magadh, in his ceremonial armor, had appeared with a group of soldiers. Next to Magadh, rode Captain Caraid.

"Bacach! What have you done? I will have your head for your treachery!" Magadh shouted, not slowing the canter of his horse or paying any attention to the goblins.

"How is he alive?" Uiall spun on Bacach.

Bacach turned pale. He was a rabbit caught between wolves.

"How am I alive, you ask?" Magadh responded, pulling his horse to a stop with his soldiers behind him.

Uiall looked upon him with seething contempt.

"I am alive because I was not in Kingsford at the time of the attack. I am alive because the horde of goblins I assume were yours failed to kill me. I am alive because my brother is a coward and deals death like he deals every other doing of his life, by using someone else's hands. Maybe if he had the use of both, he would have been able to complete his chores," Magadh sneered.

Bacach flushed and a crazed look came over his face.

"Kill them, My Lady, kill them all," Bacach began pleading, turning to Uiall and gripping at her black lace sleeve.

She gave him a punishing look, and, with a bow of his head, he stepped back.

She lifted her hand and the goblins shrieked with laughter.

A faint rumbling could be heard and the goblins hesitated as they squeaked about the noise.

Holes began to open in the Earth and Uiall disappeared with a screech, followed by Bacach.

But Uiall had her revenge.

The goblins, in their knowledge of their duties, slit the villagers' throats and sprang upon the soldiers, Rowan, and Alder.

They fought hard. Rowan was forced to use his knife, the combat being too close for his bow and arrows. Those who had swords fared much better and the mounted soldiers rushed the goblins with their horses, cleaving heads with their swords.

A few soldiers were killed, but the goblins were defeated.

Rowan sank to the ground, staring at the people he had promised to deliver to safety. The last of the people of

Kingsford. Some still sputtered blood. Some were already gone.

Alder's sprint woke him from the darkness.

Margie.

Her plump body lay on the ground. She gripped at her throat, sputtering blood. Alder was desperately trying to hold the cloth she wore over her hair to her throat to stop the bleeding. Tears were streaming down his face. "No, no, no, no," he kept muttering over and over again.

Rowan got to her side and tried to hold pressure as well.

She stared at her two boys.

"I-I-the s-sea—" she spluttered, staring into Rowan's eyes.

She stopped choking and everything went silent.

Alder was gripping her hand and kept squeezing it and letting go, trying to get a reaction. He put his head on her chest.

"No, no, no," he was saying louder and louder. "Not Margie. Not her," over and over.

Rowan dropped his head to her chest, sobbing.

Alder continued to shake her, continued trying to get a reaction he could not be given.

He let out an agonized scream that shook the soldiers. He began to sob over her. Rowan gripped his hand and they cried together for a long time.

Rowan, remembering that they were not alone, looked behind him.

A vast network of tunnels and pits had opened all along the road and a colony of gnomes had crawled out silently. They were looking upon the dead, their plan barely too late.

Uiall was gone, along with Bacach. The earth where she had fallen was scorched. She had run back to her master, taking Bacach with her. A few gnomes with ropes and chains had moved in too quickly and now lined the bottom of the pit.

One of the soldiers screamed the same agonized scream Alder had let loose.

Rowan looked to where the man was.

He was holding one of the boys in his arms, rocking back and forth, roaring in his grief.

Another soldier found his mother and collapsed to his knees.

They had all known someone. Children, parents, neighbors, Margie.

When they had found Kingsford destroyed, there had been no time to investigate. They had seen the signs of a group heading toward the pass and had then found the slain children. They rode as hard as they could to Kingsland, hoping that their loved ones would be safe. Now everyone they knew and loved was dead and no one could do anything about any of it.

Rowan saw a gnome with a bushy beard approaching them. It was the gnome they had met in the library.

"We were too late, Elf Lord," he mourned with downcast eyes.

Alder wiped his eyes on his sleeves and made an attempt to focus on the gnome.

"We tried to catch the witch. She has brought much evil upon this land. When the people of the town were carried off, we knew we had to do something. We have been digging tunnels and pits without stopping for three days. But today, when we tried to remove the braces, they wouldn't budge. We chopped them with axes, but we were not quick enough. Your people are dead and she is gone."

"It was a noble and courageous attempt," Alder choked, barely able to push the words out.

Rowan nodded at the gnome, who only kicked a pebble over the side of a pit.

"A failure all the same," he sighed.

Magadh approached them. He had lost the look of contempt and haughtiness that he typically wore. He looked haggard and grieved. He was king of nothing. His sister's impaled body was before him, his brother had vanished with the necromancer, and his father and people were dead.

He looked at Margie's body and then looked down at his feet, not knowing what to say or how to begin. He was not used to being anything except cruel to Rowan and Alder and now he couldn't do so.

Alder and Rowan looked back down at Margie. Her eyes stared and the cloth Alder had placed on her neck was soaked with blood. Suddenly, they couldn't bear to see her in such a way.

Rowan closed her eyes and removed the cloth. Alder began rampaging through the wreckage of the houses, looking for something.

"We must have a funeral," Rowan begged, staring into Magadh's face. Magadh wanted to decline but looked at his soldiers. Many were weeping over their loved ones and, those who did not have anyone there were holding onto the soldiers that did. Many cried just the same. Magadh looked at his captain who was rocking his son in his arms. Captain Caraid stared distantly at the burned town.

A cart was found. Some of the horses were hitched. A few men left to go to the fields while the bodies were lifted onto the cart.

When the funeral procession reached the field, a mass grave had been dug. Two soldiers were already gathering all the rocks they could find to place on top of the mound.

The bodies were lowered one by one into the pit.

"Murta," a soldier called out, as an elderly woman was lowered into the grave.

"Gresha," a soldier sobbed, as another woman was lowered.

"Lorra," another called out.

"Rorrin," the soldier wailed as he lowered his son down.

"Margie."

Every person was named as they were lowered. There wasn't a person there that someone didn't know the name of. Each soldier took a handful of dirt and threw it into the grave.

Once the bodies were buried and the stones were arranged, Magadh's flagbearer stuck the pole of the flag into the mound. The wind caught it at once and set it rippling toward the east. They all stared at the flag.

They mulled for a while longer in the field, unsure where to go next.

Magadh paced angrily.

The man that had buried his son was weeping bitterly on the rocks.

Alder, with a look of determination, went back into the town. He appeared a short while later with a rolling pin. Margie's rolling pin. He shoved it into the mound without a word.

Rowan pulled an arrow from his sheath and shoved it into the mound, thinking of the boy in the pass.

The crying man removed his sword from his belt and placed it in the rocks.

The other men, seeing what was happening, took some of their own items or went back into the town to find items that represented those they had lost and placed them on the rocks.

A man began to sing. Another, hearing the words, joined him. Then they all began to sing together.

When the wind grows cold,
And the flowers shrink and fade,
You wander away,

But I remember your face.
The sweetness of your voice,
The warmth of your eyes,
But never again to see you,
Will I be given that choice.
You have gone on to distant lands,
Far beyond the moon and sky,
But you have left me with my love for you,
And I can no longer feel you in my hands.

Magadh, at the finishing of the song, took up a look of resolve and determination that Rowan had never seen before. Alder noticed this change and a look of knowing appeared on his face. The great blood that ran in Magadh's veins had finally awakened. He was ready to become their king.